STREAMSKELTER

SIMON HARDING

STREAMSKELTER

PAN BOOKS

LONDON, SYDNEY AND AUCKLAND

First published 1994 by Pan Books Limited

a division of Pan Macmillan Publishers Limited
Cavaye Place London SW10 9PG
and Basingstoke

Associated companies throughout the world

ISBN 0 330 33210 4

9 8 7 6 5 4 3 2 1

A CIP catalogue record for this book is available from
the British Library

Phototypeset by Intype, London
Printed by Cox & Wyman Ltd, Reading, Berkshire

Dedicated to Alan Lee and Brian Froud, whose wonderful book *Faeries* (Pan) reminded me about the Glaistig, and her potential followers.

A Fisherman Falls

From Grace   3

Mr Fish   9

PROLOGUES

'You stand there with your fixed expression
casting doubt on all I have to say
why don't you touch me, touch me
why don't you touch me, touch me now'

GENESIS, 'The Musical Box'

A FISHERMAN
FALLS FROM GRACE

My dreams are numbered, all right. How the hell would I keep tabs on them otherwise? Numbers in the top corner. Nought to fifty. I don't have that many but I dream a lot. The thing that really grips me is they're not all mine. Every now and again one of them slips in an extra feature, just to get me going. Lady G., well, she's a regular Dream Bitch – she'll play anywhere. Rupert's learning fast too. I picture him up in my projection room, reels of film rolling round his clippity-cloppity boots, coils of it unravelling over his thin shoulders. Chopping up the dialogue, pasting scenes in where they don't belong. Holding strips up against the light. I'll be right with you, it's around here somewhere. Numbers, old pal. Get those dreams numbered and you can't go wrong, everything falls into place.

Kaz turns herself over, she's tall and sleeps nearer the door than I do, nearer the door than I dare. I take a peep through my eyelid binoculars, listen for any clippity-cloppity coming for me up the stairs. Sure I can afford shagpile, who needs it? Keeping the noise down while she sends him up after me, sends him up to fetch me down. Clippity-cloppity on the worn worm boards, I'll hear him a mile off if he tries anything. Before I got Kaz in to hump her shoulder and sandbag my position on the posture-springing I'd string tin cans full of marbles on some old fifty-pound line I'd stripped from one of my multipliers, multiplied the odds against that skinny hoofer hooking in to me. Hooking in to me the way the bad bit-part player in dream fifty-seven hooks those little slickers. I listen out a while, eye the red digits on Kaz's alarm flicking and flexing. People ask me what I see in her, my Kaz. Figure I'd be seeing someone from the club, someone sucks long cocktails through loopy straws. Down to earth, that's me. Gone to earth, at bay behind Kaz's hunched shoulder. Katie Beardmore if you want to start prying straight off. She's a nurse at Budgworth Royal Infirmary, knows all that medical stuff, the right knots, pressure points. Unties my knots and eases my pressures, my Kaz. What more do I need so long as she stays on the perimeter and her clock keeps its neon eye out.

Dream fifty-seven, sorry I kept you. It's a B for Bummer as far as Her Ladyship's concerned. I wait for Richard Widmark or Kirk Douglas to whip around, take off a few heads. What do you call them, the Dark Ages? What do I know? Plenty. I turn up, catch my nose in D.B.'s clapperboard, I'm so keen to see where she came from. The action keeps slipping so you're hardly better off watching these repeats. Knot my fingers, he knots his hooks, hooks a worm which ties itself in slick spitty knots just the way those slickers like 'em. November, AD 876. This bit-part player's rather a small man with a crooked arm. I try and catch him out on details, maybe one day he'll forget which one's supposed to be broken, switch his sling from one arm to the other, maybe pull up his tunic sleeve, give me a glimpse of the cheap wristwatch he's forgotten to leave back in the trailer like I'm not all that hot on continuity. Get on with it, buster, I'm slicked in here behind Kaz's shoulder and a broken-down log crawling with itty-bitty insects and bug stuff. He can't see me as he sits there quiet, dangling that meaty worm knot for the slickers in the bridge pool. Yeah, D.B.'s not exactly straining her budget finding decent location shots. Hell, I played there often enough, I should recognize it now, feel safe enough you'd have thought. Our bit of stream in the old days. The stream your parents warned you about, the stream my parents warned me about. It slipstreamed him quietly, just like everything else. We'll slipstream him too, leave him to it, soon as we see what he's caught. He's typecast, he's used to this abuse. Next time he's in panto, the horse's arse, something like that, maybe you'll see my dreams numbered among his recent appearances. Does a good crooked arm, the best crooked arm there is. Those blond blokes flexing their muscles in the misty long-shot longboat hadn't come twenty miles across the marshes to eat a few fish. They'd finger their noses first, take whatever they wanted. They'd done for him in his first battle, those Northmen. Left him fit for nothing but fishing dirty streams. The axe had gone straight through his wooden shield, his dirty tunic, and most of the muscle of his forearm. They'd hardly bothered with him, left him for dead on the misty hillside with the eyeless men and the ragged ravens. Is that dry ice there or what? I, Continuity, feel a historical inaccuracy coming on. You know me for details like this. Nobody told D.B. Vikings never wore horns on their helmets. I'm not going to rock her longboat just yet, though. Wind those titles on, maybe get one of those gravelly guys to do a voice-over. They came, out of the misty fiords, they conquered the Saxon shore. Now they're settling a treaty to end the wars and they'll need a good fish supper when they've finished. You rush off and get some fresh ones you useless git. They told the Northmen straight: leave off raiding, leave us Hillstones folk to our rocky pastures. They'd left him to fish for their supper while they decided everything. Slipstreamed.

Here he is though, standing crooked as the whole world rushes past, squatting quietly by the great pool beneath the cliff with his fishing pole. In his time it was worth a visit, worth the risk. Dingle-dangling dirty feet in the cold rush. He'd catch sleek slickers up to about half a pound before they'd struggle too much and break his gut. He'd head for the shadows under the cliff so he could see them lying up near the surface, see the occasional flicks of their broad speckled tails as they steadied themselves in the brisk current, steadied themselves as the brook hurried past, dived underground. When the water's low you can see the crack in the rock layers, a letterbox at the foot of a massive grey door. The stream has eaten out the soft layer like children lick the cream between layers of sponge. The current has taken the sandy debris and filed it away like it tries to take the trout. They're too slick, too sleek for it. They slide out of the stream's cold grip, wriggle free just as they're about to be taken down for good, just as they're about to be slipstreamed too. He'd caught three, watched the leaves swirl in the current and then stood to relieve himself when he spotted the body held hard in the jaws of the cliff, held in the lips of the crack. Watched the blonde head bob in the current, hair washed this way and that in the flow, the broken waters. He could see her spine stretch the silvery skin. A woman, a dead woman in his stream. She was being buffeted against the cliff wall as if whatever force had spawned her wanted to drag her back under, drag her in. Drag me down there with them, hey nosey, stuck your neck out too far this time! He drops the willow fishing pole and scrambles down the crumbling bank into the dead cold rush of the stream. Lifts his dirty tunic above his filthy knees and wades out into the shadows under the cliff. Green weed like witches' hair slithers round his shins, slimes his thighs as he heads for the deeper water in the middle, the flow stronger, colder, pressing against his legs and shrivelling his balls. The blonde head bobbing a yard in front of him, face down. Lifeless eyes staring at the cold bright gravel on the bottom of the pool. He reaches out with his good hand, gets a grip in a slippery hank of hair, braces his legs against the current and tugs the head up. Water runs out of the slack mouth. She's convincing. She's Oscar stuff. Suspension of disbelief? She wrote the script. Chummy turns her over, slipping the legs out of the crack, delivering her. Steadying the blonde head with his awkward crooked arm, wading to the bank, dragging his prize out on to the rich red earth. He kneels, brushes the hair back and rubs the worst from her face. Lays her out on the cold grass like a fish, like a slicker he's caught. He can smell the cold water as he squats a little distance from her, half afraid still of the corpse he's dragged from the pool. He didn't recognize her from the village. She was far too fair, far too white. He looks about him, sure he should slide her straight back where she had come from. He takes her cold hand, feels the cold seep into his bones. A thin trickle of water runs from her slack mouth, ah, she's good, she's brilliant. Her pale lips. He licks his lips, thinks he'll lick hers too maybe only that's not in D.B.'s first draft. She gets a little uppity when people start taking liberties, believe me. Her neck is slim, white, blue veins stand out in the marbled skin. Small flattened breasts, pale nipples. Leaning closer, he tries to smell her breath from the parted lips. He lifts the cold hand in his dirty paw, strokes his rough thumb over the smooth knuckles. He folds her hand carefully over her chest as if he's laying her out, reaches to take her other hand, flung out on the rich red earth. The whites of her eyes roll, flick open as if he's knocked casts from her face. She's wearing contacts, those Dracula jobs they wore in the old Hammer Horrors. He's not seen anything like them though, leaps back groping for his dagger, lost in the water. Backs off like a wild dog. Her fingers flex in the red earth, her eyes, impossibly blue, sweep over him and along the bank, over the undergrowth and up the cliff to the sky framed above. She stares at the clouds drifting slowly above them, turns to gaze at him. He picks up the fishing pole, holds it across his chest. Where's your village? Asks her in the West speech, the Common speech. She stares, maybe she's not too happy with Common. Sitting up slowly she picks earth from her mouth with her long white cold spidery fingers, looks at it as if it's flakes of gold. He asks if she's fallen in. She gazes about as if he isn't there. Pokes her leg with the point of the pole and she looks round at him again.

'Where do you come from, where's your village?'

She looks blankly at him, turns and stares in the water. Maybe she's one of those silent movie queens who couldn't crack it when the talkies came along, spoke with a lisp, with a Welsh accent, something awful like that. The fisherman with the crooked arm forgets his trout and carries home his catch. Pushing her along with the stick toward the village in the gorge by the bridge with the withies. By dusk he could see the night fires burning behind the rough stockade. Old D.B.'s splashed out here, discreet lighting and dry ice so all these goddamn extras are in silhouette on a blood-red backcloth. Worried housecarles clatter down from the gate to see what he's brought home. The villagers turn out to see the sleek naked thing the fisherman's found in the drowning pool. The men rhubarb rhubarb, crudely crude, rub her hair in their filthy hands, offer bargains until their wives arrive to shoo them home. The chief's wife steps out in her best gown, sees them squalling and shoving, sees the guards prod the naked thing before the hall of the chief. Once before, a naked girl had been dragged in off the hills to his hall. Once before, he had changed his wife, taken the younger woman to his hearth. This time round she's not going to be slipstreamed by some slicker from the stream. Country Girl Teen Nympho is going to be chucked out with the fish-heads if she gets her way.

'What bait is Rush using these days, that he can catch fish such as these?' her husband jokes. Let him joke, she thinks. Wash her off? Sure, we'll get the village scrubbers to bring their scrubbing brushes, redden her up a little. Wait at the tables? As long as I don't have to. She'll watch her, dumb bitch with her feline grace and fuck me eyes filling cups like any common village slut. And so she was. Wardrobe splashed out on a simple brown shift, hair by Timor at Sushy McSushy, caught up in a whalebone clasp, it's devastatingly effective. They've had her wiggle her walk, swaying between the rows of roaring-drunk warriors carrying a tray of beakers. So she was when Jarl Raven set his glacier-blue eyes on her when he came to make the treaty and end the wars.

MR FISH

'Crank.'

'What?'

'Crank. He's asking for you, must be a crank.' The big man in the shiny suit looked up from his typewriter, glared at the youngster with the spectacles waving the receiver at him.

'Caller, Nigel,' Fish corrected him carefully. The younger man smiled, transferred the call to Fish's phone.

'Yeah?' What an actor, let me tell you about this guy. Yeah. Like we've got him under surveillance twenty-four hours a day, one of those secret-camera jobs. We really need to know his every movement, every gesture, the way he cocks the phone to his ear and leans back in the worn chair, tiny traceries of veins and rivers in the flaking leather.

'Yeah, this is Mr Fish. Yeah, I know. I heard something about it. Check out the painting? Oh . . . yeah . . . Who is this? Check out what painting? Who told you my . . . Hello? Hello? Bastard's rung off.'

'Crank.'

'Some kid.'

'What he want?'

'Wants me to check out a painting. Louis Sartre?' Nigel sighed.

'That's Jean-Paul, not Louis.'

'Well, maybe he had a brother. That's what the kid said.' Was what he said all right, Mr Fish, hey, I should know.

Lifelines 13

Lifelines II 17

Bumps 23

PART ONE

'I lingered round them, under that benign sky: watched the moths fluttering among the heath and harebells, listened to the soft wind breathing through the grass, and wondered how any one could ever imagine unquiet slumbers for the sleepers in that quiet earth'

EMILY BRONTË, *Wuthering Heights*

LIFELINES

Funny. I mean, dreaming about nosebleeds when I've never actually had one. Staring in the bathroom mirror as a tiny ruby bubble dribbles over my night-time stubble, runs over my lip. Maybe pull it fleshy and squidgy, poke at my teeth, loosen them in my bloody gums. Tug one and it slips out easily, slips out like a curtain ring. Tooth decay and then some. I turn over, run my finger over my furry snappers just to make sure, huddle down again. Nosebleeds I can live without, wet dreams I don't even remember, but Rupert – the little devil – he sticks around like he begrudges me having them, begrudges me everything. I see him now and again, strolling along behind me with a box of super-size tissues like he wants to clean up my act, smother me. I can't figure why he's so interested in my blood, my snot, and the rest of it. Sometimes he's around for a moment – watching me from the mirror as my blood blossoms in a mouthful of toothpaste foam. Sometimes he sticks around longer, say if I'm making love with Kaz. Especially if I'm making love with Kaz. Yeah, it sounds heavy but it's true. If I catch a glimpse, a breath, a whisper of him, I take a crafty look over her shoulder, the mad mane of her hair, make sure he's not pretending to touch her – maybe making funny faces behind her back, pulling his mouth wide with his dirty crooked fingers, running his tongue out like a ferret.

Gives me a grip right now, I take a look over my shoulder make sure she's not crept on out to run her tongue over the back of my neck, taken a comb to my hair. I've left Kaz's compact open beside the screen so I can see if she's ducked down behind me. Paranoid? Precautions. After all this time you'd figure I'd tell Whiteman about it, get some therapy. He's **13** been in and out of my head already, knows his way around but he's had his chance. Maybe telling you will be therapy enough. Here's hoping. Whiteman, that old quack, he knew I had beans to spill but I kept it tight. I mean, what was I then, eleven, twelve? Sure, big for my age, but he thought he was going to get it out of me, every single bit of it. He figured things the way Rupert figures now: stick around long enough and I'll crack. Somehow, though, old Whiteman couldn't stand the pace, couldn't stand the standing still, the constant repetition. The same old stuff over and over again, the woods, the pylon, Solomon. Her. Least of all her. He waved me right over, rushed me on to the next section. Whiteman didn't want to know Jack Shit about Glaistig, old D.B. Her Ladyship self. Trouble is, every other heading, every other angle, every other way of looking at it, things kept on coming back to her. After a couple of weeks he quit it, a couple of years he stopped checking up, washed his hands of me. I was free to go and get on with my teenage years, nosebleeds, wet dreams, and all.

Rupert, poor old Rupert, wasn't so lucky. They locked him up, a hand-grenade hair-cut in dead man's trousers. Missed out on his teens, on his nosebleeds and his wet dreams. On the blood and the snot and the spunk and what do you call that stuff girls make? It's no wonder I feel guilty about it, about him. Who wouldn't? I bet you're already taking his side, wondering what the hell we got up to down in the dingly old dell. Yeah, well it was nothing like that. None of that stuff, you might as well take *that* as read right now. I don't think, at least I don't get the impression, he misses me at all, just the juicy stuff. Literally. One time I expected to see him, though, one time I felt sure he'd turn up and he didn't. He left me alone down there, all on my own to face her. See, about six years ago I got into cave diving. Got into it and got straight out again, if you want to know. I've never liked heights and since I went down that fucking sink, I've not had much time for depths either. Sinks. It's such a stupid name. I mean, what's so domestic about a dirty great hole in the ground, a mile or more below the surface. This hell's kitchen's a crack in the earth, a crack brimming with muddy brown water that wants to lead me on, blind me, turn me over on my belly. I could hardly fit through the entrance chamber, I was hardly over the doorstep before I was banging my bottles on the rocks, giving the instructor a real fright. I mean, it's not my fault, I'm big to start with. By the time I'd hauled on that rubber suit, settled the tanks, and stepped into these great diver's boots I looked like the Michelin man in a size-twelve dustbin. You have to spit on the inside of your face mask, try and swallow the chunky mouthpiece like you've got a mouthful of gobstoppers. Pull the strap tight round the back of your rubber Balaclava and stick a bloody great yellow miner's helmet on your head. A hard hat with two great lamps on the side, lamps that could provide the floodlighting at the football, they're that damn bright. Up in the world that is. After an eternity of stumbling, heavy breathing, rasped shoulders, I'm ready to ease myself into the lifeless water. It's like sticking your dick in the deep freeze. So dark, if you'd dared that far down with us, all you would have seen would have been my two lamps, dim now in all that frigid murk, dim as Gollum's eyes, slowly spiralling out of sight.

Deeper, colder, clutching this daft little rope like a lifeline. It's expensive, high-grade reinforced nylon something or other, so it won't give up the ghost on me. It won't fray the way rope always frays in the movies, just when you are hanging over some cliff. It's bright orange, you can see it miles off. Up in the world that is. Down here, might as well be seaweed. Think about it for a second. Down there in the cold and the dark, with just this little rosary to hang on to. Let me tell you, I'd practically torn it in two myself, even before I dropped it. Dropped the bloody thing right down in front of me somewhere. Chas, the instructor guy, was behind me. Sure, I knew that, knew that all the time, but it didn't exactly help, if you hear what I'm saying. I was breathing my air fast those few moments. Listening to it hoarse in my head like an obscene caller through a PA system, right in my ears, catching in my throat, filling up the mask, the tiny space between my open mouth and the steamed-up glass. I don't like writing about it, I'm not really thinking about it either, not now, not right now. Picking bits out of a lucky dip of impressions, thoughts, frights, but not really thinking hard about it. I can't. It cracks me, grips me. Like she did. Oh yes, she was down there. There was just me, on my hands and knees in the murk, feeling the cave floor like it was Braille. And her, just out of my reach, waiting in the shadows, having a look at me at my worst; my shit-scared fuck the women and children get me out of here worst. I thought for a second I could even hear her laughing. I could see the bubbles rushing up to the pitiless ceiling of the cavern. Cauldroned in my dafty dustbin wrenching my neck to peer over my padded shoulders. I could almost see her, could imagine her grabbing me tight and ripping me right up close to her, staring me in the face behind the steamed-up glass. It was Chas. He'd worked his way up the rope and found me crouching there. By the time he'd got me out I had so much liquid running round my suit they had to run a hose over me. Chas was OK about it, said the best way to beat it was to get right back on the horse, turn round and go straight back down. Down there with her, down into her territory, her wet patch? Not me, feller, not yet. I kick my feet, front crawl out of there, tangling myself in the sheets and pulling the quilt from Kaz's sandbagged shoulder. Shit.

LIFELINES II

After the business in the cave I didn't catch a glimpse of the little bastard for some time. Rupert was a canary down a coal mine – keeled over as soon as she showed up. As soon as she'd swarmed up out of the murk to press her face up against my mask, glare in at me running her red tongue over the glass like some horny window cleaner, that damn bird just pegged out on me. Maybe he was embarrassed, maybe he didn't like to mince about on her territory too much. Maybe he was leaving me to the boss, the Dream Bitch. A bit later I sensed him hovering again, behind the doors, in my sock drawer, the usual places. I had a grip on him again. I thought of him the morning I had the dream about the olden-times girl.

Number sixty-seven, old pal, keep them coming there! The girl in the green coat with the little hat. It was typical Rupert art school stuff, you know, misty evening, nice sunset, popping banging old car coming along a country lane. Christ, sign the bastard up for a brown bread commercial. I thought I was in for one of those fifth-form slipstreamers, when you get to play the hitch hiker, the injured farmhand, the randy squire maybe. There was a man, though, a young man in period costume like pictures of your great-grandfather with about a million buttons down his waistcoat and shiny leather boots. He's walking along the lane, turns as the car comes up alongside. He waves and shouts something, raises his cap. The car slows and the image jumps like an awkwardly shot silent movie. Get some subtitles up there, for God's sake, I'm not a bloody lip-reader. Rupert's too busy playing with his crayons, colouring in the details. Playing about in the projection room fiddling with those hi-tech tints. Does the old-time geezer know her, the pretty girl in the watery green coat? He's leaning in, pointing on up the road, folding his hand to indicate a turn, another and another. She's nodding but biting her lip, a fuzzy close-up, white-out. The car, one of those funny old Austins, it's slewed into the rhine at the side of the lane, the door is open like a flag in a breeze, and the man's boots are sticking out. I'm tempted to laugh, it's Keystone Kops, Max Sennett or something. Moving around to peer inside. The muddy boots kicking now, Rupert must be standing clear like a news cameraman, doing his job but keeping out of the firing line. The guy in the car's thrashing about, arms braced, the car's rocking. The image slips again, he's retrieving his cap from the floor, scraping his hair back. One of her small lace-up boots has come off in the struggle and is stuck under the pedals. He pulls the white legs round, pulls her bag from beneath her body and tugs it open. He stuffs big white notes into his jacket and drops the bag. He reaches into the back, picks something from the seat, a book maybe, then drops it on the dead girl slumped in the front. The car moves off again, slowly, jerky. Then I realize he can't drive, or can't drive very well. The car bumps along, turns down a slope. Trees, branches, and leaves brushing our faces. Water. Clove brook. I recognize the neat little stone bridge, the cliff behind it, misty in the gathering twilight. He's taking off his boots, looking up now, I can see his runty, pinched features, the moustache is so big it looks false, looks false on his pinched little face. He's dragging her out now, you can see she's dead by the way he lets her head bump on the stones. Her hair's dark, auburn maybe, it's come loose, uncoiled. He hauls her by the shoulders of her coat, down the bank, down to the water's edge. He must have tipped her into the brook, he's standing now watching the water flow past, making sure she's gone for good. There's a deep pool beneath the cliff where the water swirls before sliding underground, slides under the cliff like a letter under a door. I'm down there with it, behind that wretched mask, I'm back down in the chamber under Hillstones, bloated, clumsily searching for my lifeline. Tiny brown specks, silt I've stirred up groping about on the bottom, swirls round in the lamp beam. Crawling, praying on my hands and knees. In the darkness the Dream Bitch moves in and around, lurking in the shadows just out of sight, then slides over the floor, blonde hair streaming behind her. Shimmering green dress, 'hem embroidered with spindly runes, delicate features distorted by her mad leer, the mad leer she gives me as she grabs my shoulders, nails biting through the rubber suit. Looking in at me behind my fish tank mask. She's reaching up to lift my lid, chase the little fishes around their tank with her furry pads and shiny claws. It's Kaz now, it's Kaz rocking me gently, bringing me out slowly as if dreams could give me the bends, as if my dreams of water and witches could burn her if she's not careful. She's a nurse, used to sudden screams, and my nightmares don't cut much ice with her. Too matter of fact to be bothered by my ramblings, she gives me a second to get a grip.

'Lay off the cheese,' she says flatly, turning over and tugging the covers up over her bare shoulders. Lay off the cheese, I ask you. With anybody but Kaz you'd get annoyed, feel like hitting out. With Kaz it's different. I look at her, dropping off with her long lashes fluttering. I make a face, a big mean mouse, hold my cold hands up to my chest and pretend they're little paws. Eeek Eeek my lovely cheesy curled up warm thing. Eeek Eeek I'm the big mouse to chase you back up your hole. She's a big girl, hit her and she'll hit you straight back only harder. Solid, that's Kaz. A damn sight more substantial than Sam, my ex-wife. Sam would always ask about my dreams, she'd want to know who'd done what to whom and why. She'd want to know what she'd said and done, what she'd worn and how she'd looked. Sam would sit up, pat her pillow, and make herself comfortable, coming out of a good sleep she'd blink a few times and she'd be right there waiting for all the gory close-ups. If I'd told her all of it she'd have gotten scared like she used to, said I ought to have rung Whiteman, go and talk my dreams out with him. Talk? I'd had enough of his talk to last me a lifetime. Sam, see, she'd been with us all through it, she'd been our little playmate at school, our first fling and Rupert's last, unless they send him the occasional auxiliary up there at the hospital. He's still got the floppy brown hair, the vacant little boy lost stare that makes some girls want to mother him, makes me want to smother him. Perhaps he has upped his score to one. He's not saying. He doesn't say anything any more, not since the night they brought us out of the gorge with our clothes smouldering and our hair singed off. Rupert prefers the subtle approach these days. Leaves my conscience to supply all his punchlines, lets my imagination set his strategies. It's OK, I've got him well sussed. I had him sussed from the beginning really. I knew what he was about, knew what he was up to with Sam and everything. His big mistake, his *big* mistake, was treating me like a fat prat. A big dumb slob. Maybe I should take it as a compliment, the fact he leaves me to decipher all his messages rather than line me up in front of a blackboard and hammer them in to me, out of me. When I'd seen Kaz off to work and settled back with my second coffee I puzzled over the car rape-murder whatever it was, tried to figure the connections. There's always a connection in the end. There's always a connection with what happened to Rupert and me.

A few nights later I had the same dream again only this time I missed most of the action, came in on ratface with his sleeves rolled up, holding her under in the rushing water. It took me a moment to realize it wasn't the same man. This guy's hairier, he's not wearing a shirt it's some kind of tunic thing. He wasn't pushing her under and holding her down, he was pulling her out, getting his arm under her head. The blonde hair swirls in the current as she sinks again. Wades to the bank, dragging her on to the wet red earth, smearing her white skin, clogging her hair, filling her eyes and mouth. He crouches beside her, scrapes the worst away, clambers out to squat beside his prize. I don't know. It's the stream again, slipstreaming me maybe. My dad used to tell me they'd had the men from the ministry down our brook one time, back in the fifties before I was born. The white coats wanted to find out what happened to the stream between Clove and the big marsh to the south. What went on under Hillstones, what's the big idea? The brook diving under the cliff like a fragrant letter slipped beneath a lover's door, never to be read again.

That's what bothered them, not knowing. I bet they looked at their geological charts, got annoyed at all the blank bits, the white spaces. Wanted to fill them in, get everything mapped out nice and neat. If they could have gotten pipes down there, I bet they would have done. Lay them out, nice and straight. Dad said they'd poured bucketfuls of dye into the cliff pool, turned the whole lot dark blue. Then they had jumped back in to their Land-Rovers and motored on down the gorge, came out where all their maps, all their readings and reckonings told them they'd see the dye emerge.

'Where'd it come out then?' I asked him impatiently. He sucked on his pipe for effect, then pointed the chewed stem at me.

'It didn't,' he said triumphantly. What, didn't come out anywhere?

'Not a trace. They looked all along the levels, all along Hillstones. Not a trace.' I knew this was leading up to something. 'So just you mind out when you play down there,' he warned me. 'Kids have been drowned down there, you know. Your mother's concerned.' All that dye, enough to turn a whole army a different colour, enough to turn the white coats blue. 'There's the Rec. Why don't you play down the Rec?' A million reasons. Reasons dyed bright blue. Crystal chambers full of transparent blind fish, blundering about in blue water. That's why we played down there. Down in the gorge, in the heart of the woods, deep down in the dingly old dell. Clove brook we called it, our bit of the stream. The stream that swallowed dye and shopping trolleys. The stream that had a soft spot for children, somewhere. Didn't leave any traces, any stain. The stream that ran down from up Budgworth way, ran through the village and into the gorge by the neat little stone bridge. Doubled back on itself a couple of times before running up against the cliff, swilling around like mouthwash in a sink before diving down the plug hole, into the Hillstones' disposal system. It had chewed me around a few times, chewed me up and spat me out. I've been down there, I've squeezed through the sinks and pots and pans, dived the caves and groped my way along chambers a mile below

Gibbet peak where only lost sheep and the most determined fell walker ever go. Fell walker, I ask you. What's so special about eyeless ewes and jabbing ravens. Come to that, what's so special about hidden chambers and secret journeys and transparent blue fish. What's so special about our bit of stream? I'll tell you. I'll tell you when I wake up. That damn girl's drugging my drinks, I'll swear it.

BUMPS

Whatever it was it woke me up, dragged me right back to my nice warm bed, my nice warm Kaz. I reach over to switch the reading lamp on. You know what it's like, though, you lie there straining to catch every sound, every squeak. Your brain must leave something on guard, listening out for the bump that's going to wake you. Kaz is hunched over, she's taken most of the quilt again. White back black hair and let me tell you she gives off some kind of heat. She's so hot I don't usually mind her taking the covers, grasping them to her like they're her own special worry blanket. I cool down a little, listen out a little, then drop back off. Maybe I'll just grab a little corner back to cover my balls. You read any of that Stephen King guy? He says people don't like sticking their feet out of the end of the bed in case the bogeyman gets them. Me, I don't give a shit about my feet, but the green bastard can't have my balls. I'm not about to leave them unprotected, like a couple of covered wagons hunched down for the night on some Arizona badland. I'd sleep easier if I could retract my undercarriage. Kaz tells me off, tells me to stop playing with myself. I'm not playing, I'm protecting. She usually says something cruel and turns back over, sandbags me like she's supposed to. She can't complain, she knows why she's here.

Anyway, here I am, taking a peek out over the perimeter of the quilt. Maybe working too hard, imagining things. Foxes bark right here on the estate sometimes, and the wooden panelling under the window gets rattled all night if the wind's in the wrong direction. No wind, though, and no foxes. Not tonight. By the time I've registered the silence I realize the light in the hall has been left on. It's streaming in through the grille over the bedroom door like a torch beam, like I've **23** aliens landing in my hallway. A few seconds seem longer, I lay there listening to Kaz's heavy breathing. I spend another second feeling annoyed with her for lying there out of it while I'm wide awake. She works damn hard at that hospital and by the time she hits the sheets she's usually out for the count. Her breathing and the light. I mean, think of the bill. It's hopeless trying to get anything out of her before about noon, but I roll over, shake her anyway.

'Did you leave the light on?'

'Uh . . . wha sa time is it?' It was something like that, and I'm not trying to be funny. I tug the covers over her, slide my legs off the bed, and stand up. The floorboards are cold under my squeaky feet. I pad out to the hall, yeah, I'm a regular ghost for a big bloke. You won't catch me clippity-cloppitying around waking decent folk from their honest rest. You can tell the big hundred-watter's been on some time, practically taste the burnt ozone, feel the heat of it. Girl's going to burn the place down one night. There's the switch, off you go. The rest of the light is coming up the hallway from downstairs. What, she been down to fix herself a midnight feast? Leave the fridge door open as well? If she needs to go to the bathroom she's usually in and out and back to sleep, leaving me listening to the dripping cistern. Like you could bury your head in the pillow, fill your ears with porridge and you'd still hear it, plop, plop, plop. I clamber down the stairs, a little unsteady although I've hardly drunk a thing, one or two cans maybe, before we went to bed. I look around the familiar living-room. The fish aren't giving anything away, the light's on so it's free swim time I suppose. They look happy enough chasing each other's tails and mouthing their own shit. What, can't they recognize it by now? There's my leather jacket, my Filo, my wallet. Video present and correct. Back window is intact and the fat sausage thing Kaz made to keep out the draughts is lying by the back door keeping out draughts. Both the lights are on. The standard lamp is a bugger, anything but standard if you ask me. You have to reach up inside it, practically limbo dance underneath the rim to switch it on or off. There's no way she did this in her sleep, she'd have knocked the thing over no trouble. I'm walking on down to switch it off when the telephone rings. Made me jump, the bastard. Gave me another of my grips, right there and then. Ever have those? That feeling you're going to fall just after you climb into bed, that feeling there's somebody out there, dressed in green, ready to throw a hank of her hair round your neck and throttle the daylights out of you? I had one right then. It rings twice more before I pick it up. My hands are steady, pretty steady considering.

'Hello, David? Were you awake?' It's Samantha, my ex. The one I told you about. I feel myself deflating as if she's thrust a needle through the earpiece. Yeah, she rings what, once, twice a year. Any time she needs to really.

'Were you awake?' she repeats.

'No . . . yes . . . don't worry about it. What's up?' I ask her, real friendly.

'My dad just called. He's had a guy on from Budgworth.'

Really? What is it, conversation she wants? At what, 3.46 a.m.? Typical Sam. Spends years living with you barely saying a word, moves out and she can't leave me alone.

'One of his old mates on the late shift. Listen, David. Rupert's dead. He killed himself. Left a note, everything.' The voice is quite steady, I'm not sure I am. I'm loose, cut loose, the telephone cord's my lifeline, holds me in there.

'One of his old inspectors gave him a call. Dad thought we needed to know.' What do I know what I was thinking? I'm telling you what she said, what I said, what, you want my thoughts in brackets, would that help?

'David, you still there?' Sounds a little shaky now, wanting me to answer. I could make some ghosty noises, really fuck her over. Do my scary mouse face at the receiver.

'What kept him?'

'Pardon? Speak up, David, I can hardly . . .'

'I said, what kept him?'

There's a disturbed silence on the other end of the line. God, the girl must be twitching. She was never that good at it, keeping things in. For her, this is Zen calm. I remember her having the raging ab-dabs if we forgot to get something at Sainsbury's, if I farted during a dinner party. To be honest, she's not as frazzled as I'd expect her to be. In the circumstances.

'I know you were close . . . despite everything. Had you seen him lately?'

'Not since we split.' Uh-oh. To her, see, I left. Abandoned her to her nightmares. For Christ's sake, I was having enough of my own, without having to try and blow the whistle in hers too. Can you blame me? Christ, I have enough trouble butterflying my way out of my own without dipping my big toe in her mysterious rock pools. Lift a stone there see what you'll find, see what comes skitting out to stick its pincers in your pinkies. Not even her dad could bring himself to blame me, not for long. He'll be ringing me himself in a minute. He knew I gave her my best shots. Of course I knew Rupert would do it. Would in the end. Maybe all these dreams I've been getting again were like Rupert burning out, burning up his life through my nightmares. Frantically signalling me while he still could. Perhaps I'll get a little peace now. Is that too much to ask, a decent night's kip? A guttering candle, flickering beyond his locked room, snuffed out with a thick paddy thumb. Somebody got careless. I know the Institute. It makes Colditz look like an open prison. Somebody will be getting a bollocking, a real bollocking, right now. Whiteman will be chewing them out. The reports, the press, the families, the friends. Friends like Sam and I. I suppose I knew, sooner or later, somebody would fuck up and he'd do it. Finish it. I knew from the moment they brought us in that night, smouldering, clothes singed and smoking. Third-degree burns on our arms and legs. I can see him staggering in the smoke, the headlights, the firemen shouting. I can see the big guy with the blanket rolling him up like a bit of pastry, tugging him toward the ambulance. I could see through the soot, the muck. I could see there was no one home. I couldn't speak, my throat was raw, I'd run about two miles and I'm no athlete. I couldn't say but I could point, nod my head. They were asking questions right off, questions all the way to the hospital. What were we doing, where was Solomon? Had he tried to touch us in the cottage? Ooh, Matron. Touch us, yeah sure. Nod, let them think that's what he'd been up to. It could wait.

Zodiac Boy	29
Picture This	34
Drips and Drabs	38
Tommy Guns	43
Two boys, one girl	49
In Church	56
Prince Burning	60
Bedroom Scenes	64
Embraces	68
Gobstoppers	71
Doctor Doctor	80
Offerings	84
Trouble	88
Red-Handed	93

PART TWO

'I have spread my dreams under your feet
Tread softly because you tread on my dreams'

W. B. YEATS, 'He Wishes for the Cloths of Heaven'

ZODIAC BOY

I first saw him when he rolled up with his big brother, mum, and dad in the spring of 1971. That Ford Zodiac had seen better days – at least a million – coughing and pinking under the weight of the Jones family and assorted suitcases, cardboard boxes, and pets. The long-awaited return of Mr Silas Jones, long-lost Water Board official of this parish. They moved in three doors down from us on Cliff Drive, right there on the new estate above Clove. Do you know Clove? It's OK. Even now, after all that's happened, I still feel quite good about being there, the people you know. The quiet little High Street is pleasant enough when the day trippers have gone back up the gorge to Budgworth, taking the old road up alongside the brook, turning over the neat little stone bridge. That's the way Rupert's dad came in the hissing Zodiac, ticking and clicking as they waited outside the principal pub rendezvous in the town, the Blue Boar. Silas left them there while he ducked under the low door to collect his elder brother. Old Solomon had been hibernating in the back room of the Boar for as long as anyone could remember and the plan was for the whole lot of them to move in together, now Silas was back in town. It meant Rupert had to share a room with his brother, and thinking back on it now, I can't imagine Mrs Jones was over chuffed to have been saddled with the miserable old git either. Solomon looked as if he'd been sharing a bed with half a dozen goats. I mean looked, because once you actually got up close to him he had a warm, friendly kind of smell, reassuring somehow. As if he belonged in that old overcoat in that old town. Part of the scenery, same as the cliffs and the caves. He spent most of his time on his allotment out on the hill, looking after his chickens, pushing a creaky barrow **29** up and down the lane. Once a month he and Andy Ham, the other town volunteer, would drive up to Budgworth for Fire Brigade training. Kept him out of mischief, out of people's way. Never found it necessary to say much to anyone. Great big bear of a bloke, must have been fifty or sixty but looked older. Weather-beaten and wrinkled. Worry lines, my mum called them. Worry? More like blind bloody panic, I'd say. There were all sorts of rumours about him, of course. Half the kids reckoned he was a child molester, the town strangler. He'd never touched me but he was a bloody-minded old cuss. He'd hardly nod to my mum and dad as they took me down to the Rec or anything. If I was alone I'd walk right on past him, but he didn't even seem to see me. Big bear of a bloke shambling along in his feisty old coat never mind the weather. Looked as if he needed a shave straight after he'd shaved, if you see what I mean. Could have seen his face in his shiny sleeves. His cheeks looked like cracked bindings of old books, his teeth discoloured and his hair rusty wire-wool, bristling from beneath a battered grey felt hat. His eyes always gave you a start. Amber and beady, just like his chickens. If you got close enough to look in them, though, they weren't mean or anything. Kindly, sad almost. Then he'd spot you and bristle up, ask you what you thought you were staring at. Rupert told me he hadn't offered as much as a bag of sweets although he hadn't seen his nephews since they'd been toddlers. Just ruffled his hair and said, 'Hello, young un,' something like that. All our bucolic country bullshit came as a bit of a shock to a big city kid like Rupert. He brought down all his toys, the latest High Street stuff. Johnny Seven, Action Man commander, the works. The fucking thing talked, for Christ's sake. I mean, our collections were obsolete, worthless junk.

We went home from Rupert's house with faces like fiddles, worried our parents. They thought maybe he was getting us on to drugs or something. Calling us country bumpkins, hayseeds. I didn't like it. Sounded too close to Fat Bastard to me. I'd never felt any great affinity for our part of the world anyway. I mean, you don't realize what you've got till it's gone, do you, especially at twelve. I think of countryside, think of farms round Clove and think of baling twine. Yeah, baling twine. The wretched stuff's everywhere. Farmers wouldn't be able to hang their gates or keep their trousers up without it. Their crappy fall-apart machinery would fall apart, the cattle would wander off just like the good bit in *Far From the Madding Crowd* when the dog chases the flock off the cliff. Yeah, that bit always sticks in my mind. Those daft sheep trotting over the edge to their deaths. Poor old Gabriel Oak. Wait till the others have shot each other dead and move in on the bird. A few years later they had us set our own essays for O-level English. Bathsheba Everdene was a fucking prick-tease, discuss. Roberts, I suppose you think you're above all this, nicely nippled Miss De Plechon wanted to know. I smirked back at her, me, I smirked a lot when I was sixteen. Reading Hardy – then and now – reminds me strongly of old Solomon. He was a farmer's son. Old Jubal had owned most of the hill one time, they named places after him, shook their heads and sipped their scrumpy, said there weren't many of his sort left. They still told stories about him down at the Blue Boar. Right old goat he must have been, snug there in his old rocker by the fire like Gaffer Gamgee and about as tall. God knows how he'd managed to father a strapping great bloke like Solomon. Must be something in the water, huh? I'd heard his mother had left Solomon with old Jubal some time during the War. Ran off with a Yank or something. Taken little Silas and upped sticks to Budgworth. Perhaps she'd gotten tired of Jubal's salt of the earth ramblings. Funny really, I mean, you stuck with your man through thick and thin in those days. To take the kid and scarper, well, she must have had a bloody good reason, no matter what my parents won't tell me. Rupert always clammed up if I tried to ask him about it.

'Listen, David, don't go quiet on me, OK?' Sam. I'd forgotten all about her. I'm standing bollock naked freezing my balls off, remembering.

'If you want to cry, cry.'

Where does she get this stuff? She must have been watching too many BBC2 plays. Sure, we were friends, we were friends before it all went wrong. Before we lost touch. Rupert, poor bastard, he'd lost touch with everything. I could see that the night they brought us in off the hill with our hair singed off. Up at the Institute they would do it for him these days. Sit him there in those turn-up trousers give him a quick Gulag flat-top and lead him back, docile and shorn like that Samson guy. They'd led him away that night, shaking, walking funny, staggering. I walked away. Walked away on my own two feet and stopped visiting him. Being with him was like it had been before, only he didn't talk. Never changed his faintly surprised expression once, the whole time I was there.

'Listen, if you want to call Dad, I know you two always got on.' Yeah, we'll chew over old times. The copper and the kid, just like the old days, eh? This woman down the line, down the lifeline from me. The times we had together. The times I'd watched her do all her personal things, washing her hair, waxing her legs. The way she'd chuck her head forward, uh uh uhhing as she came. I lived with her as long as I could stand it, as long as I could stand her missing him the way she did. She was my hollow victory, my joyless triumph. The winnings I could never spend. I'd won her fair and square, but only won half of her. I'd won her slinky hips, her thrusty tits, her mouth. I'd bought myself as many nights with her as I could handle without getting that sore feeling as if you've been kicked in the balls by a rhino. Trouble was with Sam, all the time I was there, I never got her mind, cornered her thoughts. She was always in an adjoining room. I could hear her moving about but I couldn't go in. She wouldn't let me, I didn't try that hard maybe. Laughing boy was in there with her, locked in comfy. And now he's dead. Gone for good, all the guilt, the nightmares. Yeah, well I'm getting there. We're getting there. I'm halfway back there, to tell the truth, it's all coming back, flooding back. I was halfway there when I'd woken up with cold balls listening for the bumps I'd already heard. Before we go right back though, I'd better mention the note. Make any coroner's eyes gleam, a good note.

'He left a note. David, do you want me to tell you . . .'

'Sure . . . go ahead.'

'He said he was tired of waiting. Might as well get it over with. No point in keeping her waiting,' she recites from memory. I wait for her, listen to her breathing.

'He says she's waiting for us, you and me, David.'

What did I expect? You get caught speeding, sooner or later the brown envelope's going to fall on your mat. She must be on something, she must be taking something to keep the hatches battened down like this. She must have taken some of her blues because if she hadn't she'd be howling like a banshee, like a little flicky-eyed goblin creature swallowing his own spit, just waiting to get me the way me and Rupert, the way me and Rupert

PICTURE THIS

got the painting. OK, stole the painting. It was a mistake, I knew it would be, no use trying to fool you. I said no, should have meant no, stuck to my guns. I should have walked off and left them to it. Only if I had left them to it, what would I have got? What would I have been? We started it. We woke the slumbering giants from their cold graves, raised them out of Hillstones, blasted them out of their catacombs the way they blast stones over in the quarry. All we did was steal the picture, the picture that was holding up all the weight, all the wrath of the hills and the stones, the long barrows and the circles. We didn't realize we were robbing a grave, looting a tomb. We thought we were playing games, up on the hill. Bony knees and flinty elbows wearing holes in the green mantel. Jutting crags, old skulls crowned with slippery scree. Cleaned and polished by the wind and the squalling rains. Hillstones. Because that's where we are, that's where all this shit went down, right in the heart of Hillstones. We live in the middle of the range, right down in the big split in its belly, Clove gorge. The hills march from the Dun Downs in the east forty miles to the sea, petering out westwards in a series of stone islands, seagull crowned. A vast green carpet caught in an immense door, ruckling and rippling across the belly of southern England. Cliffs overhanging picture postcard villages, sudden gaps in the beds of stone that seem to go all the way down to the vitals of the planet. People drive down from Budgworth and beyond, risk the traffic jams in the gorge, just to spoil people's picnics throwing themselves down the cracks. Let me tell you they never get any of those bodies back. They haven't got ropes long enough. Their lifelines don't stretch that far down into the nothingness. They leap off and hang like seagulls for a split second, then down they go, dashing themselves against the rocks like storm petrels lost in the mist, skimming the wavetops towards battleships. Blood and brittle feathers. Playing on those cliffs two million years before we'd have had some real fun, watching a great brown river sweep over the flatlands to the north to come up fast against the terrible wall of rock. Terrible but tottering. The hills came tumbling down and the mad brown water rushed in to wash the rocks away for ever. Crunching massive boulders like sherbert pips. Forming waterfalls which would have made Niagara Falls look like rain leaking through a hole in the guttering. Two million years on it's tired, relaxing. Meandering over the lowlands, bogs of sedge and shifting mires. Sliming the shallows where moorhens scuttle and herons spear minnows. Where frogs are legion, slimy buddhas. It's sulking now, this great river. It's had its day. No longer needs to force its passage down the gorge, it can take it steady, bubble and burble and talk to itself about the old days. It tinkles round boulders it could have tossed in its youth. The Kyle, it's called on maps. Clove Brook, we call it round here. The little trickle that wanders up to our bit of cliff. Perhaps that's why it ganged up on us, picked on us kids, all down the years. Picked on me like it picked on you, like it took your younger brother, took your little sister. Thought we should have worshipped it, like they worshipped it in the old days. The Mightylode, the Stonechewer, O Rio Magnifico. Kyle indeed. Maybe it decided to send us something, teach us some manners, a little respect. But hey, don't pick on me, Mightylode, Stonechewer. I could never bring myself to stand on the treacherous mossy rocks with the other boys, aiming arcs of urine into you. On my own, maybe with Rupert, I'd sit and stare into the dishwater-dead flow. I knew something far more dangerous than two-day-old Tizer flowed in your old veins, swirled in the sadly waving tentacles of weed, caught in the aimless current in the pool at the foot of the cliff. Where did it breed its fetid vapours, why was its breath so bad? From the moment I first splashed through it in my shiny Wellingtons, I knew something was wrong down there. No matter where I'd taken my nylon net I'd always managed to catch something. A bloodworm, a little water-boatman or a beetle with a tiny human face. Not a sausage. Not even an old Coke can. Just water that went cloudy in your jam jar and stringy weed like witches' hair pulled out of the plughole with stinky fingers. Looking over my shoulder from my quiet explorations I'd see the mist had sidled in over the gorge, tattered banners caught on spears of beech, ash, and elm. Twined round pikes of oak and sycamore. A cheerless dismal mist, drenched with flavours of old dustbins. As if the stream had been choked with corpses after some terrible battle and had never been able to pick the bones from its teeth. Clouds and mist packed down in the gorge like cotton wads thrust into the holes on sinking ships. As if the sky wanted to soak up the seepage, soak up the watery discharge. And Rupert and I were down there in amongst it more than most. It was our territory, Rupert with his funny name and notes to excuse him games and me with my weight. What a combination. He abided me, I abided him. His name, my weight, taboo subjects. He hated his name the way the river hated his.

Maybe that's why the stream let us run along its slippery banks without having them crumble in on us, send us with windmilling arms into its chilly embrace. The big boys who had more than enough imagination when it came to teasing me had a field day when Rupert arrived. He was Princess Rupert, our boy from the big city, pansy, patsy. It struck me as particularly pointless, teasing him about his background. I mean, his roots went as deep as ours. There had been Joneses on the hills since the Civil War. He had as much right to be there as any of us, as any of the old guard clipping hedges down in the village, regulation check shirt and hacking jacket. The stout brogue brigade. I suppose heavy duty footwear helps them keep their feet on the ground, keep things sensible. They get indoors and kick them off, maybe dance a little jig around their rooms, scare the Pekinese. Silas had itchy feet, just like his mother. Gone and gotten himself some of these here new-fangled qualifications. He dealt in water. Water was what he knew, he knew his business. Too little or too much.

Too acid, too alkaline. Water that ran all ways in our drainpipe gorge. Draining the high plains to the north, soaking the southern flatlands, sucking and splashing under a thin veil of mist. He'd come to help it on its way, a river midwife. Caused quite a deal of talk in Clove, Silas coming home. About as much as his mother's unexpected departure with him under her arm, thirty years before. Why the hell she do that, take Silas and leave Jubal and Solomon behind, toiling away on the hill? Anyway, he'd returned, he'd returned and he wanted his brother with him. There was nothing wrong with that.

DRIPS AND DRABS

Nothing wrong wanting your brother with you, after all that time apart. Whatever had split the family up Silas obviously wasn't worried about it, or he'd decided to bury the hatchet. Felt it was high time Solomon was rescued from the back room of the Boar. He'd been there years, ten, twenty at least. He'd come back from the allotments, from the chicken shack, have a meal in the back kitchen, then take his seat by the fire. He liked that seat, liked the crackle and snap of the pungent oak logs glowing orange in the seventeenth-century grate. Most people couldn't stand it so hot, couldn't stand the skin-stretching heat. Maybe he knew he'd be left alone, let alone as long as he stuck up close to the flames. Sometimes the tourists, ducking down under the beams, would stumble on him, crouched there steaming, staring. They'd imagine he was some kind of wood demon, some kind of local celebrity they could crush up against, take turns to be photographed with. He'd look up, study them with those bright beady amber eyes, turned damn near red in the fireside glow, until they took offence and stamped away, knocking their heads on the low beams as they went. He wasn't rude, never made trouble, but his face didn't fit. Did he lack something or know something? He had been in the same class at the town school, worshipped at the same chapel, fought in the Somerset Light Infantry during the war. Maybe there's a clue. I've heard my parents, relatives, mention him, then mention the war. Some woman, Margaret or something. These hill folk, they had long memories. They wouldn't talk to him, pretended he was part of the furniture up there by the grate. What had he done, desert, run away? Hide up in the hills till it was all over? I can't see it somehow. Up close you knew he wasn't going to back off from anything. He hadn't backed off when little Annie Duckett's grandfather had fallen asleep in his armchair after a particularly friendly evening at the Boar. Fallen asleep with his pipe smouldering in his lap. He'd gone up like a torch. Might as well have been drinking petrol, the stuff they brew round here. Set the house alight with little Annie asleep upstairs. By the time Andy and Solomon had arrived the whole place was going up. By all accounts Andy was for standing back playing a hose over the front until the brigade arrived from Budgworth. Not Solomon. He'd tugged up his scarf, wrapped that old coat about him and ploughed into the smoke billowing out of the front door. Up the stairs breathing hot soot, heavy tread through a rotten plank, hand down on the burning rail to steady himself, the narrow landing thick with the choking smoke. Kicking open doors till he spotted her smouldering teddy and huddled body. Tucked her under his coat, bear-hugged, and back the way he had come. He'd singed most of his hair and one eyebrow, flayed both his hands before blundering out into the blessed cool of the evening and the throng of folk with handkerchiefs held over their mouths. He had laid the girl carefully on a neighbour's bench and stood by as they crowded round to help. Billy Duckett had been away at a sale in Taunton. When he heard how Solomon had saved his daughter he bought him a drink. Walked over that invisible dividing line by the fire with a tumbler of whisky, placed it on the table in front of the old boy. Nodded and left him to it. Not a fucking word. Can you believe it? Solomon had looked up from his pint, nodded, and taken the drink. I got this in drips and drabs from various people. Like I said, Rupert would clam up if I asked too many questions about his funny uncle.

Come to think about it, Rupert didn't say much about anything. For friends I mean. Me and him, best mates. You see those American movies these days, all the little buddies discussing the meaning of life over a shake and a dirty book? You seen them too? Yeah, well Rupert and I weren't like that. We were different. It was like being alone with somebody else. I'd sprawl out on his floor reading comics while he tried to play 'Smoke on the Water' on his new guitar. He always had better stuff than me. We'd spend whole evenings at each other's houses, hardly say a word. People figured we were close, time we spent together. He abided me and I abided him, that was about it. I'd call him Root, he liked that. Made him sound like a bit of a slicker. He wouldn't call me fat, porky, or anything. I'm not too fat now, I'm quite thin. Well, not too fat. Our real playground was the allotments, the winding lane, the woods and the chicken shack. A low shed with high wire fencing all round, tacked to splintering wooden posts. Here Solomon supplemented his income with the occasional boiler and frequent baskets of warm brown double yolkers, feathers still stuck to the drying dung. You have never tasted eggs like it, I tell you.

He was more often than not the only person we'd see as we rode our Mustangs over the purple sage, hunted Tiger tanks in the frosty Ardennes. (Although I did have misgivings about calling it the Battle of the Bulge. I looked at him when he suggested it, to make sure he wasn't taking the piss, but he was already assembling his plastic Schmeisser, so maybe he wasn't.) We'd sit in the wrecked old car, Fort Sahara, and pick off Tuaregs as they milled round impotently. It was an early Austin, pre-War, my dad said. Which war, I asked? He'd given me one of his looks. The doors had gone, so had the wheels. It had rusted into the brambles a hundred yards from the pylon. Rupert said once it had belonged to Solomon before the War. What, a farm labourer in a car like that? He said sure, he'd crashed it and never bothered to move it. The gorge had plenty of momentos of the old man. The car, the shack, and down in the middle of the gorge, right down in the dingliest part of the dell, their old cottage. Jubal had raised his eldest there after his mother had left. Farmed the hills where they'd built our estate. Must have been a regular hive down there once. Now it was locked and barred. The stone walls long neglected had collapsed under an onslaught of ivy. Our patrols often led us way down there in the wild wood where the trees and bushes seemed to be rising up trying to blot out evidence of human habitation. It was only minutes away from the main road, minutes from our dirty great estate, and yet you could have been in another world. Fallen though some hole in time, come out in Fairy Land. Not that we stuck to the road. We had our shortcuts, our tunnels. We'd dash out of our garden into the lane, whooping like Comanches. Dodge PC Bell as he manhandled his heavy Polish motorbike out of his garage. Over a broken stile and past two rows of old dustbins where the men put their garden refuse, thin trails of blue smoke bitter on the sweet breath of the hill. The warm stench of the chicken farm. Over another lane and down the slope, shot here and there with wild chicory, oniony smells. Under the boughs, through the brambles, we'd spent the best part of a summer cutting that tunnel. Our escape route from the outside world. From shouting adults and big kids with sticks and stones to break our bones. Solomon had come close to catching us down there by the cottage, came close but never caught us. He never told, but he glowered at us. He'd cornered us once sitting in the old wreck. Crept up on us like a hairy old spider. He'd shaken his fist, clutching the stiff yellow legs of a dead chicken, a necklace of rubies wound around its throttled throat feathers.

'Have you two been down my cottage again? There's a board missing,' he'd growled, thrusting his great leonine head in through the door-frame. I noticed his discoloured teeth, as if he chewed tobacco, something like that. I'd been in the driving seat for once. I leaned back, away from his feral breath.

'Just stay clear. Those tiles could come off at any moment. You could be killed, and who'd get the blame again?' He stared at Rupert, then me, then thumped the top of the car. It felt as if we'd been torpedoed. We watched him trudge off down the lane toward the main road. Rupert sighed.

'He won't tell. Hardly says a thing. Dad's beginning to wish we'd left him at the Boar.'

'I can't understand why he wanted to be cooped up down there anyway,' I said cautiously, 'not when he had the chance to live down in his own cottage.'

He gave me a quick glance, knew I was fishing for details

again. Ignored me. 'Tomorrow morning then, seven sharp. Battle of the Bulge.'

Was he taking the piss again or what? I took a quick peek at him, the skinny bastard, as he climbed out of the car, loped off after his uncle.

'Seven sharp,' I said to his back.

TOMMY GUNS

Our back lane leads to a row of garages behind the last houses on the hill. Rupert trotted along at the appointed time and I left my lookout post at the back window picking up my gloves and replica Kalashnikov. Replica sounds better than toy, doesn't it? I suppose it amounts to the same thing though, really. I close the door quietly behind me, Mum and Dad still asleep in bed. We're off. Doubling past the ratty hedge that divides lane from allotment. Brambles and bushes loaded with the last of the season's fruit, food for the thrushes. The rutted lane bends around the garages where we normally pause to catch our breath. They are all shut down now. Left open they remind us of Spitfire hangars or U-boat pens. It struck me the other day that if we climbed up on to the roof we could look straight into the back rooms of the nearest houses. I mean, we could play snipers or something. If we lay there long enough, quiet enough, we'd maybe catch a glimpse of Samantha Bell, the policeman's daughter. She goes to school with us. Maybe we'd catch a glimpse of her in her Scooby Doo pyjamas, the ones I've spotted on their washline.

It's so early the mist is still shredded over the floor, cast-off costumes of night things. It rises slowly from the water butts alongside the allotments. The only other time I get up this early is to go fishing with Dad, out on the moor. That's spooky enough, watching the sun rise over the hills, the mist spilling out over the fields and the cows blundering about, lowing quietly. Big wide pungent river, bright red float nosing through the green waters, maggots in a small green container, crawling over each other as they crawl under each other. Rupert hates fishing, won't touch maggots. He's looking at me now, giving me one of those superior stares. 'You should have brought your Tommy gun,' he whines. It's too small for me.

'It's broken,' I lie. If he starts going on I'll leave him to it, I've got better things to do than wandering about making funny noises with a plastic gun. I stare at the silver pylon, dripping in the morning mist, dew glistening on the drooping cables, the Martian legs. Crackling and humming to itself. When we were younger we'd run beneath the spread legs and pretend to fall into other worlds. We got too big for that around the time we graduated from *The Hobbit* to *Lord of the Rings*, from that to *Dune*. The chickens are waiting for their first feed, you can hear them humming like an old fridge in the still air. Humming and clucking until Solomon pulls back the rickety gate and lets them out into their wired run, red earth scored by hundreds of horny chicken feet.

'It's no use bringing a Kalashnikov if we're doing the Battle of the Bulge, is it?' he asks, smarmy face and floppy hair. I could do him sometimes, going on.

'So we'll do Vietnam,' I suggest. I'm more than tempted to go AWOL, stick there listening to him moan all morning. What difference does it make which plastic toy I lug about? Rupert frowns. He's gazing up at the back windows of the houses. Something's gone wrong with our games lately. When the other kids go bird-nesting or something I'd rather be lounging about or kicking a football. Yeah, guess what? Rupert hates football. The big kids won't usually let me play, not unless they're short. Fuck off fat bastard, you see the advantages of running about up to your Wellies in the stream pretending to be cut off behind SS lines. I look up, follow his gaze. The badly painted council houses are hung with cheap bright curtains. Look like a row of chocolate boxes. If we climbed on that oil drum we could lie flat and spy on them. I'm about to suggest it when I spot his eyes flicker back along the row. I look over my shoulder just in time to see Samantha Bell pull her curtains open as if she was in a TV advert for breakfast cereal. You should see her hair, it's all over the place. She's spotted us. Lounging by the stile, sawn-off urban guerrillas. Pokes her tongue out and pulls her curtains to again.

'She'll tell her dad we've been spying on her,' Rupert says, shouldering his replica US Army carbine and vaulting over the stile easily. I clamber on over and fall in behind him, wondering if her dad will tell our parents. We were looking, is all. By the time we've crossed the lane and ducked down through the tunnel our jeans are soaked. We slide down into the stream, stand there enjoying it a moment. It's really misty down here, down in the crack of the gorge. It's like dry ice, sidling round us, swallowing us up. We move off like timber wolves, listening out for the tell-tale squeal of tracks, the hoarse shouting of the Panzer Grenadiers. Despite the realistic weather though, our Ardennes adventure is no more successful than Hitler's. Rupert straightens up first, carbine hanging. 'Bollocks to this,' he says.

'Bang, you're hit,' I say half-heartedly. He ignores me, clambers up the bank, flops down on the mossy tumbledown wall round Solomon's orchard. I drag myself up next to him, hold the Kalashnikov between my knees and rub my hands together.

'We must be getting too old for it,' I suggest. He raises an eyebrow, could mean anything.

'What else could we do?'

'Dungeons and Dragons.'

'Did that Tuesday.'

'What about the Rec? Martin Lawrence might be down there with that lot.' Rupert doesn't like Martin Lawrence. I don't like him much either come to that.

'He's just another big mouth,' Rupert says. I nod. He's right. If we were like Martin Lawrence we'd be heaving rocks at the cottage there, knocking tiles from the roof, sticking matches through the cracks in the planking over the windows. Rupert is staring moodily at the old place, contemplating some mischief. Solomon's abandoned home. Hard to think of his family doing chores, relaxing, laughing. Hard to think of them laughing down here.

'Let's go in.'

That's it. That's what I was telling you about. I could have stood up, washed my hands of the whole business. Then where would I have been, eh? On my bloody own, that's where. He glances round at me, smiles a little.

'Come on. Let's have a look.'

I could have left him to it, could have walked away. He couldn't make me, couldn't blame me. I could have walked off and left him to it.

'Come on, he's not even fed the chickens yet. Won't be around for ages.' He's keen now, his green eyes as bright as marbles. I'm still not sure, in two minds about it. My dad's easy-going most of the time, but petty breaking and entering; I'd be in deep shit if we got caught.

'He'll not even notice we've been in, if we're careful,' he encourages me, getting to his feet. His eyes are flicking over the cottage. I glance about. The green trees, shrouded with mist, the pylon on the cliff above rising out of the murk like the crow's nest of a sunken battleship at low tide. He gives me a tap with his trainer.

'Come on, you're not scared, are you?' Getting pretty near 'You're not scared, you fat bastard,' I think. I can see the words piling up in his mouth, can almost hear them scrambling over his tongue, wanting to get out. I can—

'Hey! What you doing?' I practically fall off the wall, slip and bark my shin on a fallen stone. Rupert crouches, looks upstream. Samantha Bell has somehow managed to man-handle her bike down the path leading from the main road. Through the tangled undergrowth, over broken-down old logs. She must have gone the long way, down the hill, and then turned along the path by the bridge. She struggles along cluthing the red grip handlebars. Her hair is in a bob. I used to like it when she had it long but the bob gives her a tomboy, impish appearance. She and Lorraine Lamb sit three rows in front of us. You can see the little hairs curling on the back of her neck. She leans the bike against the wall and wipes her hands on her jeans. We're too astonished to speak so she gives us a good look, nose in the air.

'What are you up to then, breaking in?'

'What are you spying on us for?' Rupert is the first to recover but he's already on the defensive.

'I thought you two were spying on me,' she says archly. I'm sure she's not been down here before. How did she get the bloody bike over the fence? We've never thought of bringing our bikes down here.

'Why are you playing down here anyway, why don't you go down the Rec?' In the summer the playground is full of day trippers. The big kids go down there to smoke fags, kick cans, crucial stuff like that.

'We weren't spying on you,' I say. I can feel myself blush as soon as I've said it. Girls can detect a blush through a crash helmet, I reckon.

'Yes, you were,' she snaps. 'You always do. Every time you go down the lane you look back, I've seen you do it.'

Rupert and I exchange looks.

'We don't like the Rec. All those kids,' says Rupert, picking up a stone and throwing it at the boarded windows of the cottage. Makes a sort of hollow thump. I don't like it, stuck here with her.

'Perhaps you prefer playing soldiers,' she simpers.

'We were wargaming,' Rupert says. She's not interested in the terminology.

'Are you breaking in then, or what?' she asks him.

'We'd tell you? You'd tell your dad.'

'Well, what are you doing? Looks pretty suspicious the way you two flit about. My dad says he's going to follow you one day, see what you get up to.' We are struck dumb by the chilling prospect. She notices the way we look at one another. She must be watching us all the time. It had never struck me before people could know as much about us as we knew about them.

'Why don't you go on down the Rec then,' Rupert challenges, still trying to shake her off.

'At this time, you must be joking. I normally sleep till ten anyway.' Rubbish. She feeds her rabbits at 7.30 a.m., just before the milkman comes. I've seen her.

'Well, go back to bed and leave us alone,' he says.

She pouts. 'Think you're clever, Prince Rupert?' Weighing up some fat boy insults for me too, I bet.

'Cleverer than most of the pricks in our class,' he answers.

Samantha's one of the brighter ones too, so she knows this isn't aimed at her. It's a sort of peace offering. He's being nice to her. I'm lost. She changes tack.

'You go in, I'll come in with you,' she offers. Her voice drops to a whisper. 'My dad says he died in there, Old Jubal.'

I stare at Rupert. If I'd said it he would have slunk off home in a sulk. Instead he shrugs, looks as if it doesn't bother him. I peep at the locked cottage as if Jubal could appear at any moment, tilt his cap back over his eyes to study the clouds scudding up over the hill.

TWO BOYS, ONE GIRL

'Scared of ghosts, David?' It's the first time she's called me by my first name, to my face.

'First I've heard about it, Jubal died in there,' I grate, trying to look as unruffled as possible. Old Jubal died in there, in that horrid place?

'Jubal always said he'd been born there, he'd die there. So Dad says,' Rupert chips in. 'My nan left in the war. Took my dad to live in Budgworth.' Tell me something I don't know.

'She ran away with her lover?' We're both shocked. I mean, old people, doing it. That.

'I didn't hear anything about any lover,' says Rupert stiffly. Me neither.

'They weren't getting on. They decided to split up, Solomon stayed with my gramper, Nan took Dad.' There's got to be more to it though. We're talking Somerset, 1940 something. Country folk didn't just agree to differ like a bunch of Kensington Bohemians, for Christ's sake. Samantha sits on the wall, Wellingtons swinging forwards and backwards. She looks gorgeous. I'm still blushing.

'David could be the lookout, we could go in through the window,' she suggests. 'Those boards don't look too secure.'

'There's no need for that, we'd spot anybody coming up.' As soon as I'd opened my big mouth I knew I'd put my foot in it.

'Well, you didn't spot me, did you, Davy Crockett?' Sam's on to me like a flash. Rupert giggles. There. I told you. They're already ganging up on me. I'll be forced out. He likes her. Look how he keeps glancing at her, swinging his hair out of his eyes. Trying to squeeze me out. That settled it, right there and then.

'We'll all go in. Move the bike behind the wall,' Rupert says. She hurries round, wheeling the bike behind the tumbledown stones. Into the orchard. Solomon would have known it neat, clipped. Ewes and lambs and Granny Smiths falling.

'Come on, it'll be a laugh,' Rupert says. A new excitement in his bright green eyes. I can remember him so clearly. I hated him a little then, because Samantha liked him more than me. It was obvious. Body language, looks. She reacted to him, waited for him. I was their shadow, bulging, misshapen. I walked off, they both stopped, watching me. I climbed over the fallen stones and strode up the overgrown path as if I was posting a letter. Picked up a broken bough and snapped it over my knee. Got it in behind those planks and yanked them off. I suppose it was my anger, my resentment, all boiling up in me. Could have towed a bus out of the stream just then. I could hear them coming up behind me. The loose boards were cracking, bucking under the pressure as I jemmied the bough under, rammed it home, levering rotten wood and rusty nails. I stood back and let the foul air flow out. Dust motes settled in the cold air. I peered inside. The kitchen, as it had been left. Cupboard doors hanging drunkenly on rusty hinges. Enamel pots leaning on sloping shelves, everything coated in a shag-pile of grey dust. The pile of green and grey velvet must have been a loaf of bread once.

'Bloody hell.'

'It stinks,' Samantha says, holding her pretty nose. I'd have held it for her. Her nails are painted pink. The sink is ancient. An old handle rises out of a pile of cracked crocks. Jubal's washing-up. All cracked and crooked, draped in filthy webs.

'Are you going in or not?' She nudges me, I pull my belly tighter. I still do it now, anybody touches me. D.B. coming out of the icy green depths, clutching my face mask, turning off my oxygen taps. She's choking off my air supply but I'm throwing out my chest and sucking in my gut. Got to be at my best, when she comes calling in my dreams. Christ, that room, its life cut off so suddenly. Her fragile fingerprints were all over the place, if I'd known where to look, known who I was looking for. I'd stopped dead in my tracks, peering into the dark depths. Rupert shoulders me aside. His head is swallowed by the shadows as he springs up and jack-knifes into the room. Samantha looks at me.

'I'll help you up,' I offer.

'It's OK.' She copies Rupert, folds herself into the room like a little gymnast. I get my belly over the ledge and heave myself in. The floor is disgusting, dry and wet at the same time. Smells awful. Rupert steadies me and I hate the skinny bastard for it, hate him so hard I want to run my hand on a rusty nail, tear my skin open. Teach myself a lesson. Sam has moved off into the murk. A small flight of steps up into the main room. Stone jars are stacked against the peeling whitewash along the right-hand wall. I bend over one of them and poke a finger into the mushy cork stopper. Something hisses through the powdery blockage and I back off. Rupert's nose wrinkles in disgust.

'What the hell's that? Didn't they have an outdoor toilet?'

I've seen jars like these in the cellar at the Blue Boar. 'Scrumpy,' I say triumphantly. 'They probably brewed their own.' There's enough here to blind an army. The best stuff's almost clear, just a breath of pissy colour. My dad had a bottle once. I stood shaking it one day, making all the little itty bits swirl about like one of those snowstorm-in-a-jar jobs. Damn near blew his head off. Sam's not interested in my apple juice archaeology.

'It's all furnished. All his stuff's here,' she says, picking her way into the Tutankhamen-period lounge. We press behind her, look round the cramped room with its low ceiling, thin beams of light filtering through the cracks in the boards. Looks like a bloody hobbit hole, only the windows are square, planked up. People must have been smaller in those days. Had such big families too. There is a window to our left with a small bench pushed underneath as if someone was fond of sitting there watching the stream go by. Next to the window the front door, smothered with planking, rusty nails protruding like some Dark Age cavalry trap. Light bores in through the holes where the nails have given up the ghost. The facing wall is bare grey plaster, lighter squares where the pictures hung. Scratches and tears up in the top corner as if something had got itself trapped, wanted out. We stood there staring up, D.B. leans in over my shoulder, pale reflection on my green screen, turns slowly, mocking leer. All her own work, we didn't know shit. We figured whatever it was had gotten trapped, probably dropped down dead in the corner by the smell of it. Warm, fruity. There, she's shaken her head, wagged a long white finger, eased herself back into the flowery wall-paper. Soon as I finish that stuff's coming off and I'll paint the room white. No corners, no hidey holes here. The rickety stairs climbed steeply to the pitch blackness upstairs. There is no way on earth you'll get me up there, clippity cloppity crash. An overturned armchair, guts blossoming through rusty springs. A Welsh dresser, drawers pulled out and plates cracked. The whole lot is covered in at least an inch of dust. We stir up little eddies as we pad about. A sneezy shagpile. I glance at Samantha. We could grab her and shag her on it. She's looking at the fireplace, coals grey with dust. A poker stands in a bucket of fossilized ashes.

'How old was your gramper?' Samantha asks him.

'Must have been at least eighty,' Rupert says. 'Solomon didn't go to the War until he was about twenty. I don't think he stayed too long afterwards.'

After what?

'If you cleared it up it would be quite nice,' she says. She's found a small photograph or something on the mantelpiece. I look over her shoulder, get a whiff of her. She smells nice in all this dirt. She's found a small watercolour. Ballet dancers. '*Swan Lake*,' I say. She looks round, she's close to me. Smiles a bit. Smiles for the first time.

'It looks like it. This green one . . . that's the horrible one, isn't it?' Like we're a couple of critics in the middle of some gallery. I wrack my brains but I'm not too hot on watercolours. The *Mona Lisa*'s about my limit when it comes to art. If I could have thrown in some details, if I could have come up with a name, I could have got one over on smarmy Rupert, looking down his nose at it as if it's on the tip of his tongue too. I'll find out, I'll look it up, beat the bastard to it in case he's thinking the same as me.

'Fancy that old man having something like this. Do you think it's worth much, then?' I take it from her. The frame is heavy, looks like tarnished gold. It is covered in tiny etchings, leaves twined all around the picture as if they are growing out of the foliage in the background. It's beautiful, anybody can see that. I go to replace it on the shelf but she takes it back, gives me a little look. Hey, if it was mine, I'd give it to you. Maybe she wants to dig up some details too, beat the both of us. Rupert has wandered away, looking at the marks in the ceiling. Some bird or something must have hung there upside-down, clung on with its claws and scratched like mad. Right up in the top corner there.

'Rats,' is Rupert's verdict. I look around nervously. Winston Smith's got nothing on me when it comes to rats. Give me a grip just looking at their horrid tails. Samantha shivers. She tugs her ski-jacket tighter round her as if they are going to start popping out of the beetled woodwork.

'What, they put a ladder up, did they?' I ask him, regaining a little confidence. A little bit more each second. I'm in there, hanging in there. They've not got rid of me yet.

'What else was it, then?' he asks sharply, sticking his bony chin out a little. We gaze at the claw-marks. Horrible. Frenzied. Something wanted out of here pretty bad. The bare grey stone beneath the shredded plastering is rent with white marks. A shadowy arm flexes in the wallpaper, long fingers lost in the flowery fronds. I remember Samantha standing there, picture clutched to her tiny chest, grinning at us.

'Nobody's going to miss it,' she says.

I shake my head. Oh no. 'Solomon will,' I tell her.

Rupert shrugs his thin shoulders. 'Let her have it,' he says easily. 'I don't suppose he's got an inventory or anything.' I glare at him.

'Someone walks into your room, takes your Bowie poster down and you won't notice?'

'He hasn't been in here for years,' Rupert chides. 'Don't be such a wally.' It's like all this dust is turning to quicksand, sucking us all in.

'We could hammer the boards up, he'd never know we'd been in,' Samantha says, does a little jump of delight making the dust eddy round her Wellies. He smiles at her, Mr Cool. So that's what we did. They sent me running home to get a hammer from Dad's shed while they looked around. By the time I had returned Rupert had tried the stairs and put his foot straight through a board, given himself a nice nasty little cut. She was dabbing it with her handkerchief. He was making a meal out of the whole thing. I could just picture her holding him, staunching the blood. She presses the hanky to her lips. Any minute she's going to drop to her knees and lick the bloody cut for him. Kneel at his feet, run her tongue over his smooth skin. I twitch a bit, glance round for those nails again, wonder about running myself in on one. It'll hurt. I hop from foot to foot, itching to be out of there.

'There's some meat under a net thing in the kitchen. It's so old it doesn't even smell bad,' she announces, still clutching the painting to her boobs. Now she's had her present. Rupert winces to his feet, flexing his knee. She's all nice now, nice as pie now she's got her precious present. It's a waste of time arguing now. Those two against me. I wonder if they've been kissing or something while I was running for the hammer.

Perhaps he had tried to get her to go up in the dark with him. Fallen through. Served him right. Maybe Rupert was right, though. Solomon didn't go into the cottage. Just checked the boards now and again. Samantha could have her picture, he'd never know. We got out of there and nailed the planks back on the rotten window frame, then I tugged them back a bit.

'Forgotten something?' Rupert asks.

I pick up a handful of dirt, peeled paint, powdered rust, rub it over the shiny nails, freshly splintered wood.

'He's going to smell a rat if he checks it out, finds it's nailed up tighter than Fort Knox,' I say. Crafty little bastard, see? They thought I was thick, I was already thinking ahead. Looking so far ahead, looking back now.

'They were loose when we arrived. They're loose now.' I glance at Sam. She looks pretty impressed. 'Let's cover our tracks in the dirt,' she says. It wouldn't take an Apache to work out three kids in boots had been scuffling about here.

We fetch sticks and brush our way back up the path. Samantha collects her bike. She must have stuffed the painting down her jumper. She tugs the handlebars free from a grasping bramble.

'Come on over if you like, we'll play some records,' she says, manhandling the machine down the track. She hurries off and we watch her bright ski-jacket disappear into the greenery.

'I saw her first, Fatso,' he says. Yeah, that's what he said all right. And now he's dead.

'David . . . you still there? You all right?'

'Yeah, I'm here. You OK? You handling things all right?'

'I know you said . . . can you . . . I mean, can we can meet, just for a drink? Drink would be nice, we could talk. We need to talk.' It's demands already she's making.

'Sam, you know what I said last time.'

'Jerry's in Milan till Thursday. I really need to talk. I'm sure Kitty wouldn't mind.'

'It's Kaz.'

'Sure. Kaz. I'm sure she wouldn't mind.'

'I've told you.'

'Maybe you could give Whiteman a ring. We could talk to him, talk it through.' What the hell do I want to talk to him for? I spent six bloody months talking to that bastard. He was hoping to deliver a paper on us, the three screwy kids who used to hang around the wacky gorge. Make a real name for himself. All he ever did was shake his head and doodle in the margin of his notebook. He told my parents once he thought we'd all been doing mushrooms. Found a big stash down in the dingly old dell and zonked out on the stuff. Magic fucking mushrooms. Yeah, can you believe it? I had to prove him wrong, try them one time. Like drinking ten pints of lager only your senses were sharpened, not dulled. You could tune in to people's conversations, see things happening you wouldn't see otherwise. Like I tuned in to Whiteman one time, telling my parents just behind the door, 'I really don't think there is anything wrong with him medically, but then, you can never be sure after such a hurried diagnosis.' He didn't see much wrong with Rupert either, and Mistah Rupert, he dead.

IN CHURCH

Five days after her call, five days after I'd woken up listening for the bump that was going to wake me, I watch Samantha climb out of Jerry's red BMW. Yeah, she's looking good. Lost a little weight, makes the most of her elegantly cut black suit, stockings, small black hat and short veil. Can hardly see the girl's eyes at all as I stand, awkward as ever, to shake hands. Funny really, shaking hands with someone you've done just about everything with. I mean, some of those videos you can get, I wouldn't want to do anything like that. Some of that nasty stuff. The mouth moves under the veil, red shape under smudgy eyes.

'You didn't ring,' she says quietly. Her boyfriend, Jerry, smart in his Italian-cut suit, lingers at her elbow looking round the countryside, taking it all in.

'What could I do?' I'm already apologizing. 'I wasn't any good to you before, why should I be now?'

'Just to talk, that would have been help enough,' she says shortly, looking away over the church wall, the clump of willows and the fields beyond. Behind the wall, behind the fields, the grey slopes of the gorge, a giant with his arms flung about us, hemming us all in, all these birds who want to fly off and hide. Here's her father. Police Sergeant Malcolm Bell. Puffy pale face, shiny and neat in his best uniform. Strides up and clenches his daughter to him like an emotional wrestler. He nods at Jerry, nervously passing his keys from hand to hand, then me.

'Good drive down then, Jerry?'

'Pretty good.' Doesn't say much, does Jerry. Kind of like the guy. He knows this is none of his fucking business for sure. This is her old life, all he took her away from. Cured her with daily doses of money. The mourners are drifting around to the front of the small Norman church, opposite the Rec we never used to play in. Rupert's mother is being supported by a friend, Silas having died several years ago. Unlucky kind of family, you'd have to say it. He'd died on the job, if you see what I mean. Had a heart attack down at the Axeheads Reservoir taking water samples. Clutched his chest and toppled in. One minute he's beavering away with a test tube, the next he's floating belly up like a dead roach. They dragged him out by one of the main water filters. Rupert was in no state to care by then, but his mother took it hard. Kind of ground her down even more. She was all broken up inside when Rupert went first time, a cup dropped on a stone floor, never quite the same even though all the pieces had been stuck back together.

'He's alive,' she'd screamed at me when they'd brought us in off the hill. I hadn't actually heard her, but I could see her mouth forming the words in strings of spit. That night they'd smothered us in blankets and pressed mugs of hot soup against our blistered lips. I'd nodded, eyes streaming with all the smoke and the soot, as the ambulance men hauled her away by the elbows. I hadn't told her what I'd been thinking, that I'd seen more life in a dead roach bobbing in the shallows of a reservoir. You could tell, one quick look at his eyes as he stumbled along beside me, picked out in the torchbeams. Staggering away from the glow in the gorge. She tugged away, hunched over him as they folded him on a stretcher, dragged another blanket over him. Now she was going to hunch over his coffin, cry some more. Cry reservoirs full of dead roach. Bell nods again, and takes Jerry by the arm, leading him away from us and into the hushed church, hunched over its quiet brood of gravestones. Samantha stops me.

'You could have rung.' Earnest, determined now Jerry's slipped inside the cool vaulted doorway. I shake my arm free. 'I wasn't asking much.' Oh, yes you were, way too much. You were asking me, inviting me back down the gorge, inviting me to roll down the slope, right back in there. She tries to handle things from the outside, lets all her feelings out and then rushes round trying to rein them all back in again. I keep things tight. Right up close, close to my chest. My arm on her shoulder can't help what's going on in her head. It didn't then, it won't now. The blurred blue eyes film over so much I can barely make them out. I don't like the veil, I'd rather see her eyes, see how she's taking it. She looks away again. Her high heels crunch the gravel as she walks ahead of me into the church. I'm about to follow her on in when another suit slips alongside me. I look round, recognize the face. He's smaller, no, I'm bigger. Two feet bigger. His hair is grey, nicely cut. Let me introduce you to Dr Arnold Whiteman, yeah, the one I told you about. I find myself shaking hands with him while my mind flicks through his file. Remembers. Remembers all those moments. Strung together, taken apart as if my thoughts were bits of Lego.

'David, you're looking well.' I raise my eyebrows, smile a little.

'You were with him . . . at the end.' At the end. The language of the funeral parlour. When he hanged himself. Topped himself. Pinched a sheet from some careless auxiliary's trolley and got out of it.

'Total catatonia. Failed to respond to any stimulus, chemical or electrical. He took us all in, I'm afraid. I saw him every day, you know.' He looks over his shoulder, nods toward a heavy looking bloke in a shiny suit who's hanging about the car park. 'If I were you I wouldn't say anything about . . . the case to chummy there.' I recognize him now. It's Fish, that reporter feller. Let me tell you about this guy. He smiles a little, nods. I nod back. I remember him. Oh yes, I remember Mr Fish. Whiteman sighs.

'You would have thought he'd have the decency to leave the family alone at this time,' Whiteman says. Whiteman, he's got chips on his shoulder a mile wide about old Nicky. It's funny, if you looked quickly we could almost be cousins. He's coming over.

'David, I want to tell you, we did our best for him. I may not have been much help to Rupert, to either of you come to that. If you do feel you'd like to talk things over though, give me a call. I'm usually up at the Institute. Now if you'll excuse me?' He nods and stalks off into the church. Fish comes over like a bad smell, looks awkward. It's almost like looking in a mirror only he's ten years older. He's about the same size as me, same hair, similar eyes. We always saw eye to eye, Nicky Fish and me. His suit's too tight, he pulls it about a bit, making himself comfortable.

'What did he say, not to talk to me?'

'What's there to talk about?'

'How it happened,' Fish says, raising his eyebrows.

'He got hold of a sheet, tied it over a door, and hanged himself,' I say. He nods, rubs his chin. He could have shaved. 'That's what they said up at region. But how'd it happen? You were mates, you want to know.' Do I?

'Look . . . the ceremony's about to start . . .'

'Sure, sure. Just going through the motions. No offence meant.' He says it flatly, as if he didn't give a shit whether I took offence or not.

'Still on the *Clarion*, then?'

Now he looks a bit put out. Nods. 'Still on the *Clarion*.'

'I saw you on the TV, everything.'

'They didn't like my face.'

'Well . . . anyway . . . see you about.' I turn to go into the church.

'There was a note,' he calls. I stop.

'There was a note . . . wasn't there?' he asks. He's fishing. 'I mean . . . I wondered if it shed any light on your . . . little escapade down in the gorge?' Man's got a cheek, mind.

'You'd better speak to Whiteman about it,' I say.

'Only the Coroner didn't read it at the inquest on Tuesday.'

'They don't usually read notes for the benefit of the press.'

'Did it mention anything in particular?'

'This and that.' I leave him to it, hopping from foot to foot as the breeze picks up, picks up speed along the gorge. I wander on in with the rest of them.

PRINCE BURNING

Whiteman had sketched out his game plan the day they took us up to Budgworth, up to the Institute. He told me straight away, you can't be cured unless you face up to what you've done. OK, I told him what I'd done. What we'd done. Stolen the painting. I came straight out with it, told the police, told Whiteman, just like I've told you. We stole a picture from the old cottage. So chop off my hands, feed them to the sniffer dogs you had nosing over the hill, searching out our hidey-holes. I knew they couldn't just send me back to school, wash their hands of me. I knew there would have to be some kind of treatment, for my own good and all that. I knew they couldn't just let things slide. I mean, you can't have kids missing games because they'd spent the morning hanging out with water witches, could you? This creep, worse than witchy Whiteman, holding on to me like that. Shaking hands with him, a piece of wet fish, squid fingers. Leading me along like I'm one of his lunatics, has to be helped along to the lavatory. We take our places in the pews, which are surprisingly full considering the limited social intercourse Rupert's been enjoying lately. Wasn't exactly open house up there, was it? Must have been a popular kind of cabbage. The Reverend Reginald Lamb thinks so. Way he goes on, you'd imagine he'd actually met the poor bastard. He concludes Rupert had wandered from his path, but had now been gathered unto God. Amen to that. You wouldn't like to think of him stuck in the stream for ever with her, would you? You wouldn't wish that on your worst enemy, am I right? Sorry if I'm rambling. I mean, it's pretty hard to remember all of it, all that happened. Some of it I only got second-hand, some third-hand. I even believed the things I read in the papers about it, realized with a sort of shocked resentment they were talking about me. Everything filtered through someone else's memory, sieved through their own complex web of emotions, reasons, hang-ups. Bit like me really, sieving all this before I write it down. Way I figure it, though, I'd better be straight with you otherwise you'll be taking their side against me. You'll take their word for it. Reverend Lamb bleats a final goodbye, and we watch the shiny coffin slide under the velvet curtain. I hate the stuff, gives me goose flesh. We file out into the watery sunshine, breaking through the cloud cover as the wind rustles on up the gorge. Trying not to look up at the tall smokestack, the crematorium they've built behind the church. Belching what's left of Rupert out on the breeze. I turn my collar up and aim for my car, spotting Fish in his battered Cortina reading a music paper. Whiteman's trotting alongside, hair ruffling in the wind.

'If you'd like to talk about it, maybe make an appointment.'

Sounds like he wants to double-glaze my mind. Does he want me to like him or something? He stops by his Jaguar, wipes a grain of soot from the bonnet. A little bit of Rupert, Prince Burning. Is he worried I'm going to blab to Fish, make some complaints, call for an inquiry? Try and find out how a patient who hadn't moved of his own free will for fifteen years and more managed to top himself? Top himself in the secure unit of the local psychiatric hospital? No wonder old Fish is sticking around. Way I remember it the regional health authority were ready to sue his ass last time. You just can't keep a good man down. Maybe he thinks if he sticks around long enough he'll spot me throttling Whiteman. He gave up on Rupert, we all did. Wouldn't you? Wouldn't you have had something better to do? All Whiteman wanted to know about was the sex angle. Tried to find it from the first day we were in there. Had we. Had they. Could I. Couldn't I? He couldn't get much out of Samantha. She'd crack up and bawl as soon as he flicked his notebook open. Besides, her dad was a copper with connections in Budgworth. What a surprise, she gets packed home to rest after a week or two. Rupert, well, I wasn't the only one who figured there was no one home. That left me.

My parents were too much in awe of Whiteman and the rest of them to protest. He was the doctor, must be right. I had been playing up after all. The business with the chicken and then the teacher. So they ordered a full check, a psychiatric assessment.

'To be honest, Doctor, I think I've had enough talk.' I'm not rude or anything, but he bristles up straight away, just like he used to when I was a kid.

'You never could accept that we were just trying to help you, could you?' he says curtly. 'You know, in a way you were worse than Rupert. He'd gone from all of us, but you . . . you didn't change, and you haven't changed now. There was always so much anger in you.' He thinks better of whatever he was going to say. I fish for my keys.

'I was sorry to hear about you and Samantha. Do you see much of her?'

'Not much. She travels around a little.'

'And you've stayed here.'

I nod, shrug.

'Ahh, Mrs Jones.' He looks round me as Rupert's mother is guided along the path by her friends, Italian crones in some gangster movie. She hasn't spoken to me since the night they brought us in and I'm not betting on her rushing into my arms now.

'I'm to wait for the ashes,' she says as if she's learnt some lesson.

'He would have wanted them scattered on the hill he used to play.' She wipes tears from her blotchy eyes. Is that what he would have wanted? You don't get many twelve-year-olds making wills. There's that phrase about being sound in mind and body, kind of lets Rupert out I reckon. Whiteman nods reassuringly. 'You've done everything you could, we all did. I'm sure he would have liked it.' I hear Samantha's heels crunching the gravel as she walks up to our little encounter group, eyes averted. Jerry's fiddling with his keys again, wants to whisk her out of there. Whiteman is prattling with Rupert's mother and Nicky hasn't budged from his foxhole Cortina. Maybe he's going to follow me, see where I go, which pub I'll visit to drown my sorrows. I nod to nobody in particular and head for my car, straight into Sam's dad. Just like the day we went round her house for the first time. Went round there to court his daughter.

BEDROOM SCENES

Rupert had his Gary Glitter LP, I took an armful of comics. Well, I didn't know, did I? PC Bell had been sitting at the kitchen table reading the *Clarion*, checking Nicky had got his facts right. He was just a junior then, of course. He looked up and did a double take, figured our parents had sent us round for a clip round the ear. They did a fair bit of that in those days. Now they'd have him up on a charge before you could say police brutality.

'What do you two want?' he snorted. Never could stop being the village copper, that bloke. Up at the Boar they always lowered their voices as soon as he turned up for a drink. They hadn't issued him with a car yet so he was always riding around on this old boneshaker of a motorbike. You could hear him coming a mile off. When the bloody thing broke down he had to walk. Detection rate must have rocketed. Samantha's mother steps back from the door, lets us in to the snug.

'They've come over to see Sammy.' I noticed her raise her eyebrows at her husband, his pale bristly hair already receding from his freckled brow, his pale puffy face.

'Going to play some records, aren't you, boys?' No, we're going to stake her out on the bed and sacrifice her to the sun.

Rupert nods, taps the album he's brought over. I haven't got a record player. Next Christmas, next Christmas. PC Bell frowns at the comics.

'And read,' I add lamely. We stand there fixed expressions for about a year and a half before Sam pokes her head over the stairs, waves us up.

'Hiya. Come on up. It's OK to play some records, isn't it, Mum?'

'Yes, dear, not too loud.' We gallop up the stairs five steps at a time and follow her into her room. We're in. The bedroom is small, pink, and smothered in posters. The narrow bed where she sleeps is pushed against the left-hand wall, a rack of books and her small stereo opposite. I cross to the window and damn near fall through it. Christ, she can see everything from here. The lane, the stile, the allotments, the tangled undergrowth under the pylon. It stands in the middle of the brimming treetops like an H.G. Wells space machine. The window is the perfect observation post, a sniper's delight. She could have picked us off on our patrols, brought down a mortar barrage on top of our positions, gunned us down as we sneaked along the hedgerows. I can even see the brambles folded cunningly over our secret tunnel. Our secret's out. All of them. She must have watched us hundreds of times. Firing toy guns at one another, tossing pebble grenades into the old wreck, crashing to the ground in simulated death throes. It's a good job I'm looking out, they can't see me blushing. I can hear them jabbering behind my back, they've forgotten I'm here already. I glance over my shoulder. They are squatting on the floor with their legs folded beneath them. I'd rupture myself trying to sit like that. I pick the bed instead, notice the purple leg of her Scooby Doo pyjamas sticking out from beneath her pillow. Remind myself she's got secrets too. She sits as if she's double jointed, legs splayed in her tight jeans. Her hair hangs over her face as she leans forward over Rupert to pick another record from her rack. He leans back, looks up. I can't read the expression. Maybe I can.

'Where's the picture?' I whisper. She looks up at me for the first time. Yes, that's right, fat boy's here too.

'Shh . . . if my dad finds out he'll skin me.' She levers herself up, takes a squint outside the door and closes it quietly. Drops to her knees in front of her drawers and pulls the bottom one out. I can see balled socks and what must be pairs of tights. I look away. I mean, it's not polite to peer into a girl's knicker drawer, is it? Not till you know them a bit anyway. She takes the painting out, passes it up to me. Ballet dancers in white tutus against a leafy green background. I've looked every-where, I can't find anything like it, but judging from his careless glance neither has Rupert. Look at him, lurking on the floor just like the horrible green creature lurking in the painting, sharp eyes behind a foxy mask. Dark and sinister, hunched over like it's a demon waiting to pounce. The colours are delicate, stained mists. Even I can appreciate its value. The frame is worked with a delicate leaf motif, ivy twisting and twining round the bough of a tree. I squint at the signature but can't make it out.

'Lurcher?'

'That's a kind of dog,' Rupert says, snatching it out of my hands to have a look for himself.

'I looked in the art book at school but couldn't see anything like it. The style is Post-Impressionist or something.' Rupert raises his eyebrows, nods like he knows what she's talking about. Third book along in the school library, he's had it out as well I bet.

'Maybe the reference library in Budgworth will have something.'

'I wonder why he left it there with all that rubbish. You'd have thought he would have carried it round with him, wouldn't you?' she asks.

'I would have got Bristow's to take the lot away, all that old furniture. It could be valuable, it could be antique.'

'We ought to go back and have another look,' she suggests. This time even Rupert looks doubtful. Who does she think we are, the Secret Three or something? There's no way I'm going back down there. Even if it means letting the two of them alone. I'll cut the sweets, take more exercise, make myself make some new friends. Just see me do it, OK?

'Think of all the things in the loft,' she whispers. 'Think of all the things in his drawers.' She glances at Rupert, sensing I want no part of it.

'We're bound to get caught,' I say. 'It won't take a genius to work out who's got it. I reckon we ought to take it back.'

She glares at me. Rupert frowns at me, then her.

'He's not been there for years,' she protests. 'We put the boards back up. I'm not taking it back. Finders keepers.'

Rupert sighs like he's the boss, the one to make all the decisions. I want to make decisions too.

'I don't think we need to take it back,' he says thought-fully. 'I think you can keep it, Sam.'

It's the first time I've heard him call her that. Binds them even closer somehow. Binds them, cuts me out. She clutches it to her chest, little boobs behind her sweatshirt. I shake my head.

'Solomon doesn't go inside the cottage. He just makes sure nobody else does,' Rupert reasons. It's hard to argue with that, state of the place.

'Yeah, see?' She jabs me in the arm, full of herself.

'All right, you've got away with it so far, but I'm not going down there again. I don't want the police round my house.'

'I've got them round my house already,' she giggles. Go ahead, the pair of you, go ahead and laugh at me. Outside we can hear PC Bell trudging up the stairs, coughing every other step to give us time to untie her, get her clobber back on. He raps on the door.

'Haven't you got any homework to do?' Police lingo for get those two conniving little gits out of here. Can't blame him. Can't blame him

EMBRACES

him now, taking my arm outside the church, intercepting me as I make a break for my car, collar up, eyes down.

'How are you, son?' Son, is it? I shrug, you know how it is with in-laws. Former in-laws. I've never been comfortable with him, interfering with his little girl. I reckon he thought I would calm her down a bit, straighten her out after she dropped out of college. He looks out over the fields, over the Rec. There's a gang of kids jumping up and down on a park bench, he's in two minds whether to go over and sort them out or stick around with me. The heather and bracken clinging to the slopes down the gorge turns tawny mauve then gold as the sun penetrates the clouds.

'She was in a terrible state, David. She was hoping you'd ring at least.'

'I told her, Malcolm, I told her I tried.' I look at him for a second, then look back out over the fields. His blue eyes are watering, he's close to tears. I can't handle shit like that. I've never been one of these blokes who goes around hugging his mates. Hanging out your feelings like so much washing.

'You know how I tried when we were together. There's really not a lot more I can say. She's got Jerry now.'

'That prick.'

'He seems OK.'

'He's a fucking ponce if you ask me.' He clutches my arm as I flick the lock open, get ready to escape from all of it, all the grasping arms trying to drag me down into the morass, drag me kicking and screaming into the stream. Look at him, look at Whiteman, look at Fish there in his bloody Cortina, like a jackal waiting for the lions to leave off.

'We all went through it, son, but a call isn't much to ask. For old times' sake. She'll be over it in a few days, now he's gone for good. She'd appreciate it, I'd appreciate it.' He backs this up with a reassuring nod, squeezes my arm and turns to go. He hasn't changed much. Mr Straightman, Mr Notebook. Right from the start, he'd known we meant well. Sure, he'd dog us up all right when we went round, but he wouldn't let anyone else into the garden, let alone his daughter's bedroom. We were honoured in a way, we'd earned his trust. Gruff and grudging, but trusting. We didn't go round smashing windows or letting off bangers. We hadn't helped ourselves at the corner shop when Doris wasn't looking. He'd had no cause to drag us home, read the riot act in front of our parents. When Sam returned from Budgworth thirteen months into a three-year arts diploma, we'd picked things up, started seeing each other again. He was probably hoping we'd marry, give him a bit of peace. Get her mind off of water witches and lost boys, fix it on something permanent like nappies and wet-wipes. That David, always said so, solid sort of bloke. May not be your university material, but he's no slouch. One of us, feet on the ground, drinks in the Boar. After all they went through as well. PC Bell turns back, an afterthought.

'I'm not expecting you to go back to her,' he says. 'Just a call. I'd appreciate it.'

'This note . . . it mentioned me.' The wallpaper behind me sprouts a horrid fungus of lurid green letters, pulsing and running down the walls. D.B. busy with her squirrel-tail brush, a little reminder in case I hadn't got the message first time round. I close my eyes for a second, same as Bell, blinking in the watery sunlight. It deflects him a little, forces a frown.

'Don't pay any attention to that shite. Stupid bugger stares at a wall for fifteen years and then goes off scaring everybody with all that voodoo rubbish.' I wouldn't call it voodoo, I wouldn't call it rubbish either, but I think I get his drift. 'It was the note that sparked our Sam off again, if you want my opinion. I thought she was over it. Better hearing it from me than the likes of Mr Fish there.' He nods towards the battered purple Cortina, the grinning occupant.

'You haven't mentioned it to him, of course?'

I shake my head.

'He knows there was a note, not what it said.'

'Keep it like that. I don't want her ending up at that bloody Institute.'

'This thing about scattering his ashes, can she do that?'

'She can tip the lot in the stream, it's not going to do him any harm, is it?'

You tell me.

'I'm only joking. She's going to stand on the peak and let him blow in the wind, I think.'

He shrugs.

'Come on down the Boar for a drink sometime, whatever.' He waves his pudgy hand and trots back to the knots of mourners.

What the hell is all this, be nice to David Roberts day? I mean, I'm not ice, am I? I'm not a chunk of bloody limestone. Do you think I've been above it all so far, wondered why I haven't mentioned how I felt about Rupert? I liked him. I loved Samantha once, and I got on pretty well with her parents. I can't stand here listening to all this without getting twitchy. Me, I hold on to my wild horses, keep them under a tight rein. I don't shag myself out trying to catch them when they've galloped off over the hills. What am I, the bloody villain of the piece, that what you think? Just because White-man didn't bring me along frothing at the mouth tied into a strait-jacket, doesn't mean to say I don't feel things same as the rest of them. More than the rest of them. You have to shut things up, shut them out. I do anyway. I can't go round blubbering about it. I don't want to end up wearing a dead man's trousers, one of those Institute special hair cuts. How was it on the collective today, Ivan? I jump into my bloated capital-ist car, slam the door, catch my breath. Look at the hills. They don't care what we get up to, us ants. All of this shit, it's a blink of an eye to them. Tear ourselves up, tear the planet in half, rocks are rocks. Jerry blares his horn as he drives out of the narrow yard, crunching gravel. Sam is looking straight ahead, I catch a quick profile behind the veil. Her eyes are in some kind of state. The car disappears up the gorge. I'm out of there.

GOBSTOPPERS

I stopped sucking gobstoppers the day after we went round to see Samantha for the first time. You seem to see loads of fat men with pretty women these days, try telling me that when I was twelve. All I saw were the rolls of fat over my belt. If I looked down my chins multiplied, if I tucked them into my chest flesh ballooned under my red cheeks. If I jumped up and down my belly rippled. Give me a chainsaw I'd have cut hams of my own flesh from my bones, left me bleeding, torn and sleek. A buffalo trimmed down to a gazelle. Why? Why stand in front of the mirror worrying? Why'd you think? Why give up gobstoppers, pineapple chunks, sherbert dips? Why sit hungry while my mother scraped jam rolypoly into the bin imagining I was sickening for something. For her of course. Samantha. I gave up Mars Bars for that girl, let me tell you. I avoided the sweetshop, didn't go within three streets of the village bakery, declared the burger bar a no-go area. Any chance I got I pulled on my rugby kit and went jogging down the lanes. Kept out of their way, even if it meant leaving them together, giving him a free hand.

I suppose there was more to it than Samantha. I suppose I was looking beyond her, to all the other Samanthas, all the other Samanthas who'd probably pick Ruperts before they picked me. It scared me, OK, I admit it. I didn't want to get old on my own like Solomon. Rupert never called, never phoned, but if I saw him scuttling along the lane I'd leave my lookout post, tag along. 'Hi, going round to see Sam?' I tell you, you think I'm some kind of a bastard, refusing to get upset about him now, but you think how he was treating me, cutting me right out of it. Leaving me in the lurch, stuck in my room with my mirror. You think I was going to let him get away with it?

'Hey, Rupert, taking your guitar round? How are you getting on with that "Smoke on the Water" thing?' I'd pop out of the bushes as he sneaked along, give him a real jump. Proves he had a guilty conscience, I figure.

'Hey, Rupert, that the new Glitter single? Did you see him on *Top of the Pops*? Amazing.' My best friend and my first love. They didn't dare come right out and say it. They knew one word to Solomon and we were all in the shit. They knew me well enough to know I'd do it as well. Her dad would have grounded her until she was about thirty-seven. Silas would have beaten the shit out of Rupert just as my dad would me. But I wouldn't care, because the hurt would go away. The pain would fade but loneliness wouldn't. The empty ache would go on getting worse, insulating itself with layer upon layer of fat and grease until I was a complete unrecognizable unfeeling blob. It wasn't as much her as him. At least, I always comforted myself it wasn't. He had to have her full and undivided attention. Sometimes I thought she actually quite liked me, gloomy, morose, nothing like Mr Fringe. I bet he would have been popular at college, if he'd ever got that far. Long legs, floppy hair, hacking jacket, and a pint of lager. Meaning of life and fancy a quick one. Well, old mate, old pal, you've finally left her all to me and there she goes, my new ghost. Women, huh, men! For three weeks or so our little games got sillier and sillier as he tried to lever me out and I hung on in there. The fleet three-quarter and the dumpy hooker. We tried to outmanoeuvre each other without appearing to try. Whatever I did, he'd sneer at, make out I was being childish. I got used to the simpering putdowns and raised eyebrows, the wallys, the rest of it. Stored them all up for future reference. And now you expect me to sit here in the car blubbering about him? Think I'm that forgiving? Fat boys have got to be funny, haven't they? Fat men the life and soul of the party. One time I noticed him in his back garden sticking all his old Johnny Sevens and Tommy guns into the dustbin. For a moment I contemplated sneaking in and stealing them back out again. I'd never had a Johnny Seven. Can you remember them? They were these great big green plastic multi-purpose heavy machine-gun flamethrower and missile-launcher jobs. The fucking things did everything. If they could have manufactured real ones there would have been no need for a nuclear deterrent, I'm telling you. He made sure and told Sam about it. I sat brooding about it, thinking nobody would mind me claiming it, now he didn't want it. Then the day before the dustbin men were due I saw Sam and her friend Lorraine Lamb walking up the lane with all their best clobber on, their make-up and their ear-rings. They noticed the stuff sticking up from the bin as if stuck there by a retreating army. I could see them sniggering and making comments. It's not that I've got X-ray vision or anything. Just a pair of binoculars. Well, my dad's actually. They come in handy for keeping tabs on things out on the hill. He doesn't mind me borrowing them for birdwatching, aircraft spotting, kind of stuff. After that there was no way I was going to trot out and touch them. He dumped all his comics, his model aircraft, his Hunchback of Notre Dame reading lamp. Bastard always painted his models better than I did as well. I was always in too much of a hurry to get the transfers on, smeared the whole lot. He got into David Bowie, got another new guitar and a bigger pile of records. I was still bopping round my bedroom to the innocent delights of *Rock and Roll* parts one and two so I let him make the running, let him cool himself to death. I suppose all this sounds pretty fun now, looking back. Trouble was, we were deadly serious. We never came to blows, but we got pretty stupid. Rupert got a new stereo through his mum's club book. I painted my room orange and black, gave my dad a hernia just looking at it, he went spare but Sam actually told Lorraine it looked cool. Sometimes we'd sit round in her room, look at the old picture. We'd all got books from the library, tried to place it, put a name to it. All I could make out was Lurcher, and nobody had ever heard of him. I'd tried everywhere, no joy. I'd wondered about asking her if we could sell it, make some money, but I didn't want to appear too mercenary. Wanted to convince her I had a heart under all the fat, beating still. Looking at the picture, you would have sworn the tiny leaves around the frame changed colour as the year went on.

The leaves fell in the Rec, the heather and bracken turned from gold to tawny brown. Conker time. Like everything else it had started out as a bit of a dare, a triple challenge. Me versus him, him versus me, and Sammy versus the pair of us, without any particular preference as far as I could make out. Maybe I was blocking it, the two of them. The way they were together. Anyway, Rupert's dad had promised to take us up to the island, well islet, about six miles up the brook towards Budgworth. It was only a little island but it supported four enormous horse-chestnut trees. They were so far away hardly anybody bothered to wade out there to get the conkers. There were a few scraggly trees in the Rec, so most of the kids stuck around throwing sticks. The conkers on the island were reputed to be so thick on the ground you could scoop them up with buckets. We were all looking forward to it but Silas let us down. Had some water trouble somewhere, some funny readings down at the testing station. Had to dash off, sorry kids. Sam looked pissed off, I suggested we walk.

'Walk? It's about ten miles away!' Rupert snapped.

'Not if we follow the stream. We can go straight there if we wear our Wellies. Won't take more than an hour or two.'

Sam was keen, so Rupert had to give in. Rupert called for me in his new US Army fatigues tucked into his boots. I'd put on my anorak, Sam had her ski-jacket. We hardly said a word as we jumped over the stile, filed down the lane toward the brooding woods. Past the smoking dustbins we saw Solomon over in his run, putting chicken corpses in a sack. Must have had a fox or something. He stopped, looked up as we doubled past. We got to the tunnel and paused. Sam waited for the two of us to go through and then crawled along behind. It was usually worth hanging about in case she ever changed her mind, decided to go first. Then one of us got to follow her, close as we could without her getting funny with us. We emerged on the quiet misty bank, jumped down into the rotten waters. There were a lot of leaves drifting along in the current, they tumbled and sank past us as we turned right, headed for the heart of the woods. I was still wondering what to say to break the silence when we came on the two men. I don't know who was more surprised. I mean, we'd never seen anybody else down there, and they obviously weren't expecting the Secret Three to turn up. They were wearing green waders but their clothes looked too tidy for comfort down in the gorge. They must have left their car back at the bridge. They looked up as we splashed along, stopped to have a nose what they were up to. The taller one was using a trowel to lift some kind of oily waste out of the water, put it in plastic bags. Oilslicks down in the gorge? What, a tanker gone down further upstream? The second man was taking water samples, filling test tubes, scribbling something on the labels, and then placing them in a rack tied round his neck. Looking about we could see more of the oily stuff spluttering in the mud, smearing the rocks. We stood there silent for a minute or two until they got exasperated.

'You kids shouldn't be playing down here, what's wrong with the park?' the one with the trowel asks. Rupert ignores him.

'Is there something wrong with the water?' he asks. A few balls of old sump oil aren't exactly going to have a devastating effect on the wildlife round here. There isn't any.

'There's been a leakage that's all. We're just checking it out.'

'Is it oil?' Sam asks. The other bloke looks up from his samples. Decides she's a little young for a line. Hey, wade this stream often?

'What are you doing anyway, some kind of school project? Clear off, we're busy.' We shrug, splash on past, globules of the oily stuff sticking to our boots. Rupert reckons it has been pumped out from a factory nearer the city.

'The Knot used to be dirty like this, my dad said you wouldn't believe the things he'd seen float past him when he was fishing.'

'Perhaps it was a farmer clearing out oil from a tractor or something,' Sam suggests.

'Pretty big tractor,' Rupert says, leading the way through the bubbling mess, bits of stick, old string, leaves, and debris all floating past in sticky bundles like shipwrecked sailors clinging to wreckage after their tanker got torpedoed. Another couple of hundred yards and we emerge at the cottage. Sam looks eagerly at Rupert but I shake my head.

'Let's just check the door,' she says. 'See if he's been down here.' I watch them go up to the tumbledown shack, pull at the planks on the windows. She says something to him I don't catch but he shakes his head and they tiptoe back. We stretch out on the bank for a minute, the undergrowth is thinner and we can rest without willow or elder fronds hanging down our necks like witchy fingers. I suppose that's where we got careless. None of us thought to look down at the dusty path this time, the dinky little footprints and smears of oil leading right down to the window. We waded off, forgot all about it. The sun rose over the treetops, it got warmer, stuffier down in the gorge.

Insects buzzed lazily from one horrible smelly seed pod to another. Blackbirds called in alarm, rocketed off through the branches. Not big on wildlife though, this gorge. Solomon gets the odd fox. Obviously tidying up after one this morning when we went past. By the time he hears any commotion from the henhouse the fox would be off, plump warm body clamped in his jaws, bright blood splattering on the bank. Out of our world and off into his own. We went on. Sam made the occasional comment, asked how far we had to go. Rupert seemed preoccupied with something, I was out of breath and red in the face so I was content to tag along behind. The sides of the gorge close in, it gets stiflingly hot down there. The branches tear at our clothes, scratch at our faces. We passed an old slag heap, white and grey ashy stuff dumped decades before. In one place it has spilled over the bank into the water turning it cloudy. The few bits of vegetation left are blanched, caked in dust. The stream bends to the left, tumbles over a series of rills, grading the pebbles and stones into regular little dunes. We stamp through and find ourselves in the broader part of the gorge. The cliffs retreat from the bank, the trees muscle in, big trees, choking the undergrowth out, hogging the light. It was gloomier there, under the thick canopy of the four ancient chestnuts. We gaze up at the browning leaves and shiny shell cases, split up the middle to reveal rich creamy skins and shiny brown nuts. The ground is covered with conkers and cases. The stream is practically blocked with them. With a whoop we're on them, tugging plastic bags out of our pockets and scooping them up by the handful. Shoving them in pockets, down trousers, until we look as if we've been ravaged by some terrible bloating disease. We could have filled a truck. Our boots crunch on the hard prickly shells, squeezing the conkers out with a plop. I stuffed so many into my carrier the bottom burst and spilled them all back out again like that guy's guts in *Catch 22*. It was bloody stupid really. I mean, have you ever played conkers? What, one, two goes and you're ready to take up train spotting, am I right? We took off our coats and heaped them up the way old tribes collected the heads of their enemies. God knows how we thought we were going to get them home. It was as if we had collected heaps of rubies, nuggets of gold. We had to have them all, every last one of them.

'What about the ones up in the trees,' Sam called out, pointing up into the greenery.

'Don't be daft, we can't even carry this lot,' I laughed. Rupert stopped, looked round. I suppose it was the heat, the walk, not eating. I suddenly felt sick, woozy. I sat down on a stump, splashed some water on my face. Rupert picked up a stick. I was watching him move in slow motion. All the trees were marching round him, closing in on him, raising their branches to embrace him. He looked up, head back, back bent, bent arm. Sam walked over, sweatshirt gathered up in front to carry another heap of conkers. My head was aching as if the trees had wrapped roots around my forehead, wanted to squeeze my brain through the top of my head. My mouth was dry, tongue felt too big. My eyes were watering, I couldn't see properly. He threw the stick up into the trees. I could just make it out, turning end over end, blurring, merging into the matted branches. Twigs snapped, leaves fluttered down, heralding a sudden deluge of conkers as if Rupert's stick had hit the jackpot on *The Golden Shot*. He was whooping and jumping, running round and round the trees like a demented Apache, hand over his mouth. I saw him grab Sam, swirl her round as the conkers fell, hitting the ground with dull thonks. Hitting their heads with sharp cracks. She covered her head, pulled away from him as he raced between the boughs shouting and bawling. On and on the stick shot through the branches as if Hercules himself had thrown it for a bet, tried to launch it into space. I edged away, the conkers were still coming down thick and fast. Rupert was tottering, shielding his head as the torrent built up, built up into a bombardment. Sam screamed once, ran towards the bank and tripped, sprawled flat under the storm. They fell as if we'd set up some infernal vibration under the trees, rattled them to their roots, shivered the enormous trunks. The conkers rained down harder and harder, ricocheting around us like shrapnel, catching us tighter, harder. I could hear Sam screaming and yelling as the trees tried to stone us into the stream. I could hear her shrill cries over Rupert's maniac caperings. I got up, crossed my arms over my head and doubled over the stream to her. All the trees joined in, pelted us, knocked us to the ground and ground us in as if they wanted to grind us into the mulch, turn us to compost. Mash us up and suck us in. I saw Sam crouching covering her head, sprawled over her as the storm whipped itself into a frenzy, used up all its ammunition in one last mad onslaught. The shells hammered into my back, my legs, my arms as she sobbed and yelped under me. Curled into the smallest ball she could make with me crouched over her. They caught us on the rebound, ricocheting off the stones, off the boughs. I suppose our shouts carried downstream, carried as far as those two prospector guys because the next thing I remember was the two of them, wading and splashing up the stream. Galloping awkwardly in those shiny oil-splattered waders. Lifting their legs high out of the water. I could see them as the last few conkers dropped down to the conker strewn ground. Leaves floated down gently like surrender flags as the storm abruptly gave out. They were so thick on the ground they reminded me of ball bearings in some slapstick comedy, sending the Keystone Kops crashing to the ground. They scrambled out of the water and over to us, went sprawling. They pulled me from her, sobbing and crying feebly, snot running from her nose, blood trickling from a nasty graze on her forehead. I was that close to her, I could still smell her, smell her girl smell. I sniffed it in so it wouldn't get away. These blokes are shouting and bawling, helping her up. She holds one foot up, starts crying for real, switching it on.

'What the hell were you doing?' trowel man demands, jabbing me in the arm. The other guy's rack is empty, he's dropped all his samples pounding along to see what was going on. Rupert staggers out from between the trees, wanders in smaller and smaller circles until he sinks to his knees, holding his head trying to laugh and cry at the same time.

'Must have been a bloody earthquake,' says trowel man, helping Sam trying to stand properly. Earthquake?

DOCTOR DOCTOR

Jerry's BMW's already out of sight, must be halfway back to
Budgworth by now, but I can see Whiteman's Jaguar a few
cars behind as I hit the dual carriageway, put my foot down
for the bright lights of the big city. Buttonholing me like that
outside the church. What a quack, let me tell you. What he
always liked to do was press his fingertips together and put
them up close to his mouth like he was praying. It always
struck me as a strange expression for someone who was paid
to open people up. Open up their lives like sardine cans, spill
their thoughts all over the table and sort through them. He'd
push his notebook away, lean back in his leather swivel chair.
'Let's hold it there a moment, shall we?' Be my guest, old
buddy old pal. He'd count the items off on his fingers, goods
on a psychiatric shopping list.

'The three of you steal a picture from the old man's cottage.
You know you've done wrong. You take elaborate precautions
to make sure you are not caught. Several weeks later you
return to the vicinity and see . . . what?' He's a jeweller with
one of those little spyglasses screwed into his eye. I'm the
rough diamond he's got to shape and polish, hang on a chain
nice and neat.

'The oil in the water,' I repeat for the hundredth time.

He frowns, flicks back through his notes. 'Have you had
any bad experiences with water?' My dad threw me in the
deep end to teach me to swim, but that's not what he's getting
at. It's not what I'm getting at anyway.

'Not as such, I mean, the stream never felt quite right.'

His pen is poised for the breakthrough, the big lie. 'In
what way?'

'It felt bad. It looked bad, made you feel uneasy.'

'Why? You can swim, can't you? Did it smell bad?'

'Sometimes it smelled bad, sometimes it didn't smell of anything.'

'When it did smell of something, did it remind you of anything else?'

Couldn't say it did. 'It was just a feeling, you know. Like being in a graveyard. A dead place.'

He nods. 'Why did you spend so much time down there?'

'We had it to ourselves. There were no big kids down there.'

'They bothered you, bullied you?' He's scribbling again, off on a new angle. 'Why did they pick on you then, these big kids?'

'It was mostly verbal.'

'Along what lines?'

'They took the mickey of Rupert. Made fun of his name. Called him a pansy, stuff like that.'

'And what did these boys call you, eh?'

'Fatty.'

'Fatty? Is that all?'

'Fatty, fat one, fat bastard, fat bum, fat head, fat prick . . . that kind of stuff.' His pen hovers over the page. 'And that bothered you?' No, I used to fall about like the laughing policeman. Of course it bothered me, you stupid bastard. See a fat woman on TV saying this is how I was made, this is what I am, take it from me, she's lying. She's lying through her greedy picky gnashing teeth. You hear some lying bastard say I'd rather be fat than thin, that really cracks me up. Got big bones? Bullshit. You've got a big mouth, you eat too many biscuits, too much chocolate, too many chips. Fat must have spawned more bullshit books, bullshit programmes, bullshitting bullshit than any other subject under the sun, including sex. Even now, a decade and more later, I still suck my gut in walking past a mirror. I do it even if I'm on my fucking own. Am I mad, or do you do it too? Tighten that belt boy, throw back those shoulders. Boy's got big bones, is all.

He looks up at me. 'Let's move on to Samantha for a second. When the conkers were falling . . . you . . . let me see' – he runs his pen down his margin, paragraph three, page sixty-seven –

'threw yourself on top of her to protect her from the blows, breaking her ankle in the process.' That's right, go on, laugh. I can see the corners of his mouth twitching. Go on, I'm used to it, what the hell. I broke her ankle, all right? Those prospector guys had to carry her all the way back to their car, take her to the hospital to get it set. She got to stay the night, we got sent home with a few extra plasters.

'How did it feel?'

'Being on her?' Felt damn good, Doc, felt damn good even with those conkers breaking my butt. 'It hurt. I got covered in bruises.' He ignores me trying to roll up my sleeve, show him the marks. Yeah, they're still there.

'Did it feel nice being close to Samantha?'

'I thought it was the right thing.'

'Did it feel nice?'

'Not at the time . . . not with all the conkers coming down.'

'Did you feel proud of yourself?'

'Yes . . . I suppose so. I saved her from being badly hurt.'

'And during this Rupert was . . . let me see . . . capering about like a maniac. Your words.' I nod. *Damn right.*

'Was it his fault?'

'What?'

'The conkers. Was is his fault they fell down like that?'

'You tell me.'

'I'm asking what you thought. Did you think at the time, did you blame Rupert for the conkers coming down like that?'

'I suppose so.'

'Why?'

'Because he threw the stick. There was no need to do that.'

'What about Samantha, did you think it was her fault too?'

'Not much . . . she egged him on, I suppose, being there. Made him act stupid.'

'In other words, he was showing off in front of her?' I nod. 'So you ran over and jumped on her.'

'To stop her being hurt by the conkers,' I grate. Listen to him, sounds like I'm some kind of maniac, attacking her for no reason.

'Tell me what happened after the conker business. How did

things shape up?'

'I saw him the next night . . . the night they brought Samantha home. She had her foot in plaster. Her dad gave me a dirty look.'

'You'd both had hidings?'

'The police came round. My dad didn't like having the police round, told them it wouldn't happen again.'

'That must have been annoying as you hadn't done anything?' he asks casually. I nod.

'They tanned us first, asked what had happened afterwards.'

'And you hadn't done anything wrong, had you?'

'I've just told you. We took the picture. It was a mistake, I'll admit it. I'm not saying anything else.'

'Funny the way these conkers stopped falling the second the two men from the Water Board turned up.'

'It stopped just as they got up close to us. They could hear her shouting.'

'And when they got there they saw you lying on top of her.'

'That's right,' I grate. I'm waiting for him, I'm ready for him.

'Now, David, I'm going to ask you a very serious question, OK?' Fire away, Doc. 'Have you and Samantha ever done anything sexually?' I go red. Yeah, I know, I've told you this stuff always makes me go red. Makes me look as guilty as hell and that makes me redder still. 'What have you done together? Have you kissed her? Touched her breasts, her private parts? David, can you look at me for a second?' No I can't, you bastard. It's lucky I'm typing this as well, not with you in your room, reading it out loud. Telling you about it face to face. I couldn't do that. It's bad enough like this, having you find out stuff about me behind my back. Like you're checking up on me, checking me out. What did I do with Samantha? What did we do together? That's what *you* want to know about.

OFFERINGS

What a wally I felt that night, clutching a small bunch of flowers I'd bought down in the village, clutching them in my sweaty hand as I rapped on the Bells' back door. PC Bell opened it, blond hairs twitching above his watery eyes. Full lips set in a hard line. His business look, I suppose.

'I was wondering when you'd turn up,' he says, his wife's head appearing over his shoulder like an alien growth.

'Let him in, Malcolm, he's only brought her some flowers.'

He snorts. 'I should think he has, getting her half killed like that.' He was giving me all the look, all the chat, but he hadn't hit me yet. Given me a good hiding like the one I'd had from Dad the night before.

'She's in her room. She isn't going out for a fortnight so you can tell your skinny friend,' he snaps, despite his wife's nods and smiles, tugging me in past him.

'Come on in, love, we know you didn't mean any harm. It was nice of you to . . . think of her,' she adds lamely. He stalks back to the table and snatches up the *Clarion*.

'Is Sam all right, is she going back to school?' I ask her mum as she crosses to the grill, checks his cheese on toast. If there was any going spare I wouldn't mind. I'd made do with a bloody salad and I was starving.

'Not till the end of the week. She'll have the plaster on for a while.'

'You should be more careful, lad, with your weight,' he says as she places his supper in front of him.

'He was protecting her, you can see he's black and blue himself,' Mrs Bell protests. He jabs his fork at me. 'And what's all this about an earthquake? Who ever heard of an earthquake in Clove?'

'The men said there'd been a slight tremor. They'd been getting some strange readings all day,' I say. Strange readings all right. All those maps of Hillstones, all those blank spaces. Those guys wanted something down there. So do I. Get me some straight lines, some decent pipework. I don't want to hear about pots and sinks, vast galleries like stalactite cathedrals. Deep dark water and clammy corners. Run some pipes in there, A to B, you can't go wrong. Flush the blue dye through the system, a barium meal for her to chew on, show her up flitting through the vaulted chambers. Keeping tabs on her the way I do my dreams. Numbers in the top corner. A to B. Get those readings straight, get that pipework numbered.

'That's why they were there in the first place, checking them out.'

Bell snorts, chomps into a piece of cheese on toast, and goes back to his paper. Mrs Bell smiles apologetically. Sam leans over the stairs.

'Is it all right for him to come up, Mum?'

'Just for a moment, dear.' I duck past her, avoid her father's baleful glare and take the stairs at my usual five at a time. She closes the door behind me, swivels round and pecks me on the cheek. Just like that.

'Did you get a whacking?' I nod dumbly. Have I missed something? 'I'm grounded for a fortnight. Is Rupert coming round?'

'I haven't seen him.' I watch her hobble past me to turn a record over. Couldn't tell you which one. Her right foot's encased in plaster, somebody's been scribbling on it already. Rupert I expect. Maybe not though. Maybe he's not been allowed out. I'm going to get her to myself, just her and me. Just for once she'll have to actually listen what I'm saying. I don't know what to say, though. All those things I lay awake thinking about, rehearsing, have dried up on me. I stagger over them, stagger for her. She's standing there, record clutched to her chest. She looks dead miserable. Her eyes are red, blotchy. She has a graze on her forehead and a puffy lip.

'I think he must be in trouble.' Her voice is shaky. She stifles a sob, wipes her nose.

'If he is we'd have heard by now,' I say, voicing a confidence I certainly didn't feel. Something else is there instead, something's moving in my head, in my chest, in my stomach. It's like being filled up, filled in. Little empty bits of me, little deserts all springing to life, dry wells filling up slowly till I can hardly breathe.

'What was it, what do you think happened?' she asks in a tiny voice which seems to be getting further and further away.

'They said it was an earthquake.' I open my mouth, the words make their own way out into the room which suddenly seems full of cotton wool. Jammed full. Jammed tight. She stands crushed by it, same as I am, eyes smudged, lips mushy and trembling, pale cheeks and red nose.

'My dad went mad when I told him, he thought I was taking the mickey.' Her shoulders are jumping up and down, she steps forward without looking at me, as if she wants to knock me down. She's in my arms. I close them round her in case she changes her mind. My nose is in her hair, rooting round her eyes. She's crying into my chest, getting my top wet. I suck in my gut as far as it will go, bend my head down, nuzzle her neck. Her smell comes rushing up through a rainbow of senses, I breathe it, savour it, the way a diver breathes his last few mouthfuls of oxygen. Maybe it'll be my last. Maybe she'll pull away, smack me round the face. Her tears are salty on my cheek, on her cheek as she slowly lifts her head to look at me. She's gone quiet, stiff. So have I.

'David?' PC Bell shouts from the bottom of the stairs. My prompt. I lean forward, kiss her on the mouth. Her lips squirm across mine and she pulls back. Her lips are all wrinkly like your fingers if you've been in the bath too long. I drag her back, kiss her again. It's as if I want to kiss her for ever, kiss her a million times just in case nobody ever kisses me again. She doesn't slap me, doesn't stagger across the room gagging and vomiting. Smiled a bit and said I'd better go in a husky far away voice. I think it was far away. Where are the fucking signals, where are the messages to tell you what to do? Isn't she supposed to react, say things, tell me she loves me? If I tried to say anything I know it would come out as a horrible croak. I turned and opened the door, all the furniture jumping around banging into the walls. My feet felt as if I was wearing concrete Wellingtons. My arms felt a mile long, knocking into the ornaments, the pictures down the stairs. I stagger past her parents hardly daring to speak and hear the door slam behind me. I'm halfway home before I realize I'm still clutching the flowers, all battered and bruised. And that's how we started, Sam and I. I didn't realize and she certainly didn't realize it, but that was our first time together. Rupert had been kept in, I'd been there when she wanted a shoulder to cry on. I felt as if I'd suddenly grown six inches, seemed too big for my clothes, too big for my brain, too big for my senses. I was one of the big boys. I could look at anybody and know I'd done it. Kissed a girl. Know I'd had a girlfriend. I didn't give a shit what any of them called me now, I was in there, I was in on it with all the rest of them. And I wasn't going to let it go any more than Rupert will me. Any more than she will.

TROUBLE

At school next day we had a test in the morning and games in the afternoon. Rupert had a note to excuse him because of his cuts and bruises. My parents hadn't been as thoughtful so there I was as usual, in goal. Rupert was running up and down the sidelines with a whistle, I kept on waving him over but he would shrug, ran off again as Martin Lawrence blasted the ball into touch. It was six–two to the other side before Mr Clements blew up and we all trooped in to the changing rooms, freezing cold.

'You're about as much use as tits on a fish,' Martin told me as he pulled his football shirt over his head. I shrugged.

'Where was the defence? You expect me to save every one of them?' He stalked off muttering. I couldn't see Rupert, he'd maybe gone on back to the classroom. The bell went before I'd finished changing, so I pulled my trousers over my kit, tugged my coat on and ran out with the rest of them. You know what it's like after school. Anybody within the grounds four seconds after home time's a fucking swot. I chased out of the gate but Rupert was nowhere in sight. It wasn't that I'd meant to tell him all about it, not all of it. It wasn't that I meant to crow about Sam and me. I hadn't made my mind up it had happened, let alone whether to tell anybody about it. Not till I was sure. Not till I'd seen her again, kissed her again. I ran all the way home, down the lane, and into the house. I was covered in dried mud and my football kit reeked. I'd have to have a bath before I went over.

'What are you doing?' my mum asked as I put the plug in and started running the water. What does it look like? 'I came straight back after football. I'm covered.'

She raised her eyebrows, started picking up my shirt,

shorts, socks. 'Perhaps she'll have you tidying your bedroom as well,' she said on her way out. I was about to call her back and ask what she thought she was on about but I didn't have time. I'm in there scrubbing the muck from my knees, rubbing the grass stains from my shins. Towelled myself off and spotted my mum's scales. I pulled them out and jumped on. If I suck my gut in and look up, then squint down at the glass I make it nine stone thirteen. OK, ten stone and big for my age. I've lost over half a stone already. Half a stone! I tug on fresh underpants, clean T-shirt, and the jeans my mum had just finished ironing. I brushed my hair. It's sort of half curly, half straight. Thick and dark. Tonight, it'll do. I dash downstairs.

'No tea thanks, Mum,' I shout into the kitchen. Jump a mile. There's a face at the back window. Jesus Christ, I wish he wouldn't do that. It's Rupert and he looks like shit. White shit. My mum steps back as I cross the kitchen and open the door.

'I was looking for you . . . what's the matter?' He raises his eyebrows, nods towards my mum.

'OK if I go out with Root for a while, Mum?'

She frowns, puts my tea back under the grill. 'Just for a second. You know what your dad said.'

I close the door and follow him down the path. At the gate he turns, eyes damn near popping out of his head. Who told him?

'We've got to get it back. Solomon suspects. I got home early and caught him in my room,' he whispers. The lane lurches under our feet. Oh shit. That's it then. 'Have you got it?'

'No, it's still over Sam's house.'

'We've got to get it back. I'm up to my ears as it is. Can you come now?'

'What did he say?'

He sighs. 'He didn't say anything. Said he was looking for the paper. He's been giving me funny looks the last couple of days. He knows, OK?' It's as if the stream had flowed up the hill, replaced my lifeblood with lifeless waters. I look round at the house, the kitchen light like a beacon for terrified moths, terrified children. I can see Mum pottering about getting Dad's tea ready. He told me I was grounded for the week apart from going round to apologize to Sam and her parents. I figured I could spend a few evenings apologizing. I'd be OK. But not down the woods. Not down the woods with Rupert. It's that or let Solomon check the cottage, find the picture missing, and call in the cops. Cops is curtains. I gallop down the lane after him, pull in by the Bells' garage.

'I'll go in,' he said. I shook my head.

'He hasn't forgiven you yet. I've had the public warning,' I insist. He glances at me quickly. 'How are you going to do it?' I brush past him, take a peek around the side of her garage. Luckily for us Sam's bedroom is at the back. The light's already on as the evenings are drawing in. It means we'll be going down there in the dark. I forget about that for a second, take a squint at her room. There's a shadow moving across the wall. The kitchen light's off. I creep on out and up the path, duck under the kitchen window and get my breath. It's going to have to be a stone against the window job. Jesus Christ, if he catches me I might as well pack my bags. God knows how I kept my hand steady as I groped about in the flower-bed for a stone. I find one, step back a little, lob it up against the window. Go on, break. We'll all be better off if it smashes and the whole lot is discovered, out in the open. A policeman lives in this house with his wife and daughter. The daughter has been kept off school after breaking her ankle with two boy-friends out on a conker-gathering expedition in the dingly old dell. It's like a mad fairy story playing round my brain as the stone hits the window with a gigantic clang, alerting the neighbours as far as the main road. There will be searchlights and dogs on me any second. The clouds race over the house, soaking up the twilight. I'm crossing my legs with fright, willing her to come to the window. As if by magic, she does. Opens it quietly.

'What's up with you?' she hisses, might as well shout through a megaphone.

'The picture . . . Solomon knows . . . we've got to give it back,' I whisper.

'Did he tell?'

'Just give me the picture,' I wheedle, damn near pissing myself with fright. Sam's gone so fast I think for a second her dad has caught her, dragged her back in. She's back, with the picture.

'They're in the front room, I daren't come down.'

'Drop it, I'll catch it.' Who was I trying to kid? She thinks about it for a second, holds it out and lets go. I watch it fall end over end, a small black rectangle against the night. I can't see it clearly, where's the light gone? It's gone completely. I reach up to grab it. The picture hits my wrist. I make another grab, hit the fucking thing against the wall. It tinkles into three pieces. Now we are dead. We are absolutely 100 per cent dead. I can hear her groan. I can hear him moan. I can hear PC Bell get up in the front room, ask 'What was that?' I grab the pieces, grab the frame, and shoot back across the garden as the light goes on in the kitchen. I duck round the side of the garage just as he opens the back door, sticks his head out. We squeeze ourselves into the concrete while he looks up and down, then shuts the door. We're up and running, down the lane and over the stile.

'You smashed it, you stupid bastard,' he shouts hoarsely. I ignore him, clutch the broken shards to my thumping chest. He runs alongside, looks round at me.

'Why did you want to smash it for, you fat prat?' I grit my teeth, run on down the hill, crash into the brambles. He finds the tunnel and doubles on through like a beetle. I follow. We leap over the stream, splash through the shallows, and scramble up the other bank. I'm covered. Brand new on as well. If nothing else, my mum's going to skin me. We double along the bank toward the heart of the darkness, towards the cottage. The stream mutters to itself, casts misty lines into the gloom, fireflies to tempt us on in.

'It could have fallen down and smashed.'

'Brilliant. You clumsy great prick. I knew I should have gone. You looked as if you did it deliberately.'

'Oh, sure,' I snap. Any more of his shit and I'm going to bop him one, I will, honestly. We arrive at the cottage and fling ourselves down behind the tumbledown wall. The cottage is still, no torchbeams playing weirdly over the worn plaster. 'Stay here while I put it back.' I ignore him, run over and help him prise the boards from the window. We wait. Nothing. He takes the frame, the picture, and the three bits of glass. There's a big smear of blood over them and I look down. I've got a two-inch cut over my palm and up my thumb. It's deep too but I can't feel a thing. He doubles up and slides into the gap, into the dark mouth of the cottage. Silence for forty seconds, then he slides back out.

'It's on the floor, I wiped it off and put it by the mantelpiece.'

'Right, let's get out of . . .'

'Hello, boys.' I jump a mile. There's a great heavy paw on my shoulder, holds me down, holds my skin on my quivering bones, my jellied flesh. Solomon's massive shape detaches itself from the shadows and holds us. Holds me. Rupert, the little devil, he ducks under the great paw and shoots along the path. It's like being in a vice, he swings me round as he makes a lunge for his nephew, misses. Rupert's over the wall and into the darkness.

'Come back. It's no good running, boy!' he shouts into the woods. I'm shivering and shaking like a lamb as he shakes his fist at the trees. 'Come back, where are you going to go?' he calls. Where?

RED-HANDED

I look up into his face, a beachcomber's bucket of livid colours and weathered textures. Eyelids squeezed tight over his eyes like mussels sifting a murky rock pool, boring into the darkness, the ring of tangled trees round the ruined orchard. 'Come back, boy,' under his breath. His hand's like a great weight, pressing me down into the earth. He looks down. 'He shouldn't have run like that, it was foolish,' he says quietly. Holds me upright as if I'm a fish he's tickled from the stream, as if I'm waiting for him to remove his hook and pound my brains in with a pebble. He tugs me upright, straightens my shoulders and releases his grip. The black branches reach witchy fingers over his head, lean closer as if eavesdropping on our little talk.

'Where's the picture? The dancing girls?' Voice like broken glass. There's not a lie left in me, only rank, oily fear, coating and sliming my cogs and pulleys. He could open my skull and pick whatever he wants. D.B.'s not the only one with these Gestapo gifts. Two sides of the same coin those two. Heads and tails, hearts and minds. I stand there trembling, letting the mad thump of my heart subside a little. He hasn't hit me yet, or told me he'll tell my parents. Behind the fear there's something worse. Something that might not get as far as my parents. I cast around for it, flick flies into the shadowed shallows, but my mind seems content to leave me in suspense. She's there too, a shadow in the stream, a slicker swimming slowly under the rippled surface, a fin, a flick of a broad speckled tail and she's gone down deep, watering down my wallpaper, the plaster and the cracks. It came to me, standing there: What if he doesn't want to tell my parents? What if he's got something else in mind? The thought flits in and out of the clammy corners of my imagination. I know it's there but I can't focus on it, can't picture it.

'Are you deaf? Where is it?' he demands, giving me a rough shake to snap me out of it.

'It's back. It's broken,' I blubber.

'Who had it? It wasn't in his room. You or the girl?' He shakes me again.

'You or the girl?' he grates.

'The girl.'

He relaxes his grip again. 'She had it all the time, yes?'

I nod miserably. 'I'll pay for any damage. We hadn't meant to steal it, just borrow it,' I whine. It's only a bloody picture for Christ's sake. How much could it cost? It's not like robbing a church, rifling through a tomb is it? Is it?

'I don't care about the picture. Did you touch it?' I don't know what to say. He cuffs me. I damn near collapse with the surprise of it as much as the pain. My head's spinning now, I can hardly think straight. He repeats the question.

'Yes . . . we all touched it.'

'Did she?' Another cuff. I stagger to my knees, he yanks me up again. 'Yes . . . yes . . . we all touched it. We'll pay for the damage. We always meant to bring it back.'

He scowls at me. He's got a miserably mean scowl. 'Let's get back. Where's that fool got to?' He holds my arm, guides me along the path in the gathering murk. Branches and brambles twine themselves across my face as I search for the path. I follow him dumbly, he's gazing ahead, sniffing the mist, stooping to check the ground.

'No sign of him. Where's he gone this time of night?'

If he turns his back for a second I'll find out. He's walking towards the road, maybe I can scream for help.

'I didn't mean to hit you,' he declares flatly, almost resentfully. 'But you don't know what you're doing, don't know anything,' he says. He's sorry now, he's sorry he hit me. I'll tell my dad, see what he thinks of Mr Bloody Solomon. They all think he's a lunatic anyway. He'll probably go to prison, get locked away somewhere.

'I thought we'd torn it when you dropped it. I didn't know

what to expect then.' Yes, I'm not surprised. Would have taken a bit of explaining if he'd got caught with a couple of boys under each arm.

'We'll pay for the damage,' I say, like it's going to stop him throttling me, dumping me in the stream. He shakes his head, sighs heavily. A worn-out bear who can't find a bit of peace, a nice quiet spot to wrap himself up and hibernate, sleep it off.

'It's not me you've got to be afraid of,' he says grimly. Who? The police? My parents? They might not be chuffed with my part in this but they're not going to have some old git knocking their son about, I can tell you.

'Let's get back.' Back? Back where? Where are we going now? I can hear cars slowing down to negotiate the bridge, I can see headlights piercing the misty trees ahead. We stick to the path, the scenic route.

On the Intercom   99

Second Opinions   103

Company   110

In the Fields   114

The Run   125

The Ride   130

Traffic   140

Peace and War   146

School Daze   154

PART THREE

Recruit: Say goodbye to my father and uncles too
I'm a soldier and never again I'll see you!

SCHILLER, *Wallenstein*

ON THE INTERCOM

They couldn't let it go. Same as you, same as you now you're hooked. Want to find out what we were really up to, down in the gorge. Same as Whiteman. He told everyone we were on magic mushrooms, speed, something like that. I pictured him at his case conferences, doing that thing with his hands in front of his mouth. Yes, the boys and girl from Clove. Strange case, intriguing. The elder one's catatonic, the girl largely incoherent. The younger boy (that's me) highly belligerent. He gives me bits of his dreams, for all the world as if he's teasing me, inviting me to go a little further. Most unusual for a twelve-year-old of average intelligence at the very best. It's as if he's leaving a trail of crumbs for me, leading me down to this damn wood. How do I know all this, maybe you're wondering? I mean, you know what's going on in my head most of the time because I tell you. How can I tell you what he was thinking? He had me down as a half-wit, a glue sniffer, something along those lines. Average intelligence at best. See, he used to get all these calls. All day long the intercom would be buzzing. He'd get up to take the calls in his secretary's office next door. Just got up and left his files there. Sometimes he'd switch the intercom on to speak to his secretary, forget to switch it back off again. I'd sit there and listen to him telling people all about me, like I wasn't there, like I was some kind of stooge. He'd talk to my parents in the adjoining room, leave the door ajar as if I would automatically turn away, cover my ears, be seen and not heard. 'The trouble is, Mrs Roberts,' I heard him one time, 'David is refusing to accept anything that happened is down to him. This business of dual worlds and some strange female living in the stream, well I don't need to tell you he's taking refuge in fantasy because he can't cope with the reality of the situation.' I don't know, maybe he was double-bluffing me. Maybe he wanted me to hear it all, wanted me to sit there listening when he was out of the room. Maybe he figured I'd pay more attention, thinking I was being so clever. Let me tell you, the games we played in that bloody office, that winter. 'Perhaps brought on by some kind of stimulant . . . I know he's never showed any signs in the past. The thing is . . . I know he's an imaginative child . . . I know that, Mrs Roberts, the thing is it's my job is to peel all that away. Peel it away and get down to the real problem. The real problem that he's hiding, that he's hiding from himself. Once we get there . . . maybe we'll start making some progress.' I could hear my father protesting about the time it was taking. How long was I going to be away? I hadn't been charged with anything. When was I going to be allowed home?

'Bear with me . . . he's beginning to talk about himself a little. His feelings for the girl, his weight problem.' Always my fucking weight problem. 'You would be amazed how many young people I see with these kind of problems . . . many of them simply can't cope with the strains of puberty, peer-group pressure. I think your David is on the verge of telling me exactly what happened down there. When he's come to terms with it, he's come to terms with himself,' he assures them. Finishes on an optimistic note, convincing my parents everything is hunky dory. They were already in awe of the letters after his name and the row of pens in his breast pocket. Go on home, he'll be fine with us. I heard Dad saying something about the weekend and that he'd take it higher. Whiteman strides back in rubbing his hands together, catches me slouched there picking my nose like I do sometimes. He can hardly disguise his contempt. I gaze out of the window, try and catch my parents' Viva nosing out into the traffic on the ring-road. I bet they don't even talk till they're almost home. What; concerned, embarrassed? Wouldn't you be if I was yours? He coughs, rattles his notebook to get my attention. Sit in with me for a while.

'You were describing how you thought Rupert's disappearance may have had something to do with your . . . er . . . success with Samantha?' Didn't I tell you? Oh no. Sorry. Yeah, old Rupert, that night he ran off like that. Well, he never turned up. Didn't go home. I should have maybe mentioned it earlier, in case you were wondering.

'He couldn't have known very much. Not that night. I certainly didn't say anything,' I say sulkily, falteringly. Some good teenaged angst stuff. Look at his pen go across his notebook. Is what he wants to hear for sure.

'You felt you'd won her, beaten him, beaten your rival, didn't you?'

I shrug.

'Did you boast about it, try and make him jealous?'

What, I get the girl so he runs off, that it? That what you think as well? 'He may have been jealous if he'd found out, I hadn't told him.'

'Samantha could have.'

'So ask her.'

'I did. She doesn't know if she said anything to him or not. She can't be clear on the times.'

'She either told him before he went away or she didn't,' I point out. He shakes his head.

'Let me be the judge of that. You just tell me what you know, not what she knows.' I take another look out of the window. 'I'll put it another way. If you had gone round to his house, and he started boasting about his success with her, would you have been jealous?'

'I suppose.'

'You suppose it would have made you jealous. What if she told you she liked him, liked him more than you. You would have felt jealous all over again, wouldn't you?' I nod. 'It would have made you jealous; would it have made you run away?'

'No.'

'You seem very sure.'

'I am.' I am certain. Think about it, OK? Who the hell would have been surprised if she and Rupert had hit it off, left me out in the cold? Who would have been surprised if she went for him instead of me? I was the fat one, he was the skinny one with all the stuff. Nobody would have expected me to take her from him, so how could I have lost face? If that hare had won the race, who'd have laughed at the poor old tortoise? He wasn't built for winning races.

'Were you glad Rupert was out of the way, is out of the way?'

Well, I thought I would be, to tell you the truth. I thought he'd come back with his tail between his legs in a day or so. I thought by the time he came back, Sam and I would be a nice squeaky clean little lovely couple. Just like it's supposed to be.

SECOND OPINIONS

Trouble is, nobody told Samantha. Never did. Let her go through life without taking her to one side, putting her straight. I tried my way, persistent persuasion. Didn't do me any good as a twelve-year-old, didn't do me any good when I'd grown up. She hadn't been in the mood for romance when Rupert disappeared like that. Little ingrate. Never did show any gratitude for what we did for her, saving her life like that. OK, OK, I'm getting there. Still not spilled the beans, have I? Given you a few hints along the way but still no ghosties and ghoulies. What is this, an encounter group? Yeah, well, it takes some going back to, if you want to know. Takes some going back for this adult mind, these adult eyes. It's difficult to remember that when all this shit was going down I wasn't all that impressed with it. When you're a kid you can take things in your stride, ride the knocks. It's when you're all grown up that the knocks start echoing back, bruising you deep down, inside. It seems so sinister now, but back then I'd shake it off in a few days. Nothing seemed to spook me.

Spooks me now, just tapping it out like this with D.B. swanning around the wallpaper with her sharp shears, cutting back the vegetation, the flowery borders. Stripping my walls back to the plaster and cracks. Rupert wandering out of the bare-boarded bathroom, box of tissues and a nosebleed. A pair of pincers and a grey splinter under the pad of his thumb. I push the chair back, shut the door on him, the worn wood splintering my skin so I can barely dab the keys, run the letters together, run sentences into hieroglyphic rectangles. Back then I had to eat my meals, go to bed, attend school, write my lines, same as I always had. Maybe it was Solomon kept me ticking over, kept me anchored down when everything was rushing by, slipstreaming us all. I miss the old bastard now, riding shotgun as I yank the reins of my memories. You remember him frogmarching me home that night, the night he caught us down at the cottage? By the time we'd got home I realized he knew just about everything there was to know about that damn gorge. Knew something was going on down there. He wasn't going to tell me about it, though, so I kept my mouth shut. I kept it shut when he stopped at my gate, let me trot on in without calling my parents out to tell them all about it. Just stood there in the shadows like a shapechanger. A black shape by the gate, watching me safely in through the patio doors. He never said anything about it to my parents, and I never found out exactly what he'd said to Rupert's. Sure, he'd seen us down in the gorge, but Rupert had run on home alone. Why, wasn't he back yet? He'd take another walk out if they wished. No, he'd turn up. Probably gone round to see the Bell girl, seems dead keen on her lately, too keen. At 10.15 p.m. he still hadn't turned up and Silas and Solomon had gone out, buttoned into their greatcoats, torchbeams sliding haphazardly over the allotments. Checked the lane, checked the sheds, the garages. They came round here when I was in bed asleep. My dad grumbling in his dressing-gown, no he wasn't with me. No sign. No sign next morning either. Old Solomon, I saw him shuffling along sack on his back stopping every now and then to peer into the hedgerows along the lane. He never invited me round for a chat, never tried to confide in me, sympathize with me.

He was waiting for me. Waiting to see if I could keep my mouth shut, bottle things up good, like he did. Let's face it, he was going to have to bottle up a whole lot more, next couple of weeks. He knew it was our fault. We'd attracted, concentrated, whatever it was lying in the water, breathing the mists. We'd stepped right on in there and walked away with our shoes gunked, picked up something nasty. Rupert and I, always playing in the gorge, along the stream. Running under the pylon and its singing wires, sitting in that old car. Imaginary chases through downtown Chicago. That stream, that damn thing down there was licking its lips, lining us up for the big one. It would have had us both, sooner or later, if it hadn't been for Solomon. It knew the old man like the stream knew the stones along its course. It had washed them, shaped them, moved them here and there. It had moved him down to the Boar, and then along the cliff to Silas's place. He'd realized we were treading all over its gaping mouths, tripping its trip-wires. He'd watched us labour back up the hillside as if only he could see the green filth clinging to our legs and arms, the foul weeds hanging from our hair, the slickly slippered leeches pulsing on our faces. Swarming with tiny flying creatures that tangled our hair and drowned in our eyes. What could he have done to convince us to stay away, to keep from the water? Maybe put on a white robe and try to scare us in the woods one night, like the plot they have on *Scooby Doo* every week. Hey, do you think we were going to buy something like that? He knew full well he couldn't have kept us out of there if he tried. In fact, the more he tried to keep us out, the more we'd have been in. What did he do? He waited. Waited and watched the way a shepherd watches the lambs frolic in the shadow of the wolf's den. From his room in Rupert's house he had as good a view out over the hill as Sam and I. Leaning on his rake in his allotment he'd watch us double past, paratroopers heading for the bridge at Arnhem, Cossacks on a secret mission behind enemy lines. From his chicken house he could see the roof of his old cottage, down there in the trees. Maybe he could see the stream if he climbed on an old crate, peeked through a gap in the rickety shed. From Rupert's conversations at home, talking to me on the phone, he could piece together our movements, plot our course in the plot. Man had us under surveillance and we never knew. When we took the picture he wasn't far behind, all he wanted to know was who actually had it. Searched Rupert's room, realized it had to be Samantha or me. Couldn't very well go through our things so he doubled his watch, waited. He wasn't trying to punish me that night, he was protecting me, protecting me from her. That's right, I'm getting there. You've picked her out on the breeze a couple of times, caught the green blur in the corner of my eye, the fragile fingerprints in the raindrops on the window. Followed the blip closing in on my dreamscanner. Don't worry, she'll blow up a storm any day now. Right now she's a hurricane off the Florida coast, nothing to do with us. That Atlantic's just so much salty water to her, though. A huff and a puff and she's blowing your doors down too. You'll see her just like we did, maybe wish you'd been satisfied with traces, distant thunder. Sheet-lightning crackling and popping bright white on the horizon, a fine sleet riding in on the hushed air, a lone beachcomber looking out to sea, shielding his eyes. The way we watched the police out combing the hillside the day after Rupert went. I stood next to Samantha, watching them from her window. Watching the dark line move slowly across the hillside, beaters in blue. You could almost picture Rupert leaping up with a squawk and running away from them, flapping his wings like he was trying to fly. I thought maybe it would cheer Samantha, so I mentioned it to her, a skinny white gull. She had hardly even said hello, had a face like a fiddle. Persistent persuasion, eh? She didn't think it was very funny, Rupert flying away like a skinny pheasant. Got to her. I waited a while, waiting for her to lean over, take my arm and rest her head on my shoulder. She didn't budge. Stood there staring at the searchers as they thrust sticks into bramble outcrops we'd converted into ammo dumps. Over ditches where we'd gone over the top to be mown down by the Hun machine-gunners. They reached the road, way over to our left, stopped and passed round a Thermos flask. Moved the Transits down to the bottom of the hill by the bridge and started all over again, sweeping through the thicker under-growth along the stream. A couple of them clambered down the crumbling red bank and poked about in the stillborn waters. Nothing but witches' hair weed swirling in a plughole. They lifted sheets of corrugated zinc, found snails and slow-worms slinking in the slick wet clay. They ripped the boards from the cottage, shone strong beams into the gloom. Sent dogs upstairs to sniff around. They pulled up the culvert in the middle of the bridge to get down and have a good look under there, where the stream runs deepest. Right in under the cliff they unloaded a Land-Rover and helped the diver fix

his kit. Heaving those heavy tanks from the back, paying out orange rope and breathing lines. He'd bob to the surface in a cauldron of bubbles, hold up whatever he'd found. An old tyre, coils of rusty wire. Rummaging there among the shopping trolleys and rotting armchairs. No sign of the boy, though. We could see a senior officer with his ear to a squawking radio, directing his troops around our battlefields. Boy's got to be here somewhere. Had no money, just took off into the night. Boy had broken some picture so he may have been upset, frightened he was going to be punished. Now they were counting days rather than hours. What if he hadn't run off. What if he'd been snatched. Widen the search, check the petrol stations along the main road. Seen anything funny? Get out the well-worn picture books, Budgworth's top hundred molesters. Check 'em out all over again. Used and strangled, bundled down the muddy red slope into the stream. Floating there with his thin white arms sticking out, floating face-down over the bright pebbles and shopping trolleys. While Solomon had been grilling me over the picture he might have been clawing at a car boot, choked down in there with a worn spare tyre and a bag of oily tools. Stuffed in there with the rags.

'That's Inspector Macall from Budgworth. Dad says he's in charge.'

It's the first thing she's said without being spoken to. Something's gone wrong with her. I can see she'd be upset with him gone like that, but it isn't my fault. I didn't knock him over the head and roll him into the stream, did I? Why is she treating me like she doesn't know me? She knows me now, doesn't she? I try and hold her arm, she pulls away like I'm covered in mould. Stands there biting her lip, staring out of the window.

'He'll be back,' I reason. Trying to get back in her good book. He ran off, not me. He's the one acting the big kid, the sulky brat. Forget about him for a moment, maybe cuddle me. Kiss me. That's what I'm here for, not to stand here staring like a scarecrow. I want to taste that taste on her lips again. I want to run my tongue over those tiny dunes of skin, rippled silk. David Roberts, human fruit pastille. Let me soothe you. Her face is reflected in the window. I reach out, dab her glass eye with my finger. She looks round, frowns.

'He'll be back,' I repeat, wheedling, smiling.

'Perhaps he's gone under the cliff,' she says shakily. 'Perhaps he fell in and got dragged under by the current.'

I shake my head. 'He was quite a good swimmer' – not as good as me by the way – 'and the current's not too strong at this time of year. If the stream was in flood . . .' I shrug. The stream runs into a crack not more than six inches above the normal water level. He couldn't fit under there.

'Well, he's got to be somewhere,' she snorts, exasperated with me. Why me?

'Sam, you know the other night . . .'

'You pulled the wood from that window like you're some kind of bloody Tarzan.' What? Sorry, have I missed something? Pinch me a second and I'll remember where we were.

'If it hadn't been for you showing your muscles he'd never have got the bloody thing in the first place.' While I'm still working this out she brushes past me and crosses to her drawers. 'And you dropped the picture, you clumsy prick.' She swivels away from me as if she doesn't want to say it to my face, but she might just as well be pissing on my grave. I'm standing there by her window, rocking forwards and backwards, trying to get my bearings. What the fucking hell's all this got to do with me? I'm the one who didn't want to get involved, I tried to talk them out of it. She's so sure of herself, I have to keep running it over again, make sure I remember things right. You heard me tell them to forget it, didn't you? You remember? She stands there with her back to me, shoulders shaking as she sobs into a handkerchief. She hugged me in, she kissed me. After we held each other I thought we'd carry on nicely, like couples are supposed to. Our minds would carry along nicely, two sets of tracks running along a tunnel. She's derailed herself, set herself right on another track going in the opposite direction, like all her points have given up the ghost, gone crazy. She's two feet away from me, but the gorge opens out between us, a dirty great chasm come to swallow all my hopes. I'm still reeling as she turns as if she's made up her mind. Says, cold and spiteful:

'You don't even care he's gone. Your best friend. I bet you're

just jealous. I'll tell my dad you know where he is, I'll tell him, see if you like it.' I stand there, slack mouth, defeated. A poor know-nothing peasant bowed before his empress. I'm thinking of things to throw back at her but my tongue's given out on me. She sits on her bed, snatches up a book and slings it down again.

'Oh, why don't you just get lost?' I'm holding a holed umbrella against a hurricane. Back off. Back off she's upset she didn't mean it. It's like a throb going through my brain. Give her a chance to think about it, she'll realize what she's said.

She'll be crying, saying she's sorry all over. I shut the door on her, walk downstairs quietly. PC Bell looks up from his paper. Figures I'm worried over my dear little rat bastard playmate.

'Don't fret yourself, son. He'll turn up. In the mean time, watch yourself, OK?' If he turns up I'll strangle the slimy little creep myself, that's what. He rises, lets me out of the back door into the gathering darkness. Guess who I bump into in the lane?

COMPANY

'Have you heard anything?' Jesus Christ I'd wish he'd stop doing that. Lurching out of the shadows at people. Solomon, buttoned tight into his overcoat. I shrug. My heart's beating like that fat guy sits in the front of those ancient galleys, beating out a rhythm for the rowers. Beating out a rhythm on me all right, pounding away as if he's got his fat thumbs behind my eyes. That would teach her, wouldn't it, if he came out and clobbered me as well, dragged me off to the henhouse where he'd dragged Rupert, covered him in red dust and chicken shit. Smeared him all over. If they found me in a ditch with the baling twine from his belt bitten into my neck, maybe that would make her think, the selfish little bitch.

'You don't want to go down there,' he says, nodding his head toward the fields, the gorge. I stop, look around me. Say something to let me off, for God's sake.

'Come on down the henhouse with me. They want feeding.' He holds up his big zinc pail, glittering dully in the twilight like a gun barrel.

'Keep me company, I'll see you all right. Always lock 'em up this time of night, foxes will have 'em else.' I knew he was going to tell me something, I knew he was going to fill me in. He'd never spoken that many words to me before, not in one go anyway. I look at his rugged old face, those amber eyes in the sickly dusk. His wiry hair, this way and that like the fur on a goat's behind. They won't miss me yet. They thought I was safely tucked in with Sam. She won't miss me at all. Serve her right if he did strangle me, roll me down the slope, splash me into the dark stream.

'I'll go with you, perhaps he's hiding in the chicken run,' I say quietly. He studies me for a moment as if he can read the thoughts reeling off my mind. Pick around as if he was examining a tin of nails.

'I checked. They checked. They checked up on me right enough,' he says gruffly. He grunts something.

'Come along anyway. Two pairs of eyes are better than one.' What difference does it make if he kills me or not? If Sam's thrown me off like an old bone who'll have me? Lorraine Lamb? She goes round with Martin Lawrence's lot. She kissed me once, and it's worse missing it now. I follow him down the lane, over the stile, into the deep gloom of the allotments. The mist is out, the dustbins fume quietly to themselves. The water troughs are full of what looks like blocks of emerald water. I walk behind him, the gruff old git, take a look at the back of his head, the battered grey hat, the rusty hair. If I'm not careful I'll end up like him, chickens for company, staring at the fire. Chickens will take feed from anyone, take it from strangers well as from him.

'Why did you want to know who had the picture?' I ask as we turn along the track toward the shadowy chicken shack. The warm cackling of the hens guides us in the still air.

'I know about the picture.' Yes, fine. 'I know why it came to me, I know why I left it there, I know why you brought it back.' He doesn't sound angry about it. He's not blaming me for something, is he? 'You brought it back to get me back,' he declares.

'Get you back for what?'

'Get me back down there. Down in the cottage, in the stream.' I trudge along in silence weighing it. Doesn't make any sense to me, buddy.

'She's caught me once with that picture, she knew she'd catch me again.'

'She? You mean Samantha?'

He chuckles a little. A sort of chuckle anyway. A grumbling chuckle. 'Glaistig.'

'Glass stick?' What the fucking hell's that?

'She's Glaistig. The Glaistig. The Lady Glaistig,' he recites.

I shiver a little, half expect him to turn round and bare his fangs, dribble all over his coat.

'Did she live in the cottage?' There's that chuckle again.

'Here and there.' The stream. Tumbling conkers and still-born waters connect circuits that had been lying around gathering dust on forgotten shelves. He stares round at me.

'Don't stand there gawping, boy. You know damn fine there's something wrong in the water,' he tells me flatly. 'You've felt her, you can feel her now. The mist coming up now, that's her breath. The stream burbling down there, that's her chattering to her followers.'

Oh, right. Sure. I didn't know shit back then.

'Don't look at me like that, lad, think for yourself. Is the stream right?'

'Right in what way?' I ask politely. He frowns.

'If the stream was right, boy, you wouldn't be walking along o' me here.' He unlocks the rickety gate and holds it open for me. I step into the run, dry red earth scratched for ever by hundreds of horny chicken feet. The chickens flock around our feet like feathery footballs.

'You mean she's got Rupert?'

He pours the bran from the pail into the dull grey trough, straightens up.

'I know what I think.' He looks down at the mass of brown bodies swarming round the food.

'She's the stream. She's all the bad things washed down the centuries. Washed down and washed together. She's all bad things clinging to a raft, washed up down there.' He nods with his head. No wonder he's an outcast. No wonder the village has cut him off like a leper. He's just a lonely old man, living out some daft fantasy. You think I'm bad enough, going on sometimes. I didn't have a thing on Solomon. He believed it all, took her as read, this Glass Stick creature. What did she look like anyway? Where did she appear in his picture? She was his picture, his whole picture. He moved in the background of her portrait. He was the peasant toiling in the field as Brueghel's Icarus falls. I eye him curiously, expecting at any moment a nudge and grin, good one, eh? You looked like a ghost coming out of the Bells' back there. Thought I'd give you a bit of a fright to cheer you up. Is that what he's going to say?

'When I was a lad, bit older than you, there used to be a stone over there,' he says, nodding toward the immense silver pylon standing above the trees. 'There used to be seven, but they'd dragged them away, broken them up for walls, slates. There was just the one left.' He opéns the door and steps into the warm reek of the chicken house. 'Hasn't always been like this you know, this hill.' There are two rows of nesting boxes along each wall, each compartment has its own cosy patch of straw worn smooth by warm chicken breasts. Occasional white egg, stuck with dung and fine feathers.

'You're not scared of the Glass Stick, then?' I ask.

'Glaistig. GGG.'

'That's what you call the bad things in the water?'

'Is what she calls herself.' Oh. 'She can't really do me any harm, apart from in here.' He taps his head. 'I'm of no interest to her any more. If she can do me any incidental harm she will,' he remarks. In other words . . .

'So she's interested in us . . . Rupert and me?' Pretty calm about it, aren't I, considering there's a watery witch thing out there with my name on her number-plate. This supernatural dream bitch bearing grudges from the Stone Age, to listen to him.

'Watch yourself, is all.'

Watch myself? That it? 'It's already got Rupert, is that what you reckon?'

'She might have. She might have someone else who's got him.'

Like an evil spirit, I figure he means. Like she makes other people do bad things for her? 'What makes you so sure, what's she done to you?'

'What's she done to me,' he chuckles, wipes his chin and studies his nails. They're

IN THE FIELDS

chips of flint, chipped from a stone by the slow strength of some Neanderthal Clove man. His hands are calloused and scaled from years of toil and cold water, hard soaps hardly lathered in his hairy paws. They were his tools, these vices, these pincers. For tearing and pulling, digging and hammering. Farmer's hands and none the worse for that. You can't expect to work your father's fields and have hands like some penpusher from Budgworth. Honest toil, day in day out, with just a few hours between to meet your cronies at the Blue Boar, drown your thirst with still cider. Back home a hard bed in a small room he had to bow his head to walk around. Lie awake listening to the creatures moving in the thatch. Sleep till dawn and Jubal, coughing on his first cigarette, shaking him awake, lantern swinging in his liver-spotted hand. Rising from his warm pit to pull on his trousers, the shirt that told its own stories of toil and sweat. He'd hardly given his hands a second thought, till now.

'Well, what do you think?'

'Well, 'tis . . . beautiful Miss May. Beautiful.' It wasn't a word that came handily to Solomon, squatting there awkward with the picture clamped in his great scaly hands, Caliban's claws. He'd never had much call for the word, until he'd met Miss May. Like a little flower she was, a little blossom in her silky finery, leaning back to let the breeze play in her fine hair. The frame had been etched with infinite care and precision, a skill he could appreciate. The picture itself reminded him of butterfly wings, petals crushed in tissue paper. Dancers. Ballet dancers fleeing from the mysterious green creature that lurked in the bullrushes, peering out at them like a greedy fox. He'd see dancing girls enough if he got a Middle East posting. He glanced at her again. Couldn't help himself. A tress of hair had fallen over her peachy cheek, he longed to reach across, tuck it gently back behind her ear. She sat on the best blanket he'd been able to find, waited on him like an angel. Picking daisies and threading the stems to form a delicate chain. She looked up smiling, lifted the chain over his bony hands.

'You can't get away now,' she said quietly.

'No, miss.' He could have torn her in two without missing a breath. She folded her hands in her lap. The heat must have been getting to him, he felt as if the hillside was shifting gently under him. The sun overhead cast a golden glow around her as if her head was resting on a giant dandelion. Her eyes were deep blue, languidly following a pair of cabbage whites as they dipped and fluttered over the blooming field. Her nose was small, rather pointed. Her cheekbones were high but not Asiatic. High forehead and smooth blonde hair, swept back over her long neck and caught in a green velvet headband. Her dress seemed to change colour as the sunlight shifted, change in sympathy with the shimmering heat haze. High above in the eggshell-blue sky three Spitfires roared toward Budgworth. He shielded his eyes, watched them. Summer, 1940. Those few Spitfires were all that stood between them and Hitler's tank armies. Jubal had taken down their shotguns, collected up their cartridges.

'Let the bastards come,' he'd tell the regulars down at the Boar. 'Let 'em come and see how many'll get out of my gorge.'

'No call to turn the signposts round down there, if these 'ere paratroops drop in on us,' Crutty Mungo told him, sipping his pint and chuckling with the rest. Two hundred miles east the RAF were fighting it out tooth and nail with the Luftwaffe. They might as well have been flying round the moon, sitting here on this hillside. Away yonder a pair of skylarks were hovering in full song, annoyed at the couple who had invaded their cliff. He'd pointed them out to her, told her how his father would set a lure, a bright spinning lure, to catch their tiny souls. He laid the picture on the blanket with unaccustomed reverence, a Russian peasant with an icon. Folded his hands behind his head and lay back to gaze at the sky.

'My mum can paint, after a fashion. Got an interest in books and sichlike,' he said. She nodded, gazing over the clifftops, breathing the breeze.

'It's wonderful, your little hill,' she said dreamily. He propped himself up, followed her gaze out over the cliff, the gorge, the trees.

'I bet you bring all the girls up here,' she said softly, making him twitch.

'Why no, miss . . . not all of them.' He'd brought Mary Lamb here though, after chapel on Sundays, hadn't he? Up above the cliff, the gorge where the trees held sway. Somewhere behind the belt of trees the stream twisted round boulders and rocks, chattered beneath the stone bridge which carried the road off the hills and into sleepy Clove. Miles away from the gathering war clouds. Light-years away. This was his place, he felt it without thinking, as if his bones had been cut out from the cliffs. Down there to the right their cottage, a curl of blue smoke from the chimney, and in the foreground newly dug allotment strips where Jubal was busy cultivating more vegetables for the War effort. Get the field ploughed, lad, he'd ordered his son. No good letting it lie fallow while there's folks a-starvin' and a-dyin' up in Budgworth, and soldiers out in the fields making do with slop from rusty cans. They'd never dug the top field before. Rough grazing for goats was all it had been good for. And that great stone they'd shifted. It made him prickle to think of it. Chilled him even as he lay out there in the sun. Had to be moved, his father said, get it moved, get the plough up there. Couldn't plough round it. Solomon had objected, told him it had lain there hundreds of years, they'd best leave it be.

'We've moved the bleeders before,' Jubal pointed out, raising his cap and wiping his steely grey hair from his bronzed brow. 'We moved all that was left, save this one, when me father was a tenant here, after the first war.' Solomon hadn't been convinced.

'There's folk that have come a studyin' these stones, down from Budgworth. They won't take kindly to us a-shifting it about.'

'There's a bloody war on, son, who's going to object to us clearing the bugger off?' So they had called Lamb up with his new tractor, damn near burned the motor out dragging the slab off. With a final screech of the engine the tractor had lurched forwards taking the great slab with it. Jubal had trotted forwards and then bent double covering his mouth. Solomon thought at first his father had been hit by a chipping, the way he'd tottered. Then he smelt it for himself, tore his shirt out of his trousers and stuffed it into his mouth, over his nose. He was a countryman born and bred, but the smell that rolled out from under the stone was the very worst thing he had ever caught wind of. It took him a few moments to clear his eyes, they'd run that badly. He looked up to see Lamb standing on his tractor, hat held over his face.

'Good Christ alive, what the hell's down there?' he'd called, muffled, to Jubal. Jubal had inched closer to the pit, peered down, jumped back a foot or two in alarm. Solomon strode over, grabbed his father's shoulders. He felt him leap in his hands as if he'd electrocuted him. Jubal was shivering and sweating though his bones felt cold. Solomon held him as he peered over the rim. The stone had been about seven feet long by four wide and three deep. The pit was deeper. About ten feet deep, with sheer sides, strata of chalky soils, flints, and seams of richer red earth. The bottom had been flattened down by many feet, roughly paved with flatter stones. The bones he took to be human at first. Solomon could see the ribcage, but couldn't make out what had happened to the legs. Perhaps they'd been crushed, broken, eaten. He strode backwards, pulling Jubal away.

'The Beast with Two Backs,' he croaked. Lamb had jumped down from his tractor, peered over, lurched backwards.

'My Christ, we'll pull the bloody stone back,' he shouted. Jubal shook himself free. Solomon had let him loose. He looked over to Lamb. 'There's no call. 'Tis only bones.'

'A beast with two backs?' Jubal had waved his hand.

'Old customs, old stories.' Solomon hadn't heard any about a beast with two backs.

'An old ritual,' Jubal said, peering over the edge of the pit, **117** wiping his face with his bright red neckerchief.

'In the old days they'd do this. Warning off others.' Lamb was shaking his head. 'We ought to put the stone back, it's not right now, Jubal,' he argued.

Jubal grunted. 'What do I care for a few old bones and a bad smell? We've brought 'e up here to move it, not bend your knee and worship it,' he'd snapped.

'What did they do? What ritual?' Solomon had demanded.

''Twas for whores and sichlike,' Jubal growled. ''Twas for them that had stolen hearts of husbands. The womenfolk would bring 'em out and do it to 'em, make 'em a beast with two backs.'

'How?'

'See for yourself. Can you not see the bones down there?'

Solomon reeled away from them, dashed to the hedge thinking he would bring up his dinner. Lamb stood by, ashen, while Jubal lifted the spare fuel can from his tractor. Solomon had looked up, focused on his father as he tipped the fuel into the pit.

'Are you going to burn it out, then?' Lamb asked shakily.

'Of course we're going to burn it out. Would you have me scuttle away now, now we've found her? Stand back, move the tractor away.' He watched Lamb climb back into the driver's seat, start the engine, and haul the slab away from the pit.

'Father, don't—' Solomon called. Jubal brought out a match, cupped his hand, and knelt beside the pit.

'Burn in hell, then,' Jubal called, and dropped the match. The fire rushed out of the ground like the German flame-throwers in the newsreels, gushing over some Polish pillbox. Here soon. Jubal staggered back, coat singed, as the heat blazed across the meadow. Lamb halted his tractor and watched the red flames climb, leap twenty feet into the blue sky, slowly curl into thick black smoke. Solomon could smell it on his clothes all week as he toiled and sweated to clear the ground around the pit. The meadow was dotted with tussocks of tough grasses, thistles even the donkey hadn't been able to manage. The whole family turned out to help, Jubal pushing barrowloads of refuse to the pit to stoke the fires they'd lit, Silas and their mother gathering baskets of heavy stones. Solomon had bent his back, hacked at the earth like a wild thing, working like a lion to blot out the image of the broken white bones. The Beast with Two Backs.

'Turn it once, the weather will do the rest, it'll be like cornflour,' Jubal had predicted, as his son waded into the thickest bramble outcrop.

'We shouldn't have moved it, Father, we should have left it be,' he protested, hauling great bundles of brambles away as if the thorns would do as penance.

'Are you still dirtyin' your breeches over that? What can old bones do to us that the Germans can't? We need this field for ploughin' and there's an end to it.' He paused, wiped a string of spittle from his mouth. 'Keep your mouth closed about it as well, I don't want all the neighbours causing a stink over it. They're busybodies enough already. Get on with your work and I'll hear no more about it.'

Jubal had stomped off to the cottage muttering and cursing, and Solomon redoubled his attack on the brambles. That's when he had first seen her, Miss May. Sweating bare-chested, scratched and bleeding from a dozen small cuts, he looked up to see her standing among the hacked branches and coiled brambles.

'Good heavens, miss . . . You did give me a start,' he said, snatching up his blue shirt and thrusting his bloody arms in, buttoning awkwardly. She turned her head, looked around the meadow, her face almost invisible beneath a huge straw hat.

'It's not Jubal, is it?' she asked him, looking round. She had a tiny pale face, partly hidden by the enormous hat. Her dress was a shimmery green. Rather old fashioned.

'Why no, miss. I'm his son Solomon. Did you want to speak to him? I'll run and get him if you wish.' He didn't recognize her from the village, and he wasn't a frequent visitor at the Grange along towards Axeheads.

'I didn't mean to startle you,' she said, sure of herself.

'Well, you certainly did, miss, begging your pardon. Gave me a regular turn.' She was as slim as a weasel under the shimmering gown, no meat on her at all. Down behind the gate he could see a large red car. Posh. He'd half expected to see a set of fine young gentlemen, fighter pilots, lounging in the back. Making the most of their hours without an ME 109 on their tail. Waiting impatiently as she chatted to the smelly oik out digging on the hill.

'What a lovely place you have here,' she said, looking round.

'Not what I'd call it, miss,' Solomon said, wiping his face and feeling his back shriek in protest. 'You're not from round here then, miss, not from the Grange?'

She nodded. Yes or no? 'You looked so busy up here, I just had to stop.' She smiled sweetly, looked at the heaps of brambles.

'We're clearing her, miss, clearing the meadow for plough-ing. For the War and all.' He rubbed his lower back, she looked unimpressed.

'I mean, if they start cutting our food supplies with these here U-boats, we'll need every cabbage and potato we can grow, I reckon.' She looked mystified, lost.

'Were you on your way somewhere then, miss? Took a wrong turning?'

'I know where I am,' she said simply. 'It's all changed, though.'

'Been round here before then, miss? You won't credit the state it was in. Brambles a foot thick there were. I'll have plenty of practice, if they send me out East like.'

'Out East?'

'Middle East, miss. Against the Italians out in the desert, somewhere like that.'

She looked mystified. Didn't they teach 'em anything in these fine schools of theirs these days? 'You're to be sent away?'

'Two weeks, miss. Is why I've to hurry and finish, Pa not being up to this graft these days.'

'You're to be sent East?'

'By way of Taunton first. Taunton base camp first for train-ing and sichlike.' He watched tiny zephyrs lift strands of her fine blonde hair.

'There used to be stones here,' she said abruptly, prickled his skin again.

'Stone, miss. Just the one.'

'What have you done with them?' Is that what she was, somebody down from a museum of antiquities up in Budgworth? Someone from the Ministry checking up on Hillstones monuments? He'd told her as much now.

'Just the one, miss. There were one big slab over in the other corner there.'

She gazed straight at him with her blue eyes, concentrated cornflower blue. 'You dragged it somewhere?'

He bristled, awkward. 'Well, we took it to the side of the cliff there, miss.' He nodded towards the trees brimming up out of the gorge.

'They're over there?'

'No, miss . . . just the one. We had to clear the field, see, for the war effort and all.'

She shrugged, smiled. 'Perhaps I'm thinking about somewhere else?'

'You might be getting mixed up with Dunberry Oldstones, away toward Budgworth that way,' Solomon said, relieved.

She nodded. 'I suppose I must be,' she said. He stood awkwardly, bronzed and sweating against her perfect apricot complexion.

'When do you go?'

'Two weeks, miss,' he repeated. She hadn't been listening.

'And your field?'

'Father will look after it once it's cleared. We'll have help from the village, these Land Girls and what not.'

'I hope it won't be too much of a strain for him, all this,' she said sweetly.

'You know him then, miss?'

'We met briefly . . . forget where. A long time ago.' She didn't look old enough to have been a long time anywhere. And Father had certainly never mentioned . . .

'Your name, miss? So I can tell him I've seen you?'

'May.'

'Miss May?'

'May,' she repeated. Miss May. He couldn't wait to tell   **121**

Father about her, tell the boys at the Boar. Picture their red faces as he told them.

'And there's us thinking he was sweet on Tucker Lamb's eldest,' they'd scold, jealous as magpies. Mary Lamb, yes. A man could do much worse than Mary Lamb. But she was a tractor, compared to this sleek little racing car, meaning no disrespect to Mary, like.

'Will you be here again? I do so like walking the hills now. They're so quiet and beautiful. I haven't anybody to take me.' She looked coyly at him from under the enormous straw hat. So peachy he could have bitten into her then and there.

'Would you like to drive with me?'

Was she asking to see him again? He could hardly credit it. He stammered yes, of course he would. Thought about what Mary would say if she got to hear of it. He'd made his excuses and here he was. He would have nobody but himself to blame if he was spotted up here with the girl from the big house. Nothing to lose but Mary, his sweetheart since they'd been old enough to walk. But what good was a reputation when you've to go overseas, charge at machine-guns? He could be a dead man in six months' time. Maybe if it hadn't been for the War he'd have made his excuses and stuck along with Mary, taken her up the hill of a Sunday afternoon. He was handsome enough in his best trousers, clean white shirt. For a second he'd even imagined himself worthy of her, marrying her. And why not? With Jubal gone he would have all the gorge and the top field. A dozen Frisians and more sheep. This field would be wheat, the lower pastures a market garden. He'd be rich, he'd thrive, as long as he survived this wretched war. He'd bring her home in triumph. Mr Solomon Jones and young bride, Miss May of the Great House Mays. Why not? Why not now? He glanced at her as she finished twining his great rough hands with the daisy chain.

'Will I see you again before you go?' she asked.

He stood, wiping his hands on his trousers, handing the chain to her. She took it, looked down.

'I'm busy on the farm most of the time miss,' he said, thinking of the chores Jubal had lined up for him before he went. Next Sunday was the only chance. But Mary would know something was amiss if he missed two Sundays running. There would be talk.

'Next Sunday then, same time,' he suggested.

'We'll go for a drive,' she suggested, rising gracefully while he folded the blanket, clasped his picture to his chest.

'And thank you for the picture . . . I'll have to fetch you something in return, although Lord knows what.' He thought for a moment, tried to remember her passing it over to him. That's strange now. Could only have been an hour or two since and he couldn't recall taking it. Had he thanked her properly? She looked straight at him, straight in his eyes.

'There's really no need. I'm so glad you like it.' He felt another pang of guilt, thought about Mary's hurt look when Jubal told her he was too busy to meet her.

'Sorry, miss?'

'I said same time next week then.' He watched her float across the field, her misty dress shimmering and shifting colours in the bright sunlight. Away over the gorge the Lambs' white-walled farmhouse, red roofs shining in the sun. They'd be having tea about now, bread and jam, the odd scone. A few glasses of cider and then Mary would tidy away the things while they smoked. They probably hadn't said anything to her as she fussed about them, missing him. Miss May now, you couldn't imagine her washing dishes, waiting on the menfolk like that. What would Jubal make of her? He thought about the Sunday, thought about the following Monday. Train to Taunton and then God knows what. Outside the henhouse, the night had come down like owl's wings over a field-mouse. Seeped through the rickety planking and only held at bay by the feeble glow of Solomon's lantern. The warm glow made his face look kindly but careworn. I was drained, eyelids heavier than strips of lead.

'Rambling on I was. Your parents will be worried,' he said, climbing heavily to his feet.

'It's OK, it's only half seven,' I said, stifling a yawn. He picked up the basket laden with eggs, tucked it over his arm. 'The rest will have to wait. Come round again sometime.'

Coming from that old git it was a gilt-edged invitation. He walked me back to my gate, waited till I was at the patio doors. Then he went on his way whistling. Something about those white cliffs of Dover, I reckon.

THE RUN

She never whistled for me, and I'd have come running for her.
Wretched girl winds out my string and then lets go, lets me fly
off like an over-inflated balloon. Rupert never showed up. I
hoped he would. I hoped he would then maybe she would
have forgiven me, realized her mistakes. Trouble is she
would have jumped straight at him, given him a juicy kiss
right there in front of me, knocked me aside as I tried to shake
his hand. I avoided her like the plague, of course. Spotted her
from my window now and again but she never looked up
once. I kept away from her at school, looked away before she
could look away from me. Her friend Lorraine kept raising
her eyebrows at me, then nodding toward her. I stared and
shrugged like I didn't give a shit. The worst thing about that
time though was Rupert's mother at the end of their garden,
wringing a tea towel in her wet red hands. Like she'd heard
shouting and dashed out to see if it was him. I'd seen her also
wearing her old anorak, walking the lanes peering into the
bushes as if the police had missed something, overlooked him
lying there. Silas drove off every morning holding it all in
behind set features. Holding it all in the way his reservoirs
held in all their brimming waters. She'd wander the hillside,
fetching up at quiet places like the chicken run. Hold on to the
wire with her long red hands as if she'd just been liberated
from Dachau. She'd watch us pour the meal for the chickens,
fetching water from one of the big drums, Solomon weaving
rents in the wire with long traces gripped in his gritted teeth.
Why was she staring at him for? Did she suspect something?
He was living in their back room for Christ's sake. Maybe I'm
stretching it. She didn't really look accusing, more resentful.
As if she expected him to go sniff the lost boy out. Look up to

the sun, whittle down a divining rod and point it straight at his hiding place. He straightened, tipped the battered hat to the back of his head, and looked at her. She nodded, wandered off to prepare Silas's tea. I slipped out from behind the drum I'd been hiding behind, let myself into the run shutting the wire gate behind me. He looked up again, took the wire from his mouth as if it was some kind of muzzle.

'No sign of him, then?' I think he knew I wasn't there for Rupert. I didn't bother pretending too much, perhaps that's why he let me get away with it. If I'd stood there wiping my eyes he'd have told me to piss off and bawl somewhere else. He gathered his bits of tools and folded them into a canvas sack, stowed them away in a wooden bin thing on the side of the shed. I waited for him to look up.

'What happened that Sunday, then?'

He frowned. 'Nothing. I never turned up. I'd been spotted, see.' I followed him into the warm run, watched him dithering about.

'Tucker Lamb's eldest boy Arnold, he was courting a lass over Oldstones way. He'd been coming back over the Downs. One of those things I suppose. He'd told her of course.' Of course? Bloody sneaky bastard. 'He'd told her, I couldn't complain.' He looks behind him, squats on a ledge encrusted with chicken shit.

'I had to go round of course. Da was upset when I told him. I showed him the picture and all, showed Ma. She said the girl must think a lot of me to give me a picture like that. Da lost his temper, shouted about betraying Mary, bringing up a scoundrel, rubbish like that. Said I'd expected to wed Mary, hadn't got a right to go round with some girl from the big house. He was all for taking the picture and throwin' it on the fire, tell the truth.' He shakes his old head as I crouch on the upturned pail beside him.

'So I let Da cool down on his own. Wandered round for a while then went on over. I couldn't tell her.' He breathes out slowly, wistfully.

'I told her she'd been hiring beaters for a drive. Old Tucker looked up at that, he knew it wasn't right in the season and all. He kept his mouth closed though, Old Tucker. I reckon him and Jubal had got their heads together long since, made it all up behind our backs. They weren't going to let it slip just like that. Arnold said he'd seen me talking to her, the green one in the finery, talking, not kissing or anything.' He shakes his head again, a weak apologetic sort of a grin.

'See, I was quite a catch in those days, I was. What with being the eldest and all. Fair bit of land we had then, fair bit Jubal had put by. I said I was sorry if she'd taken anything amiss, if I'd upset her. She knew it was give in or lose me for good. Wasn't a time for standing on your principles, with the War coming and all. She said if I was going to go a-swannin' off round the hills with pretty girls they'd better be her. I said all right then. She said all right then. Her dad told us off, told us to go into the parlour if we were going to row all night. Crafty old bugger. We went into the kitchen and I proposed to her. Felt a right fool with her younger brother playing about on the floor. He's dead now of course.'

I'm holding my head with all this *Mill on the Floss* rubbish. 'But what happened on the Sunday?'

'I told you,' he snaps. 'Nothing. I never met her. Went to chapel, back round to Mary's for a goodbye dinner. Dad was there with Mum, he was still in a funny mood, kept looking at me all night. Worried about the War, I thought. Thinking about having to run the farm without me. Tucker, mind, he was as pleased as punch. I forgot all about *her*.'

'You stood her up, that's why she's angry with you?'

'Stood her up, if you like. It's time we got home,' he said, clapping his thighs and climbing to his worn feet. I followed him out of the run, miserably disappointed. What a bloody ending. We tramped off down the lane, Solomon carrying his basket of eggs, whistling that tune again. Talk about taking you to the fires of Mordor only to find Sauron was a bus conductor with a glass eye. He paused, looked down at me. 'That's not it, you know,' he snapped, annoyed at me.

'What happened, then? She jumped out on you again, just like the first time?' I want to show I'd been paying attention. He sighed, nodded towards the old car.

'Sit in for a while, then,' he said quietly, ducking his rusty head in the battered hat under the battered doorframe. I darted round the other side and clambered into what was left of the seat. Twisted springs, the lingering smell of dog piss.

'You realize this was her car?' What? He's got to be joking. I don't even believe it was his, let alone hers. What, she locked in the boot or something? I give him a sidelong glance, let him know I'm no fool.

'I never bothered moving it, not after the accident. Shifted it a little, is all.' Something catches in his voice, catches me too. I stare at the smashed remains of the dashboard. He's not kidding. Possibilities explode in all directions. Rupert and I played in the bloody thing every day.

'It had all burnt out. I couldn't tow it away, and I could hardly ask Tucker, in the circumstances,' he snorts. He's speaking in a flat voice, weary, resigned.

'I didn't see her for six months. I was in camp at Taunton. Big one. Furthest I'd ever been from home. I was in the Somerset Light Infantry. Light! Fifteen stone I was, fifteen stone if I weighed a pound. Things were getting grim by then. Just after the Battle of Britain. Still didn't know if Hitler was going to risk it or not. It was hard. Hard for all of us, even those who'd been used to graft. Wasn't as bad for me as it was for them from up Budgworth way, office boys and that. They let us out one night,' he says quietly. 'We'd a bit of money put by. Bussed us all up to Budgworth.' He pauses, looking round as if pondering whether to continue. I keep my mouth shut, look straight ahead.

'I'd never had a proper girlfriend,' he says, not cryptically enough for me. 'Not a proper one, if you understand me. Mary ... we'd held hands and kissed a bit ... but nothing else.' Join the club. 'They weren't like Mary, these girls I'm telling you about. Talked to you rougher than your own father, they did. Looked at you as if you'd come out without your breeches. They said we were to call them whatever we liked. Call 'em after our mothers if we wanted. Red mouths like slits. Kissed as if they were sucking the marrow from your bones.' He gets gruff, matter of fact.

'The War was coming for us. You couldn't expect a man to go and get himself shot before he'd . . . found out about things. You know. You youngsters these days. They said it was to be Egypt, the Middle East. Gave us desert fatigues and foot powder. Made us think a bit, me and some of the boys in my section. Well, I go back to Clove and Mary hardly knows me. Smart as a razor, training up for my marksman's lanyard. Proud as Punch I was, walking in on Tucker Lamb. Ma and Da had fallen out, seemingly, weren't talking at all. Never had said much, mind you. Tucker though, he got the scrumpy out and we all sat round past midnight. He nodded off and she saw me to the door. Then she saw me to the yard, then the barn. There was a war on, she was a good girl. She was sweeter than pie that night.' He stares at the floor, quiet for a while.

'You'll find out when you're a little older.' Not at this rate I won't.

'You'll find out what it's like to love one girl but be infatuated with another. It's not like a love at all, more like a craving. Like an alcoholic craves drink. I felt a bit like that for May. I suppose I knew nothing could ever come of it, that's what gave me the alibi. I had to make the most of it. I saw a groom from up at the Grange, asked after her. Cut me dead he did. I thought it was as he had a soft spot for her himself. I was only home a day or two. Time to do a few chores for Dad, he was sickening for something, seemingly.' Here it comes. 'I was out there in the top field when I saw her again.'

THE RIDE

'Dad had gone back to the house to fetch some stakes. I didn't know what to say or where to look. If one of Tucker's lads had caught me again I knew that would have been it. She wasn't cross or anything, asked me how I'd been, did I still have the picture. I said it was at the bottom of my kitbag, never parted from it. She asked if I wanted to go for a drive. I knew I shouldn't, knew someone was bound to see us. I suppose what with Mary and Josie . . . the girl in Taunton . . . I supposed I was the Cock of the Walk. Nothing could touch me. I said I didn't mind if I did. Can't do any harm, me going off and all. I should have picked up that sledge and thumped those posts in. Should have told her I was engaged and all. I looked down yonder. Dad was out of sight. I followed her across the field to the car, climbed in. She drove up the hill, turned off over the downs, right up on the top where the track just runs out. Just grass and the sheep. Those seats were like thrones, thought I was the cat's whiskers, sitting there saucy in her car. I think I started talking saucy as well. Trying to impress her I suppose. She didn't like it, I could see that. As if she liked me as I'd been before, pulling my forelock, yes Miss May, no Miss May. I don't know. We looked at the view. There was nobody about, nobody to see us up there. She asked why I hadn't come that Sunday. Told her I'd been called away earlier than I'd thought. Looked her in the eye and lied right out. I said I'd tried to ring the Grange, tried to get in touch with her. She looked funny, disconcerted. I thought Yes, I thought, make you look a bit foolish some farm boy ringing up for you. She said she understood. I said understood what. She shook her head, said we'd better get back. I reached over and put my hand on her leg.' His voice has gone, dried out like a dirty pool in a desert. One minute he's chatting away ten to the dozen, next he's gasping, lost for words. I can feel myself trembling as he sits there, gazing out of the old car as if she was in there with us. Sounds like you do in a dream when there's a monster after you. You want to scream but you can't, you can't croak. 'She started the car up again. I'd pulled my hand back,' he says, so quiet I have to lean closer to catch what he's saying. 'I couldn't remember what she'd done, but I knew there was something wrong. She'd felt funny. Not like Josie, not like my Mary. She'd felt . . . something. She was driving fast now, driving back the way we'd come. I thought she'd go funny, go funny like Josie did, like Mary did in the barn. Go funny for kissing you and that. I thought she'd be the same, see? Put my hand on her thigh only it wasn't her thigh . . . it wasn't and it was if you take my meaning . . . it wasn't right, couldn't be right. It didn't feel as if she had skin at all.' He was staring ahead, spit on his lips. I can feel my balls going crinkly as if they're trying to suck themselves back under my belly. I stare at him, his lips are moving but no sound's coming out.

'She was so wrong,' he says at last.

'So wrong I think I must have gasped, yelped or something. I must have tried to get out of that door, scrambled for the handles. She was staring at me her eyes had changed and they were so blue and she just stared at me like a mad . . .' He croaks himself silent, breathes heavily, steadies himself.

'She stared at me like she didn't know what I was, as if I'd landed from another planet. I'd never seen anything like her. Her eyes were bulging out of her face as if someone had thumbs behind her skull. She was screaming, I realized it was her making the noise, the shriek louder than the engine. Fit to burst your eardrums. Then she let go the wheel, turned round and hit me. A real backhander, right across my face. I was crouched away from her, crouched against the door. I hit my head. We were going like hell now, going down the hill like a thunderbolt. The noise was killing, like it was crushing in on my head. Her screaming, the engine roaring, her scratching and hitting at me like a vixen. I was so scared I just sat there trying to cover my face, I was too scared to think of hitting her back. She was so busy clawing at me she couldn't see where she was going. The car seemed to drive itself. She was hissing and screaming like a cat, clutching and clawing at the back of my hands.' He looks down at them, shaking on the smashed dashboard, as if he can still make out the scars in the wrinkled skin. He sobs, sobs something back in his throat, some hard lump, same hard lump that's choking me up, filling my throat.

'Dad was coming back up the hill. Mary was with him. She'd brought my tea up for me. I only saw them like little matchstick figures on the hill, could hardly recognize them but I knew who they were. It had to be them. It was like a nightmare, looking in from the outside, as if I wasn't in the car at all. I ducked under her arm, tried to get the wheel, turn away from them. She tore at my hair, tore handfuls of it out. Raked her nails over my neck like she'd grown knives for hands. I don't know exactly what happened. I think the door must have come off. I was thrown out. Dad must have chucked himself out of the way. When I came round the car was on its back. It just went bang. Huge great orange flash. I suppose the petrol tank must have gone. It was out in a minute, as if the car sucked all the flames inside again, quenched the flames itself. I dragged Dad away from it, looked round and it was out. Just a few flames licking round the engine. I could hardly see, hardly stand. I stumbled over something, knelt down and saw it was her. Mary. Lying in the grass in her best dress, the basket in her hand. There wasn't a mark on her. Not if you looked quickly. I thought she'd be all right. There was just a little blue bruise on her forehead. I didn't think to look in the car. They all came running then. Mother, Silas . . . they thought I'd been driving, they were all shouting at me but I couldn't make out what they were saying. I pointed at the car, tried to tell them May had been driving. I think I fell over. Dad was out cold. The doctor said he'd be all right. But I'd killed Mary. Tucker had arrived then, he was going to strangle me himself. I didn't care, I'd have let him. They had to hold him back. I kept on pointing at the car, telling them she'd been driving. That made old Tucker even worse.

He was fighting his boys off, swearing he'd kill me. They carried Mary down the hill on the blanket she'd carried up for us. P.C. McNair took me down the hill, down the village. They all came running out, see what had happened, asked me what I'd done.' He's gone grey. The vivid browns and tawny hues have dribbled out of his face, left him ashen. His fire's out. Sitting in the car that had killed his fiancée, killed most of him too. No wonder he'd ignored them and gone on in that house, taken the girl out. He knew what he'd been doing, trying to save her life. Trying to pay the village back for the life he'd taken. Paying his debt. He wasn't crying but his eyes were shiny in his featureless face. He looked as if he'd been chipped out of an old block of stone, chipped from the hill, chiselled and shaped by something older than all of us. I sat still, felt as if someone had pulled my plughole, let all my innards drain away.

'And it was her all the time . . . Glaistig?' I asked quietly, giving him time to pull himself together a little. He rubbed his chin, reined in his wild horses.

'They didn't know what to do, what to think. Mother was in a terrible state. Blamed me. They all blamed me. Said I'd taken too much ale, too much cider. Got drunk and taken the car. They never found her, see, Miss May. There was no trace of her, and there's always a trace, even with a bad fire like that, some teeth, something. Not in the car, not on the hillside. It was as if the hills had swallowed her up again. Too much cider, seeing things, imagining things, they said. Scared of going off to fight maybe. I thought . . . I thought once the police looked in to it, once they asked around, I'd be cleared of it, they'd search for her, let me go. They'd find the woman and get to the bottom of it. Wouldn't bring Mary back but they'd find her. I suppose I was shocked, dazed. It was all too much for me. I could hardly understand them, couldn't connect the things they were saying with me. It was as if I didn't know myself, couldn't trust myself. The more I listened, the more I thought they must be right. I got drunk and took the car. Then I remembered the picture. Then I remembered Arnold seeing us that time up the top pasture. It did happen.

I sat there and I stuck to it, stuck to my story. Stuck to the truth. McNair came in, laid his helmet on the table.

' "A bad business, Solomon," he says. I told him. I told him exactly what I've told you. Every word. He sat back in his chair. If it had been some stranger from Budgworth he'd have beaten it out of me. But he knew me same as I knew him. He was for trusting me. If there had been a Miss May she must have been thrown clear, got away on her hands and knees in the confusion.

' "You know it then, the Grange?"

' "She said the Grange, that's all."

' "Up Axeheads way?"

' "Is what she said. I never met her there. She came to our field, all the time. Every time. I never took no car, Peter, you know that." He nodded, closed his notebook.

' "We'll have to keep you here, you realize?" He was very serious, very fair. Made it worse somehow. Maybe he should have let himself go, punched me around a little. Maybe I could have taken that. They left me quiet there in the little cell they kept for the drunks. For the odd tramp down from Budgworth. McNair came back next morning. Looked different, looked at me different. I stood up when he came in. Asked him if they'd found anything. He nodded.

' "There's some detectives coming down from Budgworth."

' "You've found her though, you've found Miss May, then?" He looked at me again, I knew they hadn't. Knew he felt the same way as the rest of them, the rest of the bloody bastards.

' "I've been up there," he said. "Met a mad old Major living in the old servants' quarters. He'd become a bit of a recluse, seemingly. Shut the place up and let it go to rack and ruin. Course, we don't go that far out usually, not our patch, is it?" He gave me a queer look. Something was wrong. Something was worse.

' "If it was our patch, I'd have known. Known not to have gone out there on your word." Now he was looking grimmer than ever. He said he'd banged on the door there for a quarter of an hour before the old man got to it. McNair explained there had been an accident. Told him the young man involved claimed he hadn't been driving. A young woman name of Miss May had. Claimed to come from the Grange. Would he know anything about it? He'd not answered for a while. McNair wondered if he had heard the question at all.

' "Is this some kind of a joke, Sergeant?"

' "A joke, sir, no, sir. It is a very serious enquiry, I am afraid. A young woman has been killed and another, who was calling herself Miss May, may be injured. As far as we can make out she seems to be missing. She may have had some kind of a concussion, certainly a shock."

' "Well, I can tell you, Sergeant, that your man's story is certainly not right. Not right at all." He'd bristled up, ragged in his old dressing-gown, his grey hair sticking up something awful, poor old fellow. "And if you had bothered to check your records before coming out here, Sergeant, you'd know why."

' "No use getting indignant with me, sir, I'm only carrying out my enquiries as best I may. Now I've had a long ride up here, sir, and perhaps you wouldn't mind . . ."

' "Perhaps you wouldn't mind giving me your name and number, Sergeant. I'll be talking to your superior. Chief Inspector Brackley, I believe."

' "Chief Inspector Brackley has retired, sir. Now if you don't mind me asking, sir, am I right in thinking you know something of this Miss May girl?"

' "I do, Sergeant, indeed I do." Maybe the way the colour had drained from the old fellow's face should have warned McNair. Maybe the way he was clenching his fists, glaring at the officer, should have alerted him.

' "Indeed I do know something about her, Sergeant. She was my daughter." McNair must have thought he was there, then realized what he'd said.

' "You say she . . ."

' "That's right, Sergeant. She *was* my daughter. If you had checked your records before coming on up here and disturbing me in this unforgivable manner . . ." McNair must have known something was wrong then, known he'd been made to look a fool. Never forgave me for that.

' "According to our man's story, sir, we felt we may have had some bad news for you . . ."

' "Well, you're a little late with your bad news, Sergeant. Eighteen years too late, to be exact. Check your files, man. August 25, 1922. They found her in a stream. She'd been strangled. As I remember your lot didn't exactly cut the mustard then. Now you come round and tell me my daughter has been involved in a car accident. It was in all the papers you know, I'm surprised you haven't heard of the case."

' "Of course I've heard of the case, sir . . . it's just I didn't connect . . . with what our man's been telling us."

' "Didn't connect, Sergeant?"

' "Obviously, sir. Obviously I would never have presumed to intrude on you. I never intended to cause distress." He muttered his apologies, closed his notebook.

' "Whatever your man has done, Sergeant, I think he's a very sick man. Don't you?" Very sick, sir. Yes, sir.

' "All I can say, sir, is that I deeply regret this unwarranted intrusion. I hope you'll accept that I had no idea . . ."

' "That, Sergeant, is obvious."

' "There was just one thing sir," old McNair said, sticking to his guns remarkably well considering the looks that old man was giving him, "only our man, sir . . . our man says it wasn't his car. I've known him a long time sir, and begging your pardon, sir, but he's never been difficult before. It might be a part of his story, sir, but I know for a fact he's never had a car like that. Said the car belonged to . . . belonged to the other party in the case, sir." Well, that was easy enough to sort out. May had taken the Austin to Taunton for a farm sale. After she was found he had no further use for it.

' "It's in the mews, as far as I know. Covered in tarpaulins."

' "In the mews, sir?"

' "Yes, around the corner. The old stable block. I'll show you." He led the way across the old yard, the cracks in the paving stones choked with weeds, the windows of the grand old house all boarded, painted out. McNair dragged the heavy stable doors open, peered into the filthy interior. The old man peered in, then looked at McNair.

' "So he's a thief as well, this man of yours, Sergeant?"

' "I must say, sir, he's never gone off the rails like this before, sir. I can't understand it, a more decent, hard-working chap you'd be hard put to find." Indeed, Sergeant.

' "Do I know the damned fellow, did he work on the estate, did he bear some grudge?" He'd sacked them all, after May had gone. After his daughter had gone.

' "He's a young farmer over Clove way, sir. Been called up recently, the SLI." A bloody shower, Sergeant. A bloody shower if that was the sort of man they were taking.

' "As I say, sir, until now I'd have vouched for him above any other in the village. Can't understand it at all, not at all, sir." '

He'd got a little colour back, in the gloom of that old car. A little colour in that battered face. The cornered fox in his foxhole.

'But why was she setting you up?' I ask. 'Why pick on the old boy?' I thought he'd finished, the way he'd floated out over the hill, then slowly formed himself back up in the seat beside me. It's pitch dark. He's just a massive shadow, hunched in there next to me, in her car.

'They never sent me back to the camp. They searched the hills, got dogs out, asked witnesses to come forward. Old Arnold, he'd had to tell them he'd seen me with her, with this girl. There had to be someone. Otherwise I'd have been looking at a manslaughter charge right there and then. Nobody had seen her, nobody had a clue. Miss May had been found in the stream in 1922. It had been in all the papers. This fancy woman, the woman who'd led me astray. They couldn't pin it all on me, not all of it. Had me in front of a military tribunal, decided on the balance of probabilities there must have been some woman at some stage but I must have been on my own at the time of the accident. I must have fetched the car from the Grange, driven it all the way back somehow. Little slip of a girl wouldn't have been able to get those doors open, let alone get it started after all those years. It must have been someone with a talent for mechanics, someone well used to getting his father's tractor working. I was guilty of this that and the other and got five years' hard labour at Shepton Mallet.'

'Shepton Mallet? Where they make the Babycham?'

'The military prison. Gross dereliction of duty. They thought I'd lost my nerve, possibly been thinking of deserting, possibly angling for a dishonourable discharge. If it hadn't been for the War, I don't know how it would have worked out. They needed everyone then, see. What, winter 1940. Things were going badly everywhere. They had me down as unsound, but that's no barrier to being a soldier. I'd been there three months when they came round, re-evaluating they called it. If you had half a mind you got bomb disposal, combat engineers. Special duties. The Germans had whole regiments like it. We preferred to spread our bad eggs round a little. All we had to do was survive. I went through the lot. Western desert, Crete, desert again, Tunisia, Italy, Cassino. The lot. Right up into Austria in '45. And do you know what?' he asked with grim relish. 'Do you know what? I never got as much as a scratch. Where's the sense of it, eh? Can you see any? Can you see any fucking sense in it at all? They were as good as their word. April, 1946, I was home. No medals, nothing. Wiped the slate clean. They hardly recognized me, six years on. The ones that did avoided me. Walked out of the pub if I went in. They'd heard all about me, all the lies, see. Me being drunk, running away, running down my fiancée. My mother had left by then, of course. Taken the young 'un and gone off to Budgworth. Couldn't stand the disgrace of it, I suppose. It was just me and Dad versus the world. I don't know whether it was the crash, or what happened after, but he wasn't right in the head, if you know what I mean. Kept on muttering we were cursed, our luck couldn't run that bad. Must be something else. Made me fetch the picture out, he was for going out and burning it. Going up and dropping it in that hole where the stone had been, setting light to it all over again. I told him not to act so daft, keep our heads down and things would pass over, we'd go on as before. Not till we've sorted it out, he said. Not till we'd sorted it out.'

'And you've been living with it ever since, the Glaistig and everything?'

He looks round sharply. 'Oh, no . . . we weren't finished yet. She weren't finished either. She's not finished now.'

What, there's more?

TRAFFIC

Come on, Doc, keep those questions coming, that's what I'd say to myself as I slumped in the comfortable armchair in front of his enormous ego-trip desk. You promised me I'd be home by the weekend, if I behaved myself, played the game. I've played along. Two and a half weeks of it. Two and a half weeks staying in one of the guest rooms. That's a laugh. Let me tell you the house-breaker who wants in here better bring an oxyacetylene torch. The bars (or window strengtheners, whatever you want to call them) are painted white, just to make you feel at home, I figure. Nice curtains too. I sleep up there on the second floor, maybe get to watch a little TV in the communal lounge, although I'd rather keep away from the rest of the weirdos in here. They must be rubbing themselves with butter to end up with spots like that. I've got all the books I want so it's no hardship staying in my room. To be honest, it's nice being a centre of attention. You know, all the staff walking around carrying bundles of orange files with your name on. It's like being on report at school. To give Whiteman his due he is putting himself out a bit over this one. Cancelled half of his engagements so he could get through with me. I watch the traffic snarled on the ring-road. All that frustration, it's almost as bad as being in here. I figured some of the kids they have here probably prefer it to being home. Three square a day, TV, couple of sessions in with the quacks, I can crack it. End of the week's in sight and I figure he's going to have to come up with some pretty good reasons for keeping me. I stick to it, tell him what he wants to hear, I'm out. Trouble is Whiteman doesn't want to hear about D.B. at all. She's *persona non grata* as far as this place is concerned. Here he is. Late. Caught in the traffic outside. I read the battered magazines in the waiting room as he chats to his secretary. That Cheryl. She goes red if I talk to her, let alone one of the junior shrinks. He waves me in to his office, stylish grey raincoat over his arm, briefcase bulging with cases just like mine. Worse. Man gets through some folders, I bet. Wouldn't like to keep him in paperclips. Magic markers, this guy chews them up. I make myself comfortable in that nice comfy chair while he unpacks and sorts himself out. Takes off his jacket and rolls up his sleeves.

'Now, where did we get to yesterday? Oh, yes, Mr Jones goes off to war.' He studies the notes he took yesterday for a while, then looks up.

'Change places, come and sit here,' he says, jumping to his feet. This is new. He's trying something on again. Never the same thing twice, this guy. 'Come and sit here for a while, listen to it from my point of view. An outsider. See if it makes any sense to you, right?'

Outsider. Hey, that's what I'll be when they let me out. I'll have to carry on where poor old Solomon left off. Go back to school and face them. I wonder if they are going to cross the road to avoid me as well, refuse to serve me in the shops. Maybe they're planning to pile the same shit on me. Roberts the recluse. Will Mum and Dad stick to me like Jubal stuck with Solomon?

'Come on, change places.' Man's feeling frisky, thrown me again, got me on the hop. Don't worry, I've got a few hops left yet. I take his place, settle down while he goes round and sits in the big chair. He's got a better view out over the fields. The purple hills in the distance. Down the other side's where I live. Down in Clove.

'I've been through the police files. The whole story,' he chirps. 'You tell me which version makes more sense, OK? No, let me finish. A young man . . .' He presses his fingers together in front of his mouth, a little chapel with his hands.

'A young man is very scared. A young man not much older than you, maybe not as quick as you, though. Maybe not as quick, but he's got just about as good an imagination. They say it's the worst thing a fighter can have, imagination. You can imagine just what's going to happen to you. And this young man's to be a fighter, a soldier. He has to go and fight.'

'He wasn't a coward.'

'I'm not saying he was. Listen. This young man can imagine himself under the tracks of a tank, pierced on a bayonet. He couldn't have been alone. I'm not saying he was a coward, but he had nobody to talk to about it. They didn't go in for counselling in those days, not for strapping great farm boys like him. Give him a rifle, he'll be all right. Same as strapping great farm boys are supposed to be. He tried to buckle down and face it out but he couldn't. He cracked. Some of them shot themselves, some ran away. Solomon comes home on leave and tries to steady himself down with a few drinks. That scrumpy they serve down at the Boar, powerful stuff, am I right?' I shrug. What, I've tried it too? I think of the stone jar stash against the wall in his cottage, the way my fingers smelt when I poked the stopper. Funny, you always know when something's going to smell bad, but you ram away and sniff your fingers up all the same. Some kind of animal instinct leftover I suppose. Whiteman isn't going to catch me with that old chestnut.

'He has a few drinks and he has some more. Walks off somewhere. Maybe thinks of making a dash for it. Finds himself miles away at the Old Grange. Decides maybe he'll sleep it off in an outbuilding. Wakes up, bumping head, it's late. Best get on back to it. Decides maybe he'll take the old car. The old car under the tarpaulin. Takes his fancy, that old car. Nobody'll miss the thing. He's no stranger to tinkering with old motors. Gets it going and drives it off across the hills. He's not used to the controls, the brakes are spongy. Somebody's coming up the path toward him. He tries to avoid them, can't. Knocks them down. Kills the girl dead. All his family, all her family, all his neighbours come rushing up to see what the commotion's about. What does he tell them? What would you have told them?' He pauses, I jump right in there.

'Arnold saw him talking to her, to Miss May.'

'That had been weeks before. He hadn't seen them that day.'

'It proves she existed, though.'

'Proves somebody existed. Somebody with a car, passing through. Stopped and had a chat, went on her way. She was no water witch though. An ordinary girl, out for a drive.' He shakes his head.

'He says she was in the car when it turned over. What she do, leap out and run for it? Maybe she was a camouflage expert? Maybe she had a magic ring, eh?' He stands up, walks to the window, looks out over the hill, the traffic.

'The trouble with old Solomon is he wasn't all that bright, was he? They come running up, ask him what happened, he says the first thing that came into his head. Miss May from up the Grange. Funny he should have said that when the poor girl went missing in 1922. That's who he was thinking about, though. Maybe he'd read about her. It was in all the papers. He needed a scapegoat, somebody to hide behind. He blurted it out, realized his mistake afterwards. Maybe her name just popped into his head, the way things do. You can sympathize with him. I can. I'm honestly not blaming him for that. It's just that he invented all this . . . smokescreen . . . to cover up his mistake.' He sighs.

'How's that sound? If you were a man in the street, somebody told you the stories, who'd you believe?'

'Say that we'd probably still think the Earth was flat,' I say, rather cleverly I thought. He wasn't having any of it.

'They'd believe me because my explanation is the more plausible. It makes sense.'

'Then why'd he give them her name?'

'He wasn't thinking straight.'

'He was thinking straight enough to make the most of it up.'

'He was improvising. Making it up as he went along. He couldn't turn round and say, "Sorry, did I say Miss May? I meant Gladys Smith of 35 the High Street." ' He makes me smile a little. He knows he's got me on the run again.

'He was brave. He made up for everything later,' I insist.

Whiteman smiles, figures he's scored another point.

'It was a moment of madness. I'm not saying he was a coward. It was all too much for him and he cracked. Maybe **143** twenty per cent of combat troops do at some time or other. I've got some figures on the Vietnam war . . .'

'He wasn't in Vietnam, it was 1940.'

He ignores me, won't be deflected now he's got me back-pedalling. 'Have you read *Lord Jim*?' I shake my head. 'It's about this naval officer who has one moment of weakness. He runs away from danger right at the beginning. He's brave enough afterwards, suicidally brave, but he's doomed because of that one moment. I think your Solomon was a little like Lord Jim. One moment of weakness and he spends the rest of his life paying for it. Covering it up under a pile of lies that mushroomed out all over the place, dragged other people in to it. Dragged you two in to it.'

'I only know the things I saw . . .'

'You saw this Miss May creature? Eh? You can read all about her from books in the school library. I asked your teacher. *Anthology of the Faery World*. She's a water nymph, protects children lost in the woods but preys on men like a vampire. And here you are telling me that's what happened. That it makes more sense. Can't you see, David, it's why you're here. They've asked me to assess your mental and emotional state. Now I think you are a relatively normal young man who is going out of his way to protect a favourite uncle. I think you are believing all this for his sake, not yours. All I want to do is get you home. Think I want you here for ever? I want you back home, back to school. But I want you to go back accepting the fact that this Solomon was not all he seemed to be. He told you stories. Very good, imaginative stories. When you can accept that . . .'

'You'll let me go home.' Yeah. I say OK, I guess that's what happened and you can pat me on the back, chalk up another miracle cure. Maybe write some paper about it.

'Not exactly, but broadly speaking yes. I don't think you are suffering from any mental illness, just seriously misplaced loyalty.' He's crossed from the window, stalked up real close to me.

'I say we made the whole thing up and I get to go home. That's what you are saying.' That's what he's been saying all along. So OK, I made the whole thing up. There, I'm cured. I feel better already, Doc. You've taken a weight from my mind. This guy, you think I've had it in for him from the beginning don't you? You think, Well, actually, David, the doctor's right. No such thing as water nymphs, vampires, whatever you want to call them. Trouble is, Solomon, see, he told me more than a few stories. So before you go taking Whiteman's side, I'll tell you what happened to him when he got back.

PEACE AND WAR

When he tried to put everything behind him and start again. When he tried to dig his way out of it, sweat his way out, back bent, head down, nose to the grindstone stuff. She stopped him. She fucked him all over. She put the stones beneath his ploughshare, strangled and stifled his crops before they'd grown clear of the rich chalky soil. Cracked the hillsides open and sucked his wells dry. It started about a month after he had returned.

'The animals went first. Fowl-pest saw off most of the chickens. Then the sheep caught some vicious worm even the vet couldn't identify. Trotting over the hillside shitting their insides out while we looked on helpless. They had to be destroyed, the bodies rolled in the stone pit and burnt. All the while little things. Churns turned over, milk soured, butter wouldn't turn. The winter came on, hard as hell. Stream froze, pipes burst. The snow drifted so high we lost the few bits of stock we had left. You couldn't walk in the gorge for dead birds, badgers, squirrels. Only the crows and rooks got fat that year. Great black vultures. Hundreds of them. So big they could scarce get off the ground. When they took off from the treetops they flapped the ice and snow from the branches, looked like the Devil was shaking the trees. There was a big rookery along the stream there. In the middle of the frozen wood. You could hear the cawing miles around. Dad and I got the shotguns down, crept up right underneath them, blasted the lot. Blasted them to bits. Fifty, sixty of them at least. Sticky black feathers falling as if we'd stumbled in on a witches' pillow fight. That sorted them out that winter, but it was one thing after another. Plug a leak in the rain barrel and the pump would fail. Cure a pig of pneumonia and he'd be out, run down in the lane. And the rats. They were everywhere. Three good mousers we had and they couldn't touch them. I watched one of them run out of the barn one time, three of the things on its back. By the time I got to it thing was half dead. We thought we'd burn them out, starting in one corner and working across. But a wind blew up, sudden like, we couldn't control it. The barn burnt down round our ears and there was nothing we could do about it. We lost all the money Dad had put by, all the money I'd managed to scrape together from the army years. It was one thing and another, grinding us down, grinding us into the ground. Dad started getting funnier and funnier. I couldn't take him to the Boar, he would sit and rave and bawl, cry, carry on something awful for him. Never shed a tear in his whole life but he shed enough that winter all right. He said we should never have moved the stones. Stone, I said, we only moved the one. Stones, he said. He and his father had moved four after the first war. He said there'd been seven once. Seven stones on the hillside there above the gorge.

He said how the old folk had put 'em there for a reason and how we should never have touched them. We'd brought a plague down on ourselves, he said. He'd tell anyone who came up, the butcher, the smith, anyone. I reasoned with him. Things would turn out in the spring. It was a bad winter, that's all. Only they didn't get better. Had to sell off the last bits we had left. Sold the top pasture to old Mungo for a song. The place was falling round our ears. He was drinking more and more. All the drink we had put by, all the cider from the orchard as should have been sold off. He got through it. Gallons of it as should have been down to the market, he put by for himself. I didn't have the heart to stop him. It was his only comfort, like. Only thing as would make him sleep nights. He got worse and worse like it was crippling him up, crumbling him from the inside. He never was a heavy man. It was wasting him away, picking away at his brain. Sometimes he didn't even recognize me, he'd howl and spit and shout and bawl till I had to hold him down. If it wasn't the stones it was her. Miss May. Morning and night. I found him out wandering one night, down by the stream. Waded right out he

147

did. I watched him. I thought about letting him go, wouldn't have taken long, not then. It was heartbreaking enough seeing him as he was. I thought about walking back to the cottage and giving him an hour. An hour to finish it and let me go, start somewhere else, Budgworth, London, anywhere but there. I thought about leaving him but I couldn't. Got in there after him. He'd waded out into the pool by the cliff, freezing cold but quiet like. He jumped like a rabbit in a gin when I grabbed him.

' "What were she like?" he said. "What were she like?" What was who like? "Miss May," he says, suspicious like, but calm. Dead calm despite the fact that water was freezing up round us. I dragged him out of it, stood there shivering on the bank like a couple of old tramps.

' "I told you what she looked like. Blonde hair. Blue eyes. Beautiful."

' "But what were she like?" he says, wizened and gasping, shivering so hard he could barely speak.

' "I never touched her." I told him a hundred times he always came back to it in the end. Did I touch her, did she run? Had I gone after her?

' "Come on in by the fire, you'll catch your death."

' "I've caught my death."

' "Don't talk so soft now, Da, come on in."

'He pulled his arm away.

' "You touched her all right." I stood there shaking my head, what could I do? Hit him with my stick? Finish him off? Wouldn't have taken much, just skin and bone he was.

' "I touched her once," I told him. I don't know why I told him. I thought maybe it would get him in.

' "And?"

' "I only touched her." I grabbed his coat, pulled him back toward the cottage. He was bashing at me, clawing at me like a mad scarecrow. "Tell me what she felt like."

' "What are you talking about, you're plain daft."

' "I know what I'm talking about and so do you. What did she feel like?" He was pulling away, wriggling like a bloody eel he was. I had a job holding on to him.

' "She felt strange."

' "There. She felt strange?"

' "She didn't feel right. She felt like . . ."

' "A beast. I knew it all along. It's true, ain't it, a beast with two backs?"

' "She felt rough . . ." I told him. I was still holding on to him, holding him off the ground I reckon. I hadn't told anyone before. It was like he knew already.

' "She felt like a goat, didn't she, didn't she?" He was hissing and pawing at me. I threw him off. Straight into the water. He landed on his back, sat up in the rush. I waded across but he rolled over, got to his feet, and pointed at me.

' "You never saw her legs but you touched them. You touched her. The Lady Glaistig, the Beast with Two Backs."

' "She was no beast."

' "She was beast beneath, she was beast beneath, wasn't she?"

'He darted away from me again, as if the stream had rushed up his freezing legs, filled him with mad capering energy. Like he was doing a little jig around me.

' "What Lady? You know her? You knew all along?"

' "Of course I knew all along, you bloody fool," he growled, standing still and pointing at me again.

' "Then why didn't you tell them? Tell them all about her?"

'He cackled at that. Cackled like an old hen.

' "I've told you, now come along in for the love of Christ," I said.

' "You touched the Lady. You touched the beast. The rabbit bit the bloody fox," he guffawed, bent double.

' "What are you blathering about?" I caught him up again, gripped him hard, shook him like a naughty child. He was all limp now, simpering to himself.

' "You know what you've done. You know why she's after us, I know why she's after us." He looked straight at me, eyes popping out like little marbles. "And we've got to get her before she gets us."

'I set him down again. Thought about it. Quiet he was then. Letting me think about it in that bloody stream there.

' "The woman under the stone. The bones you burnt."

' "You can burn her stubble but not her heart."

I shook my head, I felt as if I'd had too many as well. Played along first, but he didn't care. Just kept on.

' "How do we get her?" I asked him. He shrugged, tugged his boot through the flowing water, this way and that.

' "We call her out and burn her out."

' "How do we call her?" I was tired, I was seeing things, hearing things. I had hardly touched a drop that night, felt like I was drunk, seeing double.

' "Call her out and burn her out," he says, tugging at my coat.

' "How?"

' "Trap her."

' "Trap her, how?" I shook him again.

' "Set a trap, you'll need bait." '

'Us!' I yell at him, jumping off the bench where I'd been listening to him remember, listening to him shape the stories the way a big black spider shapes its webs. And there we were all the time, a couple of little flies, right there in the middle of it. Wrapped up, trussed up. He'd trapped me with his stories, trapped us for her. We were the bloody bait and she's out there now, prowling like a fox, silent and shimmering in the long grass, waiting for the moment when Rupert ran for it. Rose out of the grass and spread her arms, the gauzy films of silk that he couldn't quite tear his way through, couldn't quite tear from his skin, his face, his hair. Rose out of the grass and had him the way a pike gobbles up a small roach. Oh no, he's shaking his head, shaking his head sadly as I back off.

'Don't be daft, boy. You weren't the first to run on this hill and you won't be the last. You weren't my bait. It wasn't me as sent you down there.' Oh yes, he's sorry now, wants to sorry me all up. Didn't mean to set us up like a couple of live baits, cast us out into the middle of the pool. Red float bobbing in the current as the pike slides out of the rushes. I look at him, squatting in his shed like a wood demon fallen on hard times, smothered in that great overcoat tied with baling twine. He could just as easily slip it off and choke me out.

'If you knew you could have warned us,' I snap. I'm pretty

mad but not that mad. He fixes me with that live bait stare, raises his stubbly chin a notch in contempt.

'Warned you off? Told you not to go down there, the stream's haunted? I might as well have sent out gilt-edged invitations,' he barks back. 'I warned you off where I could. I told you not to go in the cottage. I told you to steer clear of the car. I kept an eye out for you like I do now.' He calms down a little, I shrug. Possibilities are occurring to me now, like a match dropped in a box of fireworks. What if this old bugger killed his father? What if he killed him that night, couldn't put up with all his blather any more? Bashed his head in with a stone in the stream, then dragged him back to the cottage, said he'd fallen down the stairs. Who was going to mourn the old bastard anyway, if he'd lost his money *and* his marbles? He's staring back at me, sometimes I reckon he can see right into my brain, read my thoughts as they gibber out of the ticker-tape machine.

'She's everywhere. She's clever and she knows her hills, knows her stream. She doesn't know it like the back of her hand, it is the back of her hand. She's the mist over the water, the cloud on the peak. We don't feel her until we're walking home late in the woods, till the light goes out in the cellar, till you drop your torch in the attic. I've read up on those old days, those old folk putting up stones and things. They weren't for decoration, you know.' He stamps around, points at my nose. 'And in any case, what are you saying, you don't believe any of it? Haven't seen enough?'

I shrug. 'I haven't seen anything,' I tell him straight. 'I'd have to see her for myself to believe you, believe anyone.' It's the truth, for Christ's sake. I'd have to bloody see her for myself, same as you, I bet.

'You want me to believe in her, I'm going to have to see her, touch her, just like you did,' I dare him. He's shaking his head like he's caught me stealing eggs.

'See her, touch her? Haven't you been listening? I didn't know what I'd touched, what I'd seen. Do you think I'd have been that keen if I knew . . . Jubal said he knew all along.' He gets angry, shouts, stamps around a little more making the hens bolt in all directions. Feathers flutter in the stifling air.

'Well, I've been warned,' I say, sticking to my guns and making him clench his fists in frustration.

'Oh, you've been warned, have you? If she stands in front of you you'll stand back and shout, "Give us a flash of your legs," will you? Is that it, you little smartarse?' I jump away from him, almost tread on one of his boilers. Now I've done it, pushed him too far. He'll throttle me the way he throttled Rupert. All those stories, all these webs. I'm standing on quicksand, not chicken shit. I'm floundering. He's knocked the lantern so it swings eerily in the smoky air, casting quick shadows and bands of smoky yellow light over his bruised and battered face, contorted in fear and contempt. He's hissing at me or he's damaged that old Tilley.

'You don't want to touch her, boy. Believe me, you don't want to feel her. I remember it as if it's burnt on to my fingers.' He holds his hands up, looks at them as if he can still see scars. Maybe he can. To see them clearly he'd hold a mirror, stare at his reflection, that's scars. 'She was . . .'

'Furry,' I suggest.

He rounds on me again, eyes flashing. 'Furry? *Furry*? Is that what you think? Furry like a little puppy dog curled in your lap? I'm talking about hard fur. Harsh fur. A badger's coat, an animal pelt. She wasn't fluffy like a chicken. She was hard, bristly, bony, and stubbly. I haven't the words . . . I haven't the words to tell you what she felt like, how she made me wish I could pull my fingers off so I wouldn't feel it any more. Cut my own hand off, my arm off. Rip the nerves out, tear the nerves out of the bloody stump like wiring so I could never feel anything like it again. So I couldn't feel it even if I dreamed about her. About Miss May beneath the dress.' He shudders like he's had a coronary. The memory rattles through him, pulls at his joints like a butcher ready to chop. It crumples him up beneath his coat. Only the baling twine holds it, holds him, all together.

'I don't want to see her again,' he croaks. Shivering a little despite the heat.

I let him stand there quiet, then say softly: 'But you said she was beautiful. You said she was the most beautiful creature you ever saw.'

'She wasn't real. She was an image, a picture. I saw what I wanted to see, a pretty little picture from the big house. She'd show you another face, another mask.'

'Then how will I know?'

'I keep telling you, you don't want to know.'

'I do now. After all this!'

'I keep telling you,' he shouts, getting himself into another tizz. 'You're better off not knowing. Why do you keep coming down here anyway? Why do you have to keep pestering me? Haven't I got enough to put up with without you hanging round like a burr? Get back home, you should be in school as it is.'

Now it's my turn to stick my chin out a little. 'I've been sent home. Suspended.'

He looks at me curiously, raises his eyebrows.

'There was some trouble at school.' Some trouble

SCHOOL DAZE

I haven't told you, have I? Well, what with all Sylvester's news I've got a bit behind. To tell you the truth my problems fade into insignificance compared with his. Poor old bugger. No wonder he wanders about, Quasimodo playing Jack the Ripper. I don't want to whine on and on about me all the time, do I? It happened what, five days after Rupert disappeared. We were all out in the playground. There's a flower-bed all round, planted with the tougher species of roses, that kind of stuff. It's been a long hot summer. An Indian summer, my mum calls it. No rain to speak of and the red soil is as hard as rock. Just lumps really, not soil at all, but it makes for good grenades, though. Since Rupert's been gone I've been hanging around with Martin Lawrence's gang. They've not exactly taken me on full time but they've stopped calling me names. Why? Because Lorraine Lamb told Martin Samantha had packed me in. You would have thought it would have made things worse for me really, wouldn't you? One more thing they could shout at me. Thing is, though, to pack me in we must have been going together. And if I'd been going with one of the best-looking girls in the class it makes me someone, damn right. Makes me a somebody, even if I'm an ex-somebody. Damn sight better than being a fat nobody I can tell you. It's like I've been reborn, been given a new start. Martin Lawrence had walked up to me in the playground as if he was going to start something again.

'Ring My Bell's packed you in, eh?' he asked, right out of the blue. 'We thought she was going out with Prince Streak of Piss.'

Wasn't really very nice to go talking about him like that but I wasn't going to bust a gut objecting. I just shrugged, looked as mean as possible. I'd had half a dozen sixteen-year-olds, what did I care?

'He was always hanging about, before like. Before he went off. It doesn't matter now anyway.' I can feel lies piling up in my throat, credibility waiting just around the next corner. I just tell him how it it was, though. Well, it was like that, wasn't it? I've told you what happened, told you how she treated me when I went back for seconds.

'Is that why he buggered off, then?' lanky Lawrence asks as we make our way in to dinner. 'Just because you'd nabbed Samantha?' He seems impressed. Almost impressed. He's going to be even more impressed if I say yes. Only I didn't, see, if that's what you're thinking. I just shrugged.

'I dunno.' Since then I've been in. One of the crowd, not one of the weedy victims shuffling around the playground hoping they don't catch anybody's eye. Now instead of finding a quiet spot to pull out my *Lord of the Rings*, *Dune*, something like that, I'm running with them, playing with the team. We'd been lobbing the lumps of hard red soil at one another. Whizz, splat, puff of red dust. If it comes too close it's whizz, crack, ouch. We'd finished, we were on our way in to the hall, when the scream echoed out of the classroom block to our right. We all froze like Elves in the Ice Queen's palace, froze for a second then dashed to the classroom window. Our classroom. Miss McNeil, the dinner monitor (monitor lizard we called her), is running, quick short steps in her tight skirt. Wouldn't catch a tortoise like that. We're all at the window miles before she gets there, peering in like it's a glass case in a museum, peering in on a frozen tableau. Lorraine is holding on to Samantha trying to pull her backwards. I thought first they were having a fight. Sam is yelling and bawling and trying to hang on to her desk, Lorraine is pulling her away as if it's going to explode or something. Sam jumps back and they both go tumbling over. Sam's leg with the dirty plaster-cast flies up as if she's a footballer going for an overhead kick. I catch a tiny glimpse of her light blue knickers before she hits the deck and brings the desks tumbling down around them. Miss McNeil's pulling us away from the window but the head Mr Abrams has beaten her to it. He's heard the scream and come lolloping out of his office and down the corridor on his great long stork legs. He dashes in with his trousers flapping.

'Samantha Bell!' Like hearing her name is going to make her stop that awful squealing.

'Samantha Bell, what is going on?' He's in there pulling them up by their arms as they thrash and kick on the grubby floor among the desk legs. Samantha's kicking and pointing at her desk. It's been knocked out of line and stands apart from the rest in the middle of the room. Exhibit A. I don't know what's going on. I'm standing there open-mouthed like the rest of them, motorists slowing down to get a good squint at an accident, the way you do. Lorraine and Samantha are pickled together, legs kicking, desks scraping. Abrams darts in like a heron, wrenches Lorraine up quite roughly. She tugs her arm away and scrambles away into Miss McNeil, who has raced in through the main door to help. He grabs Samantha by one arm as Miss McNeil barges Lorraine aside and tugs her toward the door. Martin looks at me, too astonished to laugh. I try and grin, I'm that hard, see?

'Samantha Bell!' Abrams grates. 'What is going on?'

'In her desk,' Lorraine yelps from the door. Abrams releases Samantha, she collapses into McNeil's heaving bosom. He darts over to the lonely desk, standing like an altar in the middle of the room. He wrenches the lid up and peers in. He's seen blood before, he was in Korea or something. He sucks in his bottom lip, looks up at the line of faces along the window as if we're already on the identity parade. His prime suspects. Typical fucking teacher. Whack first ask questions later. I mean, this was 1973 remember. Corporal punishment and all that. His eyes are rolling, his Adam's apple bobbing above his fashionably chunky Windsor-knotted tie.

'Who is responsible for this?'

Shouldn't that be who is irresponsible for this? He's in his element now, class detention's a racing certainty unless he gets somebody in the frame pretty damn quick. His lips are twitching, jumping about as he forms the words. We're all standing on tiptoes peering into the messy desk. I can see her exercise books smothered with blood, her hairbrush and pencil case. And the chicken's head, hanging over her Scooby Doo lunchbox, thin trickles look like red felt pen. There's something else as well, something white I can't make out. I don't know why I laughed. I told them, I told Abrams, I told Whiteman a few weeks later. It was nerves, just nerves. Laughing was all I could do. It was that or burst out screaming and bloody bawling myself. Shriek and kick in front of the teachers, in front of Martin and the rest of them. A few of the others laughed with me, joined in for the same set of reasons I bet. Not because they wanted to show off, just nerves. But I was the first, I was the biggest, I was the one Abrams clocked as he looked along the line of grinning faces. 'Roberts, in my office now.' Whiteman, he was the worst. He wouldn't let that one lie, I knew he'd come back to it sooner or later.

'You knew what it was though, didn't you, this white thing?' he asks, pressing his fingers together and looking at me over his gold half-moon specs.

'Mr Abrams told me later.'

'You didn't know what it was at the time, then?'

'No. I couldn't see.'

'And you hadn't put it there either. Am I right?'

'That's right.'

'What was it?'

'You know. It's written there in your notes same as everything else I'm supposed to have done.'

'Tell me anyway.'

'It was one of those tampon things.'

'A tampon.' He pauses, looks at me some more. 'You know what they're for . . . you knew what they were for at the time?'

'Yes.'

'That wasn't a very nice trick to play on her, was it?'

'No.' He lets it hang there between us then switches subjects while I'm staring at my hands in my lap. Hey mush, I didn't do it. Have I mentioned anything about nipping in there and doing that? Think I did it? Well, who gives a shit what you think? You imagine I enjoy you finding out all this stuff?

You think I like listing down all these things I'm supposed to have done? I could have skipped right over, not let you in on it. You wouldn't have found out any other place. Whiteman, give the bastard his due, he's taken the hypocritical oath, whatever you call it. He's not going to discuss patients with a dirty little digger like you. D.B., well, she swims on out of the screen every time I think better of something, kind of reminds me to tell it straight. Everything, warts and all.

'This was the begining of what we could call the final phase, wouldn't you say?' He's chopped his notes into four sections, I can see he uses different coloured notepaper. Makes it easier for him, not me. I just had to live through it, one thing after another. Just like old Solomon with all those things going wrong on the farm. Me, I just try and remember that I was only a little biddy bit of this, a pebble in the beachcomber's bucket.

'This is where we can start to trace the events leading up to the kidnap attempt, isn't that right?' Kidnap attempt. That's the key. He's right there, of course. It's what you've waded all this way for. It's what you swam with me under Hillstones for. It's what you peeked at my dreams to check out. 'We have agreed to differ on the kidnap attempt, I know.'

'It wasn't Solomon,' I repeat for the three-hundredth time. 'It wasn't Solomon, it was Rupert.'

'As you say. The chicken, where did it come from?' He switches again but I'm ready for him.

'An egg, I guess.' He loves me when I'm being cute, this guy. Gives me a smile. That means he's mad at me. Shows him I can still play a few aces even though I've been in here three weeks. 'It could have come from anywhere,' I tell him while he's still simmering.

'In the circumstances though, Solomon's farm would have been a pretty fair bet, eh?'

'Anybody could have put it there. They knew it would drop him in it again.'

'Why would anybody want to implicate the old man?' I shrug, finish my coffee, see my eye reflected in the heavy grey cup. You could brain somebody with one of these, I can tell you. He waits for me a second, goes on flicking through his notes. 'This chicken's head is placed in Samantha Bell's desk. A tampon is stuck in the bloody end. Your headmaster looks up and sees you laughing. Asks you if you had anything to do with it. Me sir? No sir. Just as you keep telling me. He gets a report from one of your teachers, a Miss De Plechon. She's worried about some of the stuff you're writing about in your essays.' He flicks through the stack of folders on his desk, takes a peek at an inky sheet. Ahead of my time, is all. Always had a bit of imagination. That a crime too? Christ, half the kids in our class would have failed IQ tests against a colony of sea urchins. I thought she'd appreciate me brightening her day up with something a little more juicy than 'I went home I watched TV I went to bed' kind of stuff. I should have kept my head down with the doughnuts, stayed out of trouble. Way everything gets dragged up and thrown in your face. Whiteman glances up at me.

'And when your father is called to the school the first thing he does is hit you round the head. Why was that?'

'Because he'd warned me after the business with the trees, when Sam broke her ankle.'

'When you broke her ankle.'

'Have it your own way.'

'No . . . we'll have it the right way. Who broke her ankle, you, Rupert, or a really really big conker?' He gives me one of his looks, gets me back for the crack about the egg.

'I did. OK.'

'And why did your father hit you, was it because you spent half your time down at the chicken run? Couldn't he have been forgiven for putting two and two together?'

'Abrams said he wasn't to hit me.' It was true. He'd grabbed Dad's arm, said he didn't think knocking me into the middle of next week would help matters. Said, 'Really, Mr Roberts,' as if he meant to say Mr Barbarian Shithead. Whiteman's not having any of it.

'He may not have been helping matters but he thought you'd done it. That's what it comes down to. Why did he think it; because he knew you and Solomon were like this?' He crosses his thin fingers in front of his measly face. I'd like to crack them in a nutcracker for him, right there on the joints. Crack his fingers and rip out his nicely trimmed nails. 'He knew you were down there listening to his stories about ghosties and Glaistigs, whatever she's called. The Beast with Two Backs. That's a good one. Do you know *Othello*? That's where he got that from.'

'He never read *Othello*.' He ignores me, glances through my bulging orange file. It's all in there, he hasn't been refused a thing. Not a fucking thing.

'You're pretty well read for a twelve-year-old, aren't you, David?' Another switch. 'Your stories show a very vivid imagination. Slightly sinister, unhealthy even.'

Thank you, Miss De Plechon. That's the last time I lick my lips thinking of your nutty little nipples. Got a class full of impressionable twelve-year-olds and here's Salome De Plechon strutting her stuff in a cheesecloth shirt. My God, we'd do anything for a detention with her. Writing out some rubbish a million times giving her sly looks while she wrote out her shopping list, itching to be out of there and on her way home to Horace, or whatever the hell her social worker boyfriend was called. I saw him pick her up in a battered Citroën 2CV, the back smothered with peace stickers. Should have known I didn't stand that much of a chance, even with my two-minute experience with Sam. Whiteman nods, inviting me to jump in protesting it's all in the name of art or something. OK, they might be a little bloody, a bit scary, a bit whatever. What's wrong with that? I started writing this stuff down when I was twelve, thirteen, fourteen, I should bloody know. Haven't really changed much I suppose. Hardly surprising really.

'What I'm getting at is Rupert never blamed you for anything that happened.'

'He hasn't said a word yet, has he?' I snap back at him.

'And he hasn't invented a pile of bloody bicycle shed bullshit to try and cover his tracks either,' he shouts, making me jump a little. He takes off his glasses and slaps the folder. My life's work.

'You'd be a damn sight happier if he had,' I accuse. OK, I

know it, I'm running on quicksand again, running to stand still. He gives himself a moment to calm himself.

'Take it from me, David, your friend Solomon was deeply disturbed. I won't try and blind you with science. He was cracked. Probably been that way since the War, like you told me. He'd retreated into his own little world and shut everyone else out. Apart from you. I admit he must have been convincing. He would have been convincing, he'd convinced himself, after all. I don't blame you. I loved stories like that when I was your age.' He pauses, gives me his gentle uncle look. Rupert had a gentle uncle and he poured cider over his cottage, invited us all along for a barbeque. Hey, Glaistig baby, hand the hamburgers.

'If he was here now I could try and help him, talk him through it the way I do with you. I could help him with that burden, that terrible burden of guilt he was carrying. You think of what happened to him, killing his fiancée like that. He couldn't take it so he told stories. He told stories to anyone who'd listen, anyone who'd give him the time of day. A bloody smokescreen. He'd blow it in their faces like he blew it in yours. He was lying about this Glaistig creature from the very beginning.' He's scoring points and he knows it. He isn't going to let up on me now he's got me squirming in the chair.

'If he'd let on to anyone else they would have laughed in his face. The men in the white coats would have carted him off years ago. They'd have laughed at him. The only person who listens is a twelve-year-old boy who thinks you mean *Lord of the Rings* if you mention the Bible. A sci-fi nut, am I right? A Dungeons and Dragons fanatic. When I was a lad it was girls we were after, not goblins.' He lets the remark hang. He may be going too far. He pulls up. I'm red, angry. You know me when people start on like this.

'Nobody's blaming you, David. Nobody. If you've stuffed yourself with all this fantasy rubbish it's hardly surprising you'd take to his ramblings. Take to him like he was the kind old storyteller. Because that's all he was doing, David, telling stories. Ghost stories, horror stories. The tragedy is he wasn't just telling them, he was living them. And he tried to make you and Rupert live them too, didn't he?' He leans back in his chair, day's work done. Almost.

'You know what you are, don't you? You're his suicide note. You're the one he left behind to tell us what he was thinking, why he did it. He'd been looking for somebody to write it since the day he stole that car and ran the girl down. Through you, we've got to try and read him.' Yeah, heavy stuff eh? Shut up a second can you, I'm thinking.

Prankster	165
Blame	170
Last Day	186
Streamland	192
Newsman Cometh	205
Prince Rupert drops in	219

PART FOUR

'I follow him to serve my turn upon him:
We cannot all be masters, nor all masters cannot be truly
followed'

IAGO TO RODERIGO, *Othello*, WILLIAM SHAKESPEARE

PRANKSTER

OK, maybe Whiteman was getting to me. I keep telling you, I'm not a bloody rock. Sometimes he gets me going, gets me thinking. Yeah, perhaps that scumbag Solomon was making it all up. Maybe he was a coward after all, covering his tracks behind that bullshit ghost story. Trouble is, I knew him and you just get to hear about him. You get to hear me telling you about his eyes, the way he had of looking at you under your skin, under your hair. Me, I got to look right on in. To see was to know. Whiteman didn't get to look at his eyes either. He can take any part of the puzzle and drop it in anywhere he likes, turn it on its head, turn it on its belly. He can make courage look like cowardice, strength weakness, black white. He's got all Solomon's statements and his War records, he's got files on everyone he thinks he needs, the complete works. He's got eye witnesses and forensics. The coroner came up with accidental death but Whiteman's got the clincher. He's got Solomon's suicide note. Me. Trouble is I've spilled my ink all over the pages, stuck them all together and made the ink run in crazy spiderwebs. He's got to read me first, he wants to make sense of the old guy. Whiteman's got me till the end of the week. Then he either comes out and says sure, the boy's a goddamn basketcase, or he lets me out. That's the deal, that's how he explained it to my parents. To help him make sense of the spiderwebs he's had that dopey Cheryl bring in the police files, newspaper clippings, books on teenage cults and local mythology. Figures they'll help him sift the fact from the fiction. He's got my school reports in battered red covers, lists of the books they found on my shelves, the records in the rack. They must have been over my room pretty thoroughly, I reckon. Yeah, I thought this was coming.

'What's this?' Whiteman holds it up. Hell, he's a doctor, he ought to know. I can't look at him straight when he's on to me like this. You've seen me blush before, you know what I'm like. This is worse though. This is so bad I don't really want to have to put it in, D.B. or no. Or no, who am I trying to kid? I'm either straight with you or you're not going to believe a word.

'Cruella de Come? This stuff's not available in the shops, David, you know that as well as I do. Where did you get it?' He waves the familiar pages at me.

'Rupert. Lent it. I was supposed to give it back.' I'm looking at the carpet between my feet like it's issue two or something. How'd they find that anyway?

'Rupert again, now there's a surprise. Naughty Rupert.' He stares at me like a camp actor, crooked smile.

'He got it from a kid in the fourth year. He paid for it. The other kid said he got it from Army Cadets.'

'Army Cadets? Let's hope we never have to fight another war, then. I'm not joking, David. This is hard-core pornography. It's not *Playboy, Health and Efficiency*. I couldn't buy this anywhere round here. I'd have to send away for it.' So send, so what?

'I didn't send away for it, I didn't buy it.'

'But we found it in your room. You think you're pretty clever with your little hiding places, don't you? The trouble is we're used to finding strange things in awkward places. You're playing games with the grown-ups now.' That's what this is all about, hey, Doc, playing with the grown-ups? That's what Miss De Plechon said that time she called me back to bawl me out for the story about the farmer's boy and the squire's daughter. If I squint I think I can see it halfway down Whiteman's grubby pile. My life's work.

'When did you get it? It's important. Before all this started or after?'

'He had it for a while. Lent it to me about a month ago, maybe more.'

'Before you started going round to see Samantha Bell or afterwards? Be precise if you can.'

I can be precise, Doc. 'After.'

'After the picture business?' I nod. It's a lie, OK, but this bastard's got no way of finding that out, so he can fuck right off. Well, it looks pretty bad doesn't it, going round to see Sam after spending three weeks alone with Cruella de Come for company. Shit, I didn't know you could do those things, let alone that anybody would want to. The little farmer guy in my story, he was in to the more straightforward stuff too, in case you're wondering. Lynn (that's her first name, see, keep calling her Miss De Plechon) wanted to know where I'd done all my research, gave me a funny sort of grin.

'Come on, spill the beans,' she'd said quietly, peering at me over the little gold specs she wore when she was reading.

'I've read sketchier details in a pathologist's report. Never even heard of half these things. Gray's *Anatomy*, was it?' Of course, I knew she was taking the piss as soon as she started. Trying to re-establish the correct pupil–teacher relationship, I figured. Hell, I ought to be doing Whiteman's job. She did a pretty thorough job though, I had to admit it. He coughs, gets my attention.

'About the same time your little wargames started getting boring though. Roughly?'

Roughly what? I'm lost. 'About the same time.'

'Within a month. You'd been reading this and then you go round to see her. Did she see any of it, did you try and show her?'

No chance.

'Did you describe any of it to her?'

No chance.

'Do you know if Rupert showed or described it to her before he showed you?'

'I don't think so. He never said.' Well, you wouldn't, would you? How do I know anyway? I've told you I wasn't with them every time. He'd had that book weeks before he'd even let me peek at it over at his house.

'Have you seen any other magazines like this?'

'He'd had magazines before. Bits of them. Never like that.'

'Like what?'

I nod at the copy he's replaced on my closed folder.

'What's the difference?'

'Between what?'

'Between this one and the others you've seen?'

'There's different things in that one. Not just tits and things.' He nods, flicks through it. I look away. Traffic's snarled on the ring-road again.

'Very different things, I'd say. You know what perversions are? Would you say this material was perverted?'

'I never liked it.'

'But you had it in your bedroom?' And if you think I'm telling you what his next question was, you know what you can do don't you? It was a magazine, that's all. Doesn't prove a thing. You maybe went through your teenaged years without a look at a dirty book, that right? Whiteman can mind his own business and so can you.

'I didn't like it. I never will. I can't understand how people do that stuff, even for money.' He pauses, looks at me. I'm still looking away.

'That's as maybe. The thing is, this magazine has got a spread with some girls and animals, hasn't it?' Amongst other things, yes.

'And this Glaistig of yours. This Beast with Two Backs, as dear old Jubal is supposed to have called her. She is half woman half goat. That's about it, am I right?' He lets it sink in a while.

'You see what I'm getting at, of course. That you are connecting Solomon's stories with things you have seen in this magazine. Things you quite naturally haven't been able to understand.'

'He never had those magazines. He never showed us anything.'

'I'm not saying he did. Did I say he had?'

'Rupert got them from this kid, he got them from the Army Cadets.'

'And Solomon never showed you, or you never found any of these in his possession, down at the chicken run for instance?' I know what's coming next. I've been waiting for it.

It's been churning about in his mealy mouth a few times, but he's never come right out with it. First he has him down as a coward, now he's a pervert, a child molester. One of those horrible men with dead eyes you read about in the papers. Not a chance. Solomon never made any pass, any comment like that. He didn't swear that much, only when he was remembering. Only when he got carried away. And he never got carried away *that* far, ever. OK.

'All right then,' Whiteman changes tack, sees I've got the shutters up. He goes round. 'What if Solomon had pictures like this himself. What if he had seen them. Been shown them when he went away to the Army. Been shown them and never been able to forget them? Then the whole thing can be rationally explained. This Glaistig, she doesn't have to come in to it at all.' He sits back and frowns. I say nothing.

'So the chicken's head was Rupert, the magazine was Rupert's. This story of yours the teacher passed on to the headmaster. We'll put that down to an unusually zealous interest in human biology. Then the big one. Who's responsible for that, I wonder?'

'Rupert,' I say flatly.

'You were with Solomon when you saw him come back. Followed him, stopped him in his tracks. That right?'

'Like it says in my statement.'

'Tell me anyway.'

BLAME

What are we talking now; the day after I'd told Solomon about the chicken's head. That made it almost a week since Rupert had gone. I'd been on my way down to the chicken run as usual when I bumped into PC Bell dragging his knackered Polish boneshaker from his garage.

'Here he is then,' he'd sneered, dragging the bike back on its stand so he could put his hands on his hips and gloat.

'Off to find another chicken, eh? Old Solomon must be charging you, all the fowls he's been losing lately. I saw him with another this morning. Good God, Solomon, I says to him, why don't you pluck 'em before putting them in the food mixer? He said a fox had got it. I said a fox in size seven Wellingtons.'

'It wasn't me, Mr Bell. I told Mr Abrams I didn't have anything to do with it. I was going to come round and . . .'

'Just thought it was funny. Felt you had to laugh out loud?' He stepped round the bike, I thought he was going to hit me. He'll be out the Force if he does.

'You may have pulled the wool over that old tosser's eyes but you're not going to convince me. I've seen you hanging about here. I thought you'd actually turned over a new leaf when you started coming in and talking to her instead of just spying on her. Thought you were growing up a bit, starting to act like a normal boy. Oh no. A couple of days and you're back to your old ways, creeping round like a fat ferret. If I was your father I'd have you seen to, I would.' His face is livid, his freckles look like dabs of red paint on his puffy face.

'And I know why you did it and all. Our Sam's told us all about it. Because she told you where to get off. Thought you'd
get back at her by putting that mess in her desk.'

'I didn't do it,' I insist. He's not listening. He's so red, brick red he's built himself up. Mrs Bell is in the garden, she's heard him squawking. She clutches her peg bag like a rosary.

'Malcolm . . . don't shout at the lad . . . If he says he didn't do it he didn't do it.'

He looks round at her then back to me. 'Just get out of my sight. I don't want you hanging round here. If you make any attempt to see Samantha, or hurt her in any other way, you won't know what hit you. I mean it, David. Now piss off out of it.' He swings round and throws his heavy leg over the old motorcycle. I back away, cross the stile. I didn't put that chicken's head in there with the other thing. I know we weren't talking but that doesn't mean I'd go and do a thing like that. She said I was glad Rupert had gone, now here's her father accusing me of chopping up Solomon's chickens to get back at her. It wasn't bloody fair, I can tell you. It wasn't fair at all. There's no evidence, they can't prove it was me. Circumstantial, that's what it was. Just because I laughed. I didn't mean to. Nerves. That's all. Nerves. Miss De Plechon, rolling her eyes and raising her eyebrows at me, cutting my legs from under me as I sat in on her detention. She was twenty-six and I was twelve, thinking I was big enough and man enough I'd stand a chance with her. I'd interest her in any way. Jesus Christ. And Whiteman gets to filter through it, trawl my stories and essays, those dafty poems I wrote knowing she'd get to read them, mark them. Red pen purple prose. How is this guy ever, ever going to take me seriously? How are you? Shit, you get to go through it all too. Think I'm sitting here wrapped in a dirty raincoat, drooling over the keys like some damn pervert? What have I got to do to convince you? Yeah, I thought as much. Well, she put me off the whole business for a while, if you want the truth. Put me off until I was in the sixth form anyway. Miss De Plechon I mean. Peeping up at her when she'd finished greasing me out for being a smartarse.

'Do you really think Bathsheba Everdene's a prick-tease? I've always had a bit of a soft spot for Hardy myself. No, David, that's soft spot, not G-spot. Keep your mind on your work.' G-spot? What the hell's she on about? She ducks down behind her desk, starts stuffing her files into her Afghan bag. I stare at the shelves behind her head, the formaldehyde bottles yellow and sickly, their crouching occupants giggling and chattering to themselves, making the most of my embarrassment. The little foetuses tapping their tiny nails on the tinted glass, winking at me. Shit, I swear the fucking things were twitching more than I was. I shake my head, try and focus and she jumps in right away. She leans over my desk, I can't help but stare down her cheesecloth top. Where else am I supposed to look? She freezes for a second, I can feel her eyes boring in to the top of my head. Her breasts are about six inches from my nose, a funny triangular white patch where she sunbathed with her bikini on. The smooth hollow between is covered with freckles the same colour as the ones on her nose. She straightened, packed her bloody bag, and nodded me to the door. After that you can bet I threw myself into football and fishing. You can bet I didn't waste too many maggots down at the stream. Kept well away from there and took my mind off things for a while. Pretty well stayed off things until the time I bumped into Sam down at the Boar, what, eight years later. I hardly recognized her, to tell you the truth. I was co-managing a club in Budgworth, tasteful sort of place. Remind me not to tell you about it some time. I hadn't seen her since she'd left school to go to university up in Loughborough or somewhere awful like that. I was on my way in to meet Lorraine. Yeah, Lorraine Lamb, remember her? We'd been going out for a few years, since sixth form really. Funny how things turn out, eh? Sam was at home for the weekend. They'd arranged to meet, only Lorraine's bloody Mini had packed in again. She'd been stuck at work so it was just Sam and I. Yeah, funny how things work out. She'd looked, smiled.

'David? Is that you?'

'It was when I looked this morning. How are you? How's Loughborough?'

'Don't ask. You look . . . different. You've lost weight.'

'It's going back on now. What are you doing down here?'

And there we were. Long-lost pals, old buddies back together.

We'd stayed till closing time, chewing over old times and everything. She said she was staying at her parents. I said I was staying with mine. Had I seen Rupert lately? Not lately. Not likely. Was he the same? Very likely. She'd swilled her G&T around, her eyes reflected on the glass.

'So you and Lorraine are thinking about getting engaged?' It was half true. She was. I shrugged.

'We stayed in touch, that's all.' She looked up, Christ she looked good that night. I'd had a couple of pints of Old Boar, anybody would have looked good, but she looked marvellous. Her jeans, T-shirt, leather waistcoat thing. Hair up in a bun, the way I'd always liked it in the old times.

We walked out into the brisk night air, what was it, early spring? Well.

'Not much going on down here, I suppose, not at this time of night.'

'Not unless we drive up to Budgworth. I know a few clubs.' That was true enough.

'I've had enough of clubs. It's so quiet here. I think I'd forgotten what it was like, being stuck out here. Just the hills all round, not a load of people.' We were standing there as awkward as we'd ever been. More. Where was her boyfriend, where was Lorraine? I spent a couple of seconds thinking about it before I slipped my arm round her slim shoulders. She was as warm as toast.

'Let's walk,' I said, smooth as cucumber sandwiches with the crusts cut off. She nodded, looked at her boots as she scuffed the gravel in the Boar's car park.

'Where shall we go?'

'The bridge?'

'To see the pool in the moonlight. You'd never get away with that if you'd gone up to college with me. They would have seen you coming a mile off,' she smiled.

'Ah, but these yer farm girls do like a bit of moony love talk,' I'd drawled, trying desperately to think of somewhere sheltered. Well, what are you shaking your head for? She'd worked it out the same as me, hadn't she? Maybe you think I forced her? Had one go at her when she was a kid and another when she was on the rebound from some college romance? We strolled along the road, stream tinkling away to our right, glittering and flickering round the mossy rocks.

'I'm sorry I was such a cow that time. You know.'

'Don't mention it.' Yeah, I meant that all right. Way it came out, sounded more like a threat. She looked up, eyes all blue, little curls of hair round her ears, just pinking a little in the night air.

'Or what?'

I closed my arm round her, squeezed her in tight. I was at least a foot taller than she was, had to look down at her.

'You remember that time in my bedroom? You remember how you . . . I see he remembers anyway.'

'I want you, Sam.'

'And what about Lorraine?'

'What about her? You want to run back to the pub, ring her up and apologize?'

'For what?' For the thirteen-minute kiss that practically sealed our lips. For the way she ground herself into me, shoulders dipping, body swaying. I pulled away long enough to tug her through the light undergrowth to the sheltered side of the bridge. The shadows by the stream. The bare brick wall was cold. I leaned back and pulled her on to me again.

'You've been here before,' she said, playfully punching my chest.

'Not with you.'

'With Lorraine then. Ow! If you think I'm doing it here like a bloody . . .'

'Twelve-year-old?' She relaxes again. I close my arms round her, rest my chin on her head.

'Not here. Let me fetch my car. Won't take five minutes.'

'You'll change your mind again.' Hey, I was serious.

'I'm not doing it pressed up against a bloody wall, David. Wait here.' She pulled away, straightened her top.

'How do I know you won't leave me here?' I tried not to sound too anxious. Never does to look too anxious, eh boys?

She leans forward slowly, spreads her palm over the front of my jeans, looks up and smiles.

'Just wait.' Jesus Christ. I watched her clickety-click along the path back up towards the pub lit up amongst the trees. Squinted as half a dozen cars roared past, lighting me up on full beam. Then I saw one slow down and pull in. A white Escort. She leaned over, flicked the door lever. I climbed in.

'Where to, then?'

'Better make it somewhere near,' I grated, trying to keep my eyes on the road. She drove with one hand on my leg and the other on the wheel. I grabbed her hand and pulled it higher.

'Patience, David. You've waited long enough. Five minutes isn't going to make any difference now.'

'Unless you change your mind again.' She looked round, raised her eyebrows.

'You think I don't feel the way you do? You think girls don't get randy too?'

'Nice ones don't.' She laughed. I pointed out the turning for Axeheads. Two miles along here and things get about as deserted as they can get. She pulls into a gateway, turns the engine off.

'You're not getting out?' I ask her as she levers her door open.

'Ever tried taking off a pair of Levis in the front of one of these? We'd be here half the night.'

'You've done this before.'

'What difference does that make?' None, I guess. I sit there smiling as she straightens up, tugs her top up and unzips. Christ Almighty. She's wearing bright red panties. She must have been studying videos of my wet dreams. She hooks her thumbs in the waistband and pulls them down. I blink and she's bent down, loosened her boots and worked her bloody jeans off. She tosses them in the back and jumps in. She smells warm and sweet. Her breath suggests gin, something else. Something makes you want to kiss her.

'Hurry up then.' She leans across, helps me free my belt, tugs down my zipper. It's a bit difficult. 'He's grown.'

'Not . . .' She doesn't want to hear me chatter on. I can't talk anyway. Nor can she. I tug her back up, tug her waistcoat aside. She kneels up on the driving seat, pulls it off. 'I'm not taking everything off, I'll die of cold.'

I lean over, kiss her hard belly. Girl's much skinnier than Lorraine. She shivers. She leans back, skin stretching. She's warm and smells like the rabbit's foot thing Lorraine wears sometimes. I trail my tongue down her belly.

BBBBBBBBEEEEEEEEEEEEEEEEEEEEEEEEEPPPPPPPPPPPPP

'Sorry.'

'Jesus Christ.'

'Hang on.' She's leaned back too far, sounded the horn. Now she climbs over my lap, fiddles about until she's comfortable and pushes down slowly. Oh my God. I'm in. Eight years after our bedroom scene I'm inside her. Eight years I'd almost forgotten what she looked like. If I close my eyes I can see her standing there in her pink room with her foot in plaster. 'Umm.' Her legs are warm, pressing either side of my thighs. She holds the back of the seat behind my head, rocks gently.

'This is what we were missing.' The girl won't stop talking. She's ruining my concentration, and I'm concentrating, let me tell you.

'I shouldn't have thrown you out that time. I was just upset about Rupert.' Rupert? Fuck Rupert. Fuck me. Here, here I am. 'That's nice. Oh Christ.' She's gripping the plastic seat cover either side of my head, it's crinkling and squeaking in time with our rhythm. Sitting back in the seat with her on top I can barely move. She holds me there beautifully precise. I shut my eyes again, tug her down towards me. Close my mouth over hers just in case she wants to say anything else. She pulls away eventually, she's breathing heavily. Christ, she's not asthmatic or anything is she?

'It's a pity he's . . .'

'What?'

'I said it's a pity he's . . . not . . . here . . . hang on . . . that's better. Rupert. I said it's a pity he's not here. Ouch . . . careful. I'll bang my head on the roof if you keep doing that. I don't mean with us . . . right now. I mean it's a pity he's not around. You know.'

'Just shut up about Rupert for a second, OK?'

'You're not still jealous of him, are you? What more do you want me to do?' She stops.

'Just be quiet about him . . . for a couple of minutes. OK?' She frowns a little. I twist my behind in the screwed-up seat cover. She groans softly. I do it some more.

'OK?'

'OK.'

'OK.' OK. OK? There. That proves I'm a perfectly well-adjusted young man, eh? The first time with Sam in a dark gateway up on the Axeheads road. Just in case, all this stuff about Glaistigs and goats and Cruella de Comes and school-boy wank essays had been making you think I'm some kind of a weirdo. Sam and I, that night, the other times. We never had any problems as long as she kept her mind on it and didn't start on about poor old Rupert missing out on sex and everything. Jesus Christ, the best thing I could have done with her was cut her frigging tongue out. We'd still be together, because we were good together, honestly. That day her dad caught me down the lane, though, I would have cheerfully drowned her in the allotment trough. After her dad had finished I arrived at the chicken run pretty pissed, I can tell you. I practically kicked the rickety door down, came across Solomon pouring meal into the zinc trays. He looks up, shields his eyes against the bright sun behind me.

'You look well mad.' I'm back with him. Back with Solomon. You want to know why I stuck up for him? He was the only one who really stuck by me. The only one cared to listen to anything I had to say. Him and me, we were outcasts together those weeks. We'd stick together, him and me versus the world.

'Got another bollocking, then, did you?' I nod, look round absent-mindedly as if I've never been down there before. The warmth of the shed, the constant clucking, it soothes me down a little.

'Listen, if we weren't the trap, who was?' I ask as he straightens up, puts the bucket down. He sweeps the worst of the chicken dung from an old bench, sits down. His story-teller pose.

'I was. Well, me and Dad. We were the trap. The picture was a trap, or part of it. I hung it up there in the front room, pride of place. Like a challenge, to prove I weren't afeared of her. I said we'd finish it, one way or another. I took to going out nights, wandering. Put my head on her chopping block. See if she'd do anything other than curdle the milk and leave the gates open. Dared her to show herself. If anybody saw me they must have thought I was mad. Madder than ever. Mad bloody Solomon. I was mad to see her, true enough. Hungry to see her. We were to burn her out, that's what Dad said. Burn her off the hills like they'd done in the old times.

So we waited till what was left of the crops was in, burnt off the stubble. Set fire to the fields, cleaned them with fire. We burned the stubble off the hill like bristles off a hog. All the folk in the village moaned on again, said we were spoiling their washing, setting fires like that. Have half the world on fire if we weren't more careful. Any excuse to come up and complain they took right enough. We took no notice. We went on burning. We stood on the peak and watched it roll down the hill behind a great grey curtain. We followed behind it, scorched our boots on the smouldering ground, I didn't mind it, the heat. Never bothered me, a bit of flame and smoke. We'd burned out the brambles, old trees, piles of rubbish. We'd burned old rabbits and birds' nests but we hadn't burned her. We looked till it got dark, then made our way back to the cottage. It was getting dark quick like, as if the smoke had brought the night down, choked out the sun. It had been a clear enough day, save our smoke. We could hardly believe it when it started to rain. Fizzed and steamed when it hit the ground, it were that hot. Great big raindrops, big ones so we knew a big storm was coming. It was big all right. Like a summer shower, only it didn't give out like a summer shower. It was pelting down, we had to run the last bit along the stream. I looked at Dad when we got in, a drowned rat he was and no mistake. I'd never seen him look so raggedy. You could have picked him up and wrung him out. I'd never seen rain like it. It was coming in through the thatch, streaming down the walls. Dad said we'd best get the animals locked in the barn, just in case the stream rose. I looked out. It looks quiet enough now, but you go down if we've had a good deal of rain and see it. See it how it was in the olden times when it cut its way through the hills, cut the gorge out of the rock. I've seen it up three feet and as red as blood, taking all the topsoil away down south where it's no use to anyone save a few bloody frogs. All that good soil. We had buckets and bowls out everywhere. Standing there in our soaking smoky clothes watching a puddle form in front of the grate. Dad said we should try and get a tarpaulin up over the front of the thatch, keep the worst off. We got out to the barn and dragged it out, but the wind had got up and we couldn't hold it. I couldn't do it on my own and Dad was weak as a straw. I told him to pack it in, get back indoors. I was halfway up the ladder, looking down on him. He looked as if he'd been hammered halfway into the mud. A little broken forlorn thing, I thought. He went on in as I wrestled with that damn sheet. The wind picked up and took it out of my hands. It went over the roof, got caught by a gust and blew away over the trees. Great big heavy tarpaulin as if it was no more than a lady's handkerchief. It usually blows across the top of the gorge, westerly like. This was blowing right along as if it was a wind tunnel. Blew me over, off the ladder. Rolled me over till I bumped my head against the wall there. Clinging to the cracks in the stonework tore me nails out just keeping hold. It was a hurricane, a hurricane whipped up for me and my dad. It was her wind, see, her rain. I could see it was her work as I lay there hanging on to those mossy stones while she tried to pummel me loose.

I suppose we'd challenged her, we'd challenged her to come out and fight and there she was. I just hung there for grim death while the worst of it rushed up the stream and roared on the cottage. I thought the roof would fly off. It had me off the ground, it was pulling me out of the way when it veered, sudden like. It dropped me like a gundog drops a pheasant. I crawled back toward the house but she must have spotted me from up in the storm, spied me skulking there like a wet rat. She sent me another gust to winkle me out, zigzagged past the trees, hammered the door open, and knocked me aside. I scrambled, I grasped, but she had me. I rolled over and over straight down the bank straight into the stream. You could hear the trees twanging like bowstrings. Windfalls were flying round like shrapnel, smashing windows, splattering against the walls. She bowled me right over into the stream, straight into her lap. I grabbed for a branch but she whipped it away. I bellyflopped into the stream only it wasn't the stream I knew. Wasn't the stream you know either. It was swollen, seven feet deep at least and going down brown and fast. It had me like a dead sheep, twirling me round and round. I tried to swim against it but it were like swimming in millions of snakes, all trying to hold me down, turn me around. The rain had lashed it into a frenzy so you could hardly see where the rain stopped and the stream began. The stream was every-thing, everything from the pebbles on the bottom to the clouds and the moon. There was nothing else. Just me tossed along, a piece of old rubbish. I had working clothes, my oilskin. Weighed a ton. Pulled me under, pulled me in. It was all I could do to catch a breath. Spinning like a top, weighed down by my clothes. Before I could think of anything I'd hit the bridge. I hit it so hard I knew that was it. The flow held me against the brickwork, strained and pulled at me. I tugged my chin up out of it, out of the eels and snakes that were rushing up past me, a solid block of writhing living things, wanting me dead. There was nothing I could do. I could feel myself getting sucked under, slipping away. I was half drowned and half dazed and I could hardly move a finger. The water came up over my eyes. I couldn't see a thing. I went under. Under the arch like the stream was gobbling me all up. She had me, she'd won. I tried to burn her and here she was soaking me up to nothing.' He sighs and stops.

'So how did you get out, then?'

Solomon leans back on his bench, looks at his ragged hands. When he's not talking he chews his bottom lip making the bristles on his chin rise up and down like insect antennae.

'That was the strangest of all. That was the part I've never started to understand.' He breathes deeply, looks up with his amber eyes.

'I thought the arch went straight through to the other side. It don't.'

I could have told him that. If you duck under you see the brickwork rises in a sort of double alcove. You can stand under the thing without bending your head, listen to the traffic thunder overhead.

'There was a big air bubble under the bridge,' I suggest.

He shakes his head. 'There was a gap, that's all.'

'And she was there?'

'Not her. Small things.' He looks away, then glances back at me, like he wants to make sure I won't laugh or anything. 'Small things like dirty garden gnomes. Little leprechauns. Three of them. They were hanging from the roof. I don't know how. Looked like wire cables, looked like horrible puppets some mad child had hung there to ward us off.'

Oh Jesus.

'I don't know. I'd bashed my head something awful. Maybe I was seeing things. Maybe it was dead crows Jubal had hung up to scare off the predators. Maybe it was his good-luck charm. But they looked like creatures. Little men. All dark and tatty like. I can remember floating there underneath looking at them hanging there, buffeted this way and that. Then the biggest one reached out and grabbed my hair, pulled me up. The others got me by the shoulders, by the lapels of my coat, dragged me up, held me against the worst of it. I think so anyway. I passed out. When I came to, came round, whatever they were they'd gone. I was sitting in the stream under the bridge. It was running dark and fast but it was back to about a foot deep. I was propped against the arch like a shipwrecked sailor. I turned over on my hands and knees, looked out down the stream. That's when I saw them again. The three things. They were shorter than you, stumpy things. Flat-faced, ugly little squats. The leader had these stones, I thought they must have been on some fine chain or lace, the way he had them swinging round him, looked almost comical. The leader saw me, stopped, waved me back under. They scrambled up the bank, helping each other. They seemed to be in a dreadful hurry, scrambling and slipping about. I was on my hands and knees, looking out from under the bridge like a dog in a kennel. It was her. She was floating down the water. Floating above it like green mist. The one I'd seen her . . . Miss May . . . seen her wear. All raggedy, misty round the edges. She was looking about her on both sides. Like she owned the place. Like she had a stiff neck or something. Mechanical. Floating along with the branches tearing holes in her gown, but then they'd like mist over again. Like she was a solid mist. I don't know.' He pauses, wipes his mouth with a shaky hand.

'It was her, see, Miss May, only different, sharper. Like she'd been in the car that time. Her bones were all sticking out, stretching her skin in all directions. Her hair was streaming out behind her. I think the three funny men must have moved, distracted her. I felt the bridge go cold as she passed through it, seeped through my bones. I'd challenged her and here she was, patrolling her stream like a great big misty moth with its wings pinned out. A misty great wasp ready to sting. She came right close, I could smell the cold coming off her in waves, like a fog bank moving in off the sea. She'd pulled all the mists in the gorge round her for a shawl. She came right over the bridge, I could feel her shiver through the stones. Feel the water dripping from the roof down my neck. She passed over and the stream slowed, slackened. I don't know how long I stayed there, could have been hours but I suppose it was only a matter of minutes. I climbed out, water pouring out of my pockets, pouring out of me like one of those funny statues in a fountain. I scrambled up the bank, covered in red mud. I waded home down the slippery path, legs spread apart. There were big pools and puddles everywhere, little waterfalls where they were emptying back into the stream. Parts of the bank had subsided, I had to hang on to branches to get along. As I got nearer home it got worse. All the trees were torn about, the bank had slipped away. The orchard wall was down, stones scattered about everywhere. I shouted out for Dad, realized I'd left him in the cottage. I started running, wallowing up to the front door. It was hanging off its hinges, water running out as if I'd disturbed it, running out over my boots like dribble from a dead man's mouth. I wallowed in. The room was upside-down. Everything was tipped over, washed against the walls like jetsam. The water had been in there like a pack of dogs. I found him in the corner. Thought he was a bit of curtain first, he was so small and raggedy like. I remember . . . he was all clean, clean like china. There wasn't any blood. It was all washed away, like the flood had sucked it all out of him, left him like a sucked-out lemon there in the corner. The water had held him like it had held me. Only I was young and strong and he was old and worn out. He'd been cornered in there when the flood came for him. It took me a while to work it out. How the water must have rushed in, carried him higher and higher till he was stuck there in the top corner of the room, jammed him against the ceiling. He'd scratched and pulled at the plaster like a wild thing, like he could claw his way out, claw himself some air. It didn't matter if he screamed and cursed and shat himself, it didn't matter he'd torn his nails out and ripped his fingers to the bone. The wall wouldn't give to him. It held him there for her while she got him. He must have bellowed for me, choked on mouthfuls of dirty water till it came up and stole his air. Washed and tumbled him, sucked out all his blood and left off, dropped him back on the floor like a raggy doll. Tossed him aside like fishermen drop dogfish. His eyes were open like a fish as if the stream had put its mark on him. Her mark. It must have been when she trapped me under the bridge. She'd shown me her strength. I'd called her out, she'd come.'

I'd shuddered then, shudder to think of it. She'd come all right, come like Sam had come in her white Escort, throwing her head back and crying like that. Lorraine had never cried like that. Dusk was gathering again outside the dimly lit shack. The chickens, soothed by his quiet gruff voice, had settled themselves, fluffed out their feathers and dozed off on their nest boxes. Moths were fluttering about the lantern, swinging slowly on a hook from the main beam. But how long could this worn planking, rusty nails, and baling twine hold out against her, if she came back for us, came back for more? I looked around, half expecting to see the bloody water seep under the door, start to soak the dust-dry chicken dung. He told me it had taken him a week to put it up, this last lonely fort. One wagon of timber from some bomb site in Budgworth. He'd come right out again and built his little monument, just to remind her he was still there, still playing. Still on the patch where his fiancée died on the bonnet of a car, where his father had been spin-dried to death jammed up against the ceiling of his hovel. What could I say, what could Whiteman have said? No need to tell you what he thought of streams turning to eels and snakes and little men with stones dancing on their fingertips. I'll tell you something though, I'll tell you why I believed him. I believed him because I saw some things with my own eyes, not through his amber old ones. I saw the marks in the ceiling at the cottage. Rupert that time, you remember he said it must have been rats. I knew it wasn't rats ages before old Solomon had told me what it really was. And the conkers. You remember us down in the wood when the trees went wild? He'd gone out with Jubal and blasted those crows and rooks. Blasted their nests with their shotguns till their black feathers fluttered down around them. The trees had remembered. Their black hearts had stored up all their hate for us. They blasted me Rupert and Sam the way the two of them had blasted the crows, their black children. And the stream rushed by all of it, all of us, all times. It had washed out the old man, washed him like old socks. Go on then, scratch and bawl, scratch and bawl you silly old crock. You bony old prune. Where's your spunk, old man? Bloodstains, vomit down your dirty shirt front? I'll fetch them out of you. Good as a piece of new china. Let them take the old fool's body, let them take the old fool away wrapped in a grey blanket like a Christmas cracker nobody wanted to pull. He'd walked away, watching his footing, watching where he stepped in case she had the bank slip away so she could swim with him again. Turned the stream into a big squirming snake to wrestle him down and slither round his throat.

Whiteman had shaken his head like Sam shook her head in the car that night. It was our last session Thursday afternoon. He'd already rung through to Cheryl and cancelled all Friday's appointments just to finish things with me. One more day. One more chapter. The final part of the puzzle. I'll give you a little taster, just to whet your appetite. Just tell you how we saw Rupert duck on out from under the pylon and what he did next.

LAST DAY

One day I'm out of here. I'm up early, bolt my breakfast and slurp two mugs of good coffee, dash on down to Whiteman's waiting-room. I'm edgy but not stringy. By five he's got to make his mind up. Childish pranks and an over-fertile imagination and I'm home. If he keeps me in I'm psychotically disturbed, a basket-case. Nice having things neat and tidy. Hell, he's got a chance to cure me and he's late again. It's 9.30 a.m. before he turns up, raincoat over his arm. He hangs it up, says something about the traffic on the ring-road. The man who's to decide whether I'm sane or not has clearly spent the last forty minutes chewing his fucking steering-wheel but I'm OK, I don't let it disturb my equilibrium as I make myself comfortable. He pulls my folder out of his case. I bet he was up on it at home last night, boning up. He looks a little strung up, tell you the truth. Eyes a little red, smudgy. He wipes his little gold half-moon glasses and flicks over to find his place. Like he's running his fingers along the loops and coils of my mind. That file, it's so worn you can almost see your face in it. Look inside and you look inside my brain, it's my 'Domesday Book', my testimony, Solomon's suicide note, Whiteman's paper for the bloody *Lancet* or something. It's all things to all men. It's part of all of us, part me, part Sam, part Solomon. It's part Nicky Fish and part Whiteman. It's part Jubal and part of that funny feller who fished by the stream by himself. I'm getting carried away waiting.

'Act Five. Rupert's return,' he begins, fixing his glasses on the end of his nose. I wonder what qualifications you have to have to do his job. I've never said he was a slouch, have I? A quack but not a slouch. I've got the imagination and you know I'm a good listener. Does it help if you believe people or smile and keep your opinion to yourself? Is it better for him or better for me?

'September six. A week after he went missing. You and Solomon are having another of your cosy little chats, just like we are now. You're sitting in that old car this time. What were you talking about?'

'We talked about Solomon locking up the cottage after his father got killed.'

'Died.'

'Died. He joined up again, went away as far as he could get.'

'But he came back in the end. What happened then?'

'He saw the dancers.'

'Ah, yes. He imagined he saw the dancers in the picture come to life and give him a little performance.'

Check his tone? He can't hide it for more than a few moments at a time. Like a radio announcer trying to cover up his accent. Sarcasm, it's the pits. Get a guy like Whiteman, he's always going to have a job which involves him having a big desk and everybody else a little chair on the other side. Can't do me any harm apart from recommending I be detained at Her Majesty's pleasure until I'm all better. I let it pass, smile politely.

'He said the dancers appeared in the parlour, danced all round him.'

'The dance of the seven veils, eh?'

'He didn't mention any veils.'

'They stripped off?' He's getting me going again.

'They enticed him.'

'How?'

'With their eyes, he said. He said they made eyes at him.'

He sits back, thinks I'm taking the piss again. He checks his notes. 'And this was after the business with his father?'

He can't trip me up there. Jubal drowned. It was in the papers, it was in the police report. The Coroner recorded accidental death.

'He didn't say exactly. I guess it must have been the early fifties.' He nods. 'He'd rejoined the Army for a while. Got made up to sergeant at some camp up north somewhere. You can check it all out if you want.' I suppose he'd hoped to come back and start again, from scratch. Then he saw the dancers, got on out of there fast. Locked it, boarded it, and went off down the Boar. And that's where he stayed till Silas picked him up in 1971. Now ain't that neat enough for you?

'He hallucinated.' Is he asking or telling?

'He didn't seem to think it was an hallucination.'

'People having them don't,' he snaps. 'That's the point. If you kids hadn't gone on down there we would have never heard about any of it. We would have just seen Solomon putting up with things at the Boar. You kids listened to him, you believed. He had a captive audience. He could load you down with all this guilt, settle it all on you.' He runs over it again, the guilt, the Glaistig. I'm barely listening.

'And that's when you saw Rupert? He walked out from under the pylon. Is that right?' I nod. 'You saw him walk out your side, but you never spotted him walking up to it the other side. He just jumped out.'

'He didn't jump.'

'Puff of smoke, flashing lights?' No. He stepped out gingerly, a ferret or a weasel. He slipped out from beneath the splayed silver legs of the pylon, wild eyed, sniffing the air like a fox. He didn't see us though, he didn't smell us although he stood for a moment with his head cocked to one side. Scuttled across the stony ground where the wires buzzed and hummed. The grass never grew back after they put the pylon up in the early fifties to carry the power lines across the gorge. Three guesses where they put the pylon. Yeah, right on the edge of the cliff, where the stones used to be until Solomon's people dragged them off, broke them up to build their walls. Years of water and rain, years of icy winds had cut the stones down from blocks to boulders, rocks to stones, pebbles to sand. Maybe they had fed her magic, breaking up those stones. Maybe they'd set her free from whatever ancient ban the stones stood for. Or maybe not. Perhaps you're siding with Whiteman, seeing it all from his point of view. It's OK, I'm used to it. What is it they tell you about the stars though? There are so many out there it's a mathematical certainty one

of them has some sort of life. It's how I listened to Solomon's stories. There were so many of them, so many layers, so many twists and turns, hell, some of them had to be true. Some of it must have happened like he'd said. I'm getting to sound like old Whiteman now, trying to convince you the way he tried me. Could be my way out of here. Maybe I should keep my mouth shut now, skip on out of it and out of here. Wait until I'm older, maybe find somebody I can trust to tell. Is what I'm doing now, I suppose. Rupert was covered in six shades of shit and his shirt and jeans soaked through and hanging on his bony frame. His hair is hanging in his eyes, he flicks it behind his ear in a gesture which reminds me powerfully of how he was before. Before he went away. His shoes have gone, he looks as if he's auditioning for a part in *Lord of the Flies*. He stalks closer. Walking isn't the right word for it. He picks up one foot, switches his head from side to side and then puts it down slowly. Then he takes five or six mincing little steps, a dainty wolf come to raid the henhouse. I must have gone to jump out because Solomon held up his hand, shushed me gently, so gently his breath barely misted the chill evening air. Neither of us moved. We were like mad birdwatchers, sitting there ages and awarded for our patience, a once in a lifetime glimpse of a creature on the edge of extinction. A creature back from the brink. He creeps by the car, sniffing high and low. Scurries past ten metres to our right. Solomon waits a second and then motions me out. I turn quietly and carefully avoid scraping the old crate on the rusty floorpan of the wreck. I step out and look up the lane. Rupert flits between the smoking dustbins and slides over the stile. Solomon's bulk looms up beside me and we trot on after him.

'Where's he going?'

We set off quietly, Solomon muffled in his heavy coat, his heavy breathing fogging his bristly face, and little me trotting beside him, favourite hound on the trail. I may be big but I can be as quiet as a slow-worm if I want. Rupert's not looking behind although he darts from side to side along the lane as if he's dodging puddles. He ducks down beside PC Bell's garage and pauses in the shadows by the gate. We dive down like Commandos, Solomon glances at me.

'The girl. He's going to the girl.' He's going to the girl,

that's exactly what he said. Pretty crucial point for you, for Whiteman, everyone else. We double forward again as Rupert glides over the wooden gate and sneaks up the path. There's a light on inside the house somewhere but the kitchen and back bedrooms are dark. Solomon reaches to unlock the gate, the latch clicks softly, and Rupert looks round sharply, eyes like a cat caught over a dying bird.

'Come here! Rupert Jones!' That's Solomon. He shoves the gate open and strides forward. I break right, ducking behind the garage and heading for the Watts' garden just next door. I guessed right. Rupert dashes to the fence, leaps over it and dashes down the path to their gate. We damn near collide as he leaps over their gate and I run right on up to grab him. I'm staring at his face. He's filthy, streaks of spit have cut white lines in the dirty mask. His eyes are angry points of light, teeth are yellow, bared in a mad sneer. He's punched me in the face before I can snap out of it and grab him. My head hits the garden wall and he's over me and off. Solomon has doubled back and burst out into the lane. Rupert ducks under him like a blur and he's off toward the stile. Solomon knocks a dustbin flying and trips over it, measuring his length in the stony lane. Lights are snapping on all along the row.

'What's going on?'

'It's that bloody Roberts boy again.'

The old man looks up at me, face cut open by a sharp stone. 'What are you waiting for?' he bawls. 'Get after him. Don't let him get back to her.' I dash for the stile as the doors open and PC Bell lumbers down the path to catch us.

'Come back, you little bastard! Solomon . . . Jesus wept, is that you?' I don't wait around for any more. I'm over the stile and I see Rupert in the moonlight heading back towards the cold crucifix of the pylon. He's got two hundred yards on me, I'll never catch him that way. I'll cut across the field. I leap a small trench and a pile of potato greens and crash through some canes, tearing dying vines behind me. I dash after him. He runs so smoothly, a loping wolf. It's the old hare and tortoise routine again. He's forgotten my training, he's forgotten my lonely runs round the lanes, my battle to shed the flesh

Sammy didn't fancy. He takes a look over his shoulder and sees me bearing down on him. His feral grin slips a notch and he picks up speed, heading for the pylon like it's going to whisk him out of my reach. He can't climb it for God's sake. I put my head down and arms out before he can open the distance again. My PE teacher would have been proud of me taking him out like that. Flying tackle took the legs right out from under him. All those evenings shivering in the rain watching him bully a rag-tag of twelve-year-olds. He rolls over on the stony ground under the pylon. He'd made it but not on two legs. I sprawl over him, pin him with my weight, but he wriggles and I go flying on and crack my head against the concrete base of one of the massive silver legs. He is up and ducking past me but I make one last grab for him, lock my fingers in his hair. He goes on but comes up short as I hang on, tear his head back. Something shifts beneath me like a giant turning over in his sleep. We topple down the slope thrashing together like alley cats. The wires hum overhead, the pylon seems to pulse with light against the cold starry sky. We're out.

STREAMLAND

The pylon slips away. It stands on shaky legs on top of the cliff, maybe they should have shown more sense, built it back a way. When the sun's going down it casts an enormous shadow over the fetid waters of the stream. Now the stream seems to want to cast a shadow over the pylon. As I fall I can see the mist throw a grey shawl round the whole thing. The wires hum in protest, light the grey blankets for a second before fading like a dying man's eyes. My flying tackle would have raised a cheer at Twickenham or the Arms Park but we fall in silence, grabbing at branches on our way down. Falling down the side of the cliff in a shower of dust and gravel. Falling through half light into twilight. It's a fifty-yard drop but there are plenty of stunted trees and bushes to catch us, break our fall. We tumble through hawthorns and masses of elderberry bushes. We crash through coiling brambles that shred our legs and arms without hurting, hang from creepers that burn our skin and twine round our necks. I had spread my hands out but it's like sliding down a cheesegrater. I pull them away, tuck them under my arms and fall away from him. Head over heels through the meagre vegetation at the bottom of the gorge right into the pool. I feel the bottom lurching under my feet before I register the cold. I'm up and gasping when he hits me full in the back, feet first. I'm under again, mouth full of dead water, eyes popping. My tattered knees grate against the gravel bed, I'm crushed against the stones. There's so much pain coming at my brain it can't register all at once, let's me have it in pulses. Legs, head, throat, lungs. I brace my legs, shoulder the stream out of the way and lurch away into the shallows. I topple over again, close my mouth against the stream's invasions, roll over and over until I'm lying under the crumbling red bank. I sit up, scramble to my knees. Suck in another lungful of solid air, doughy air that's been packed full of razorblades. Feels as there's a giant thumbing my eyes out, fingernails splitting my cheeks, cracking my skull. It's him! Rupert's on my back, sabre teeth sunk into my mammoth neck. He's wrenching my head back, got a finger in my eye and his skinny legs full of vile strength wrapped round my middle. He's tearing and clawing at my face, tearing my nose flat and my eyes shut. I'm choking and screaming. I can't see anything except black shadows in a red mist which flares bright and then cools. Something brushes my mouth and I clamp my jaws down hard. I damn near bite his finger off. The weight is gone and I'm foundering free towards the bank, coughing up gravel and earth in a spray of rotten water. I scramble up to the bank again, focusing slowly on the crumbling earth and dirty water. He's hurt me hard, there are bright gouts of blood swirling by. I still can't feel what he's done, feel where he's gouged me. The trees are bent over like witches round a cauldron, I tug at them, make them help me out. I roll over the bank and peer behind me into the mad mist and dancing shapes. The nearest, darkest is leaning forward like an animal dipping to take a drink. I pull myself out on some sacking, some old sack dumped by the water. I heave myself over it, pushing it down into the red soil. A sandbag with a white face and stringy colourless hair. I shake my head and squint down at it, it's never Rupert. The thing lies beneath me like a dead lover. I can feel something digging me in the belly. I pull back, reach down and feel the wooden shaft. I roll off the dead thing making it puke a little pink water. Now I can smell it. Rank, horrible. A broken arrow stuck in its guts, clutched in its bloody claws. Through the mist and kaleidoscope of firework effects I see Rupert coming toward me, back bent nose to the stream, hands hanging by his skinny shanks. I'm seeing double, treble as I try and focus, pick him out of the fireworks. Thin shapes are coagulating out of the mists, closing in on me as I scramble away on my butt. They grow features of a sort, modelled in wet clay by a backward child. There's a face against mine, black hair, bad breath rolls over my cheek and a leathery hand closes round my mouth.

'Stay still, you fool.' It's not Rupert. It's not Solomon. The speaker has been breathing bonfires for years, it's hardly more than a croak, broken bottles, broken English. His strong arms pin me to him, small grey things dance on strings in front of my eyes as if he's trying to hypnotize me.

'Hold still, fool,' he hisses in my ear with a gust of foul breath. I'm choking again, I can't breathe, the lights are dimming and the mist is stained red as blood. He squeezes me again, my shoulders, hands and legs explode in shards of pain as if I've been stung by squadrons of hornets. I go limp, feel the pain drain like boiling milk brimming over a pan. He's got me on my feet and is pulling me away with him. Away from the stream and the searching shapes.

'Leave him, Sheedatri,' he calls out to the shapes. 'Leave the other one now.' Over his fingers, his stinking hand closed over my mouth, I can see half a dozen shapes rise from the bank like horrid mushrooms, those stinking fungi that smell like rotting meat and look like entrails. I can make out red and grey shapes, sharp points and black hair hanging over dark eyes and squat noses. Wide, leering mouths with black tongues hanging out like panting dogs. They are dressed in strips of sacking, scraps of chainmail, fastened about with leather belts and straps. Each had stones hanging from his belt; rubble necklaces. Three have crude spears with rough handles and badly hammered heads, the others have bows bigger than themselves fitted with long thin arrows without flights. They hurry behind us as the leader carries me through the undergrowth like a bag of laundry in his constrictor grip. I'm looking back, the others dart from left to right and peer over their shoulders continually. I can make out the branches clearly now, outlined against the darkening sky, closing over my head as we head further into the wood. Whose fucking wood?

'Pizog. Pizog,' the one at the back is shrieking, jabbing his spear behind him.

'They're coming.' I can hear barking. Yelps, sudden hoots

that could be mad laughter. They're after us, they're going to catch us, they can't be far behind. The leader halts, I can feel his chest rising and falling with the effort of lugging me along. He catches his breath and jerks me higher on his back, his arm bent around to pin me, stopping me from crying out. His other hand is hooked behind my knee. We go on again. I can recognize the cliff and the trees although everything looks brighter and sharper now. The sky deepens to a magnificent dark blue before he stumbles to a halt under a big oak, sets me down like a bag of potatoes and whips out the short sticky sword he had stuck in his belt. The blade is dull and smeared with bright blood. He's shorter than me, maybe five foot high. An enormous stone ear-ring hangs against one bronzed cheek. His eyes glitter madly, he's dribbling between dirty sharp teeth. The rest of them wait anxiously, weapons ready, tongues lolling out. More shapes hurry in. One of them has Rupert over his shoulder. He bends and unloads him in a heap at the leader's horny feet, wrapped in sacking and strapped with leather thongs. Rupert's clothes have disintegrated, he's practically naked and the cold stream has cleaned the worst of the filth from his painfully thin body. His lips are folded back from his teeth in a foxy grimace. His eyes are open, flickering under his eyelids. I turn my head slowly, look at them. Look them up in my D&D bestiary. They're in it all right. I'm seeing double, I'm seeing goblins. One of them has a boot planted firmly in Rupert's back and a dirty spearhead resting on the side of his neck. He raises his chin and nods over his shoulder.

'They're right on us, Pizog,' he growls. Around us the small grey bundles I took to be boulders form themselves into huddled bodies. Some are sprawled under bushes, some hang from the branches of trees. Arms thrown out, skewered with arrows or crudely chopped in sections. Rough hide shields painted with crude faces. The bodies are thickest nearer the stream, as if two forces met at a crossing. Some are like these, others look even uglier, broad faces with wide mouths like children making faces in a playground. I lean against the tree and run a quick damage control. My hands are stinging like mad, my knees are cemented in agony, my legs throb. My head feels as if it's been pulled this way and that and every breath is a ball of pain dragged up through my ragged throat. I focus on the leader's pebble bracelets, the small grey stones jiggle and hop although his sword hangs still by his side.

'You, Keomalik, scout ahead. I want a way back to the deep wood. Go careful.' The deep wood? We can't be far from the road! Where's the road gone? One of the goblin archers lopes off into the bushes over a small hill of broken bodies. I turn to the one they call Pizog, the leader. He's sweating, rubbing his dirty broad face on his rough sacking sleeve. His quick brown eyes dart all over the place, he tilts his head to one side listening. The barking is getting louder. They must have brought dogs. They'll never make it. They'll never get us back to her. It's as if I haven't time to be scared, too many things are happening, too many things to stare at, too many smells and sensations. They're on to us though, they're on our scent. Pizog's claws curl round the crude handle of his sword. He looks at me for the first time.

'Whatever happens you mustn't take her,' he grates, twitching the point under my nose. 'You mustn't take her back with you. She stays with us to the end.' I don't know what he's on about but I nod anyway. He peers back toward the stream. Now I can see white and red shapes bobbing amongst the undergrowth, sticks, spears. A big banner, a shapeless field of green silk, shimmering in the dying light.

'It's her,' one of the others squeals, hopping from foot to foot in horrible agitation. His fear, his desperate fear, gets a grip in me and drains away whatever bravado I had left. Whatever she is, I don't want to meet her. Much. Solomon was right. See no evil, speak no evil, and all that palaver. Pizog strides over and thrusts me down into the undergrowth, the thick oak mulch. They drop around me, stinking like foxes, holding their breath behind their jagged teeth, eyes rolling as they hug the earth. The barking reaches fever pitch, I can make out individual shrieks of command, squeals of excitement, yips and yells. A dogs'-home chorus on gas man morning. The shouts and cackles slowly fade downstream. Pizog leaps up and tears me to my ragged feet.

'Double back, back to the bridge,' he snarls, jabbing me forwards. Back over broken beams and fallen boughs, coiled brambles and heaped bodies. Clawed hands reach for a dark sky among pools of shining gore, steaming bellies split right open. We slide down the bank into a log-jam of bodies, bobbing face down in the shallows, turning the water dark with their wretched blood. Up close, I see some of them are a sort of cheesy white colour with bullet heads and stringy hair. Battered equipment and broken weapons scattered everywhere. There must be hundreds of them. A terrible battle, carnage. I'm in on the end of some awful goblin war in our bloody bloody stream. One lot must have been ambushed as they made their way along. They don't seem overly surprised to see me, I wonder for a second, no, they couldn't have been expecting us. Could they? The white ones, more numerous down here, have red caps plastered to their heads while the darker ones go bareheaded or wear flat leather helmets. Perhaps they quarrelled over the prize. Quarrelled over Rupert and me, what to do with us. We wade in the quickening flow, back toward the cliff and the pool where the water runs deepest, where it broke my fall from grace. I can see the green waters glimmering beneath the massive cliff wall behind the bridge.

It's not our bridge. It's our bridge's great-grandfather, a long-lost cousin. Grey blocks of undressed stone, chipped flints washed with rains. I'm back with them, back with them on their hill before there were any men or any stones to keep their world away. Glaistig's world I've only glimpsed through the old man's stories. I'm in her patch. The thrill becomes a hard pulsing tightness in my guts. A new life-form taking shape in my brain, a coiling thing uncoiling from the coils. She's going to see me, I'm going to see her. She'll know me in these blue jeans, this anorak. She'll know me from these quarrelling beasties of hers. I may be torn and bloody but I'm no bloody goblin. She'll pick me out and call me to the front of the class, jibbering chimps with their flat noses and sacking trousers. Chimps thrown fast forward in a time machine hung with bits of armour and scraps of mail, jibbering and jabbering amongst themselves while I stand there and look at her. The two near the front are dragging Rupert, they look as if they'll drag the arms out of his sockets, they keep up like that. His head lolls from side to side as if they're expecting the cold water to revive him. We pass under the bridge and only I need to duck my head. Pizog calls another halt, peers back downstream. I think of Solomon and the flood that washed poor Jubal out. The creatures that hung from the roof in the wild swirling waters, and here I am with them. They saved him from her, but for whom? The scout thrusts a spear point into my belly, I pull it in tight as I can but I'm stuck there on the primitive tip.

'Kill 'em now while there's time,' he croaks. I barely make it out. Some of them seem to talk in a series of howls and yelps rather than words. Pizog pushes the spear aside with his sword, bares his teeth.

'Not till the end. Not till we've no choice,' he snarls. I feel the cold chill of the stones seep through my jacket, seep into my bones and vitals.

'If she gets 'em again . . .'

'We stopped him once.'

'He got past.'

'But not past this one.' He gives me a curious look.

'Why did you stop him? Why did you stop this one?' He nods towards Rupert, lying against the wall of the bridge between his guards.

'Stop who?' I ask.

They peer at me, nudge each other. 'Stapo, stapo,' they mimic.

'Stop him.' Pizog points his sword at Rupert, fringe flowing in the stream, slumped between the goblins. I can hear the dogs again. Pizog darts to the side of the arch and looks out. Downstream, white things spotted with grey and brown and red, a smear of colour on their cheesy bodies. Behind them their terrible billowing banner, filling the gorge with a bright light, intense emerald green flaring the night sky. It is her. The white shape I took to be some kind of skull at the top of the pole is her head framed by flowing hair. Framing her face above the shining green gown. Pizog grips his sword as her creatures scurry forward, scramble up the banks and lope around to cut off our escape.

'Piiiiiiiizzzzzzzzzooooooooogggggggg . . . ' She calls him out. The voice snaps the cold air settling in the gorge, cracks it like sharp frost cracks windowpanes. My ears prickle, I feel hollow, scooped out, pissed out. The others moan and drool, grip their weapons, white knuckled. Pizog is a small grey shadow against the green brilliance. I see it at last. I see that in her world Pizog, this miserable stinking creature bent low under the bridge, he's the one I should be running to. The ratling shape with the jingly stones clicking and clacking like caged birds, down here he's the good guy. He's here to save not prey on me. He's here to save me from the little bit of myself that wanted to see her anyway, that wanted to put my hand on the burning grate. He isn't going to kill me but she might. Like she would have killed Solomon, snapped his neck like a chicken. It's as if big chunks of my brain have unravelled themselves to leave a small tough kernel. Look at her, look at the green banner filling the stream. What did I think she was, misunderstood? sexy? My new streamlined brain doesn't stop me nearly pissing myself with fright. I'm a bug hiding under a stone from some naughty children who want to pull my arms and legs off one by one, see me rock on my bloody belly. There she is, misty murder. Solomon's Miss May, the demure sweet little thing he thought he'd try it on with. When he changed from petting to pawing she maybe changed too. He put his hand on her leg and felt his nerves jingle with wrong numbers, wrong messages. He told me, told me straight all about her, and yet I used to lie in bed thinking about her, what it would be like to meet her face-up. I crouch behind Pizog, keep my eyes on the shimmer in the glimmer. She's come out for Pizog's last stand the way she came out after Solomon. Come to see her old adversary play out his last few scenes. Trouble is I'm stuck in there with them and shouldn't be. This is no place for me, this isn't what I dreamed about. She swoops forward, enveloping the nearest Redcaps in her shifting green gown.

'Don't skulk there, Pax Pizog,' she calls, singing down the stream, soothing it so it runs like honey over our boots. She doesn't growl like a grizzly, breathe bonfire breath over lost boys. I have to keep craning forward to keep watch on her as she drifts this way and that as if blown by the breeze. Pizog, the dog that has had its day, prickles in front of me.

'Come out and talk, Pizog,' she suggests over the sulky snarling of her leashed troopers.

'I have the boys, Lady,' Pizog croaks, barely finding his voice in his stony throat. He makes me want to cover my ears, his foul talk.

'What do you want with them, Pizog? Send them trotting out and I'll let your people go,' she offers, shifting to allow another troop of Redcaps to jostle to the front with a rope of bloody prisoners. Bloody, limping, snarling, shouting. More of Pizog's stony crew. The Redcaps shove them into a line in front of her and knock them to their knees in the cold hard flow, drag their heads back by their dirty hair. The Redcaps leer and bark, daring us to come out after our friends. She smiles above them all, eyes brighter than kingfishers in her white face.

'There is no need for further bloodshed, My Lord Cloud's horsemaster,' she says. Whoremaster? Horsemaster? He couldn't master a fucking Shetland pony.

'Give the boys up to me and I will call off these dogs,' she offers. The goblin creatures snarl to each other, grip their prisoners as if they're reluctant to let them go. They want their fun, I reckon, no matter what Pizog does. He knows it too. He may be small but he's not stupid. He's eyeing the bank on both sides, searching for a way out. Just a line of goblins, jumping from foot to foot, yelling challenges and shouting oaths. She raises her voice over the noise.

'The boys, Pizog, send them along now, there's a good fellow.'

'Never.' A snarl from Pizog, ducking back in behind the stonework as an arrow plops into the water. I see the green shape flow to the left, kingfisher-blue eyes pick something out of the ranks. A yelp and a funny popping noise and one of the goblin bundles rolls down into the stream. Raspberry-ripple dishwater flows on past us.

'Hold your fire,' she calls. The hairs on my arms prickle as if they want to break off and fall away from me, get right away from everything that I am. It's a blunt knife dragged up my spine, catching and clanging on each vertebra. My balls want to slide back under my belly like a baby. I clutch them involuntarily, hold them on.

'I'll kill them both, you know I will,' Pizog grates. He will too. He'll kill us, she'll kill us.

'You wouldn't be so foolish.' I can see the green glow, Pizog's in my way. She's floated closer pushing the line of prisoners nearer the bridge, so we can see their faces, pick out friends.

'Don't let her—' One of them starts to shout something and his Redcap guard bends and drags his dagger across his throat, knees him into the water. Blood swirls round our feet again. The Redcap crouches over the body, twisting his head this way and that. Glaistig hangs there sullenly, misty gown catching in the bare branches of the trees. Is it me or is she getting bigger while Pizog dissolves away to nothing?

'We don't have to die,' she says quietly. A new tack.

'They are all to die, we are all to die,' he says flatly. His fingers tighten round the handle of his sword. Maybe he's going to throw it at her.

'No. Not all of us. You know this as well as I.' She's having a quiet chat with her old friend. She hardly notices the files of Redcaps that keep arriving from all sides as if they've been summoned from all over the wood. Cutting off any escape or rescue, flexing their muscles for the last rush.

'It doesn't have to be like this. We've fought it out long enough, you and I. Fought while everything rotted. We needn't have let things get so far. We should have talked. Together we could have found a way out of it. You say fight now,' she sneers. 'Fight to the very end of everything even when our passports out of here are by your side. Think, Pizog,' Glaistig shines extra bright, so bright it's like staring at the sun. 'We are snow in summer. We can't last. Let me have the boys. Let them do my bidding, bring me the girl. Then the boys are yours all over again. You can have them back. It's up to you what you do with them, let them return or use them yourself.'

Have us back? After what? She wants the girl, she wants Samantha. What does she want her for? Pizog is shaking his head as if he's trying to block her out. A tumpy little fungus growing under a beautiful sleek tree.

'Don't you want to live some more?' she calls as if inviting him to tea. He shivers as if settling his own mind before trusting his tongue.

'I know my place, I know my time. It is here and now, no more. You would have done well to learn this, accept your fate.' He looks up at her, directly up to her kingfisher eyes, glinting in the glimmer and the mists.

'I would rather be cut down here than spend a moment at your side, streamspawn witch daughter.'

I think I'm going to faint. The waters run cold round our feet, the bridge trembles a little. Pizog's stones hang limp on their strings. A flourish of emerald fire.

'Enough of your posturing, Pizog. Your days are done, that may well be true for your precious Trafarionath. You have certainly seen better days. And here you are deciding my destiny. Who I must be and where I must be. You sentence me to rot like you, to dwindle like an old toadstool? You who can barely stand, cowering like a rat in that hole? How much longer would you have been able to abide your own shadow, Pizog? How long before you saw your face in the stream and cut it off? How long before you and yours are running on all fours like beasts?' The Redcaps guffaw and rattle their weapons at her jokes. 'Have you looked lately? Look now! They'll go four like the rest of your family, like your children.'

The Redcaps join in a ragged chorus. 'Look now! Look now!'

He's still now, quiet. 'I have looked. Have you?'

'I have. But it does not have to be so. I must have the boys. Let them pass.' The awful whistle running through my brain, broken fingernails down a blackboard. She's teacher. She's in charge of us all. Detention means for ever. The mists have closed in, socked us in down there in our cosy little stream bed. It's mist, murder and me. I'm holding my ears but I can still hear their argument, back and forth across the ripples and rills of the stream.

'I have my own magic, Lady,' Pizog calls, as if jolted into action by her threats.

'Use it, then. Let's see what you can do. What we can do. You and I, we can live beyond this. We can live where the stream flows backwards, we can abide there. A new life, Pizog. New forms. New skins new eyes new hands to touch new lips to kiss. I'm not offering you marriage, Pizog. I'm not saying you and I must be together. Come with me, follow me there, and we will go our own way for ever. I offer you new life, will you take it?'

The Redcaps are silent and still. There's spaces on the lifeboat for three, as far as I can make out. Trouble is we're the fucking lifeboat. She wants to take over our bodies. Slip inside Sam the way I dreamt of. Pizog is already shaking his head. He doesn't want to know. He's made his mind up about immortality, obviously. No future in it for him.

'Don't be stubborn. Must I order these prisoners butchered in front of your eyes?'

'They are dead anyway. You do them no dishonour now. We have all lived too long.'

'You are so stupid, Pizog!' There's a hint of desperation in her voice now. The Redcaps pick up on it same as me, take a few steps forward, bend their bows. I look up, see a white skull atop a tattered banner, colour fading like coffin clothes. Time for the banner to fall for the last time, time for the bloodworms in the stream to unpick the smoky threads for ever.

'Pizog, I will never beg you. I know who you are. For once, forget your hatred. Forget all our past. Let us both go while we still can. We can flow with the stream.'

'We are not to leave!' he bawls.

'You push me too far, Pizog,' she says dangerously. 'Even to the end of everything.'

'Then let it be the end. Talk till your jaw drops off like the rest of you. But you will not pass the bridge. If our world must die, die it will.'

'No real Lord of Trafarionath would have been so foolish. Wise words for a stable boy!'

'No Lord of Trafarionath yet lives. I am the Last Lord.'

Where the hell have I come out? 'Tra-fah-rionath'? Wales?

'You? You're a runt, a ratling, a misbegotten court jester! Look at yourself! Look in the water and see yourself! This surpasses everything. It is unnatural to doom yourself so. No creature faced with fire or flood will simply roll over and await the end. You must run, I must run. You cannot blame me for wanting more.'

'You are not to leave. You should never have crossed before. You snapped the bonds of all our existences, brought the doom down on all of us, and now you would run from it.'

'Pah!' she shouts, looking about her in exasperation. 'I fled a night without a dawn. I paid for my foolishness, as you know well. I fled to their world once and they sent me back as I am. And now the mighty Lord of what's left decrees I must die with all. Wither, perish, blow away.'

'Even as you say, Lady.'

'I won't!' she shrieks through my skull. It shrieks round every corner and coil, every chicane of my brain. I stagger against the cold bridge.

'I WOOOOOOOOOONNNNNNNNTTTTTTTTT!' she bellows, she roars to the heavens.

NEWSMAN COMETH

Christ, I can still hear it ricochet round my head. No I can't. It's Whiteman's intercom again. Won't Won't Won't Won't. He sighs, flicks the switch, damn near breaks it off.

'Cheryl, I thought I said no calls until I've finished . . . I don't care if it has arrived . . . Cheryl . . .' He looks up, I shrug, take another peep at that traffic there, nose to tail, all the way home.

'I . . . what?' He jumps up, glares at me.

'What have you told the newspapers?' He leans forward, I can smell the mints he's always scoffing and the garlic he can never disguise. I sit back in my chair, play dumb.

'What have you told that idiot from the *Clarion*?'

'Me? Told him what?'

He straightens up and stalks out of the room. What's his problem? Talked to the newspapers, what is he on about? Christ, I've been stuck in here the past three weeks, haven't had much time for any publicity. Who the hell would want to publicize this anyway? Whiteman, though, he's shaken up good. Look at the way he bristled up just then. Maybe he's jealous, doesn't want anybody coming in and stealing his thunder, not having spent three weeks sifting through my drizzle. I pad across the room, peer through the gap in the door. Cheryl's holding out a copy of the *Clarion*, our local weekly. She looks dead worried. What is it? Who's died now? Whiteman wrenches it out of her hand so hard her hanky falls out of her sleeve. They stand there looking at it for a second then Whiteman snatches the paper up to read the front page. I can make out big black lettering. SENSATIONAL. Sensational something. I dart back to my seat, slouch back and watch the traffic. Whiteman flings the door back so hard it damn near shatters the glass, holds it up. SENSATIONAL CLUES TO GORGE HORROR. There's a fuzzy black and white close-up of Solomon and two smaller school photographs. Rupert and me. Fame at last. I can't make out the small print. You never can, can you?

Whiteman's steaming his glasses, he's that worked up about it.

'You knew all along.' Pardon? 'You knew all along . . . all this time . . . all this bullshit and you've known all along.' What is he on about? He crushes the paper to the table like he wants to impress our faces and all the nasty things they've said about us on the shiny surface. Like he wants to leave our faces staring inkily back up at him. 'You tipped this idiot off. You told him all about it. You told him and you palmed me off with all this Glaistig bullshit.'

What bullshit? You see any bullshit round here? What's got him so riled?

'According to our dear respected Mr Fish the whole thing has been obvious since they brought you in off the hillside.'

'I don't know what you're talking about,' I say flatly. They must have got a picture from my parents. My ears stick out something awful. Rupert looks as slick as ever, the little git. Solomon though, he looks like pictures of those guys trying to get out of the back door of a court with a blanket over their heads. It looks like the face from an El Paso wanted poster. 'Read it,' he barks. I drag the crumpled paper over, take a dekko:

Police are taking a new look at the bizarre suicide of elderly Clove eccentric Solomon Jones following sensational new evidence uncovered by the *Clove Clarion*.

It's bylined *World Exclusive* by Nicky Fish, which I reckon's a little bit rich, considering. I take a quick glance at Whiteman, who's glaring at me like he wants to pop his own eyes out all over my shirt.

Reporters on the *Clarion* believe they may have solved the riddle of Solomon Jones' death at his derelict cottage in Clove

Gorge. Jones died in a mysterious blaze which came within an ace of claiming the lives of village schoolboys Rupert Jones and David Roberts. The boys staggered out of the inferno after supplies of cider which had been stored in the pantry for years burst into flames, turning Mr Jones into a human fireball and sparking a bushfire which raged to within feet of a nearby housing estate and toppled an electricity pylon blacking out homes as far north as Budgworth. This week the *Clarion* believes it may have uncovered a link between the incident and a murder in the gorge fifty years ago. The *Clarion* believes it has pinpointed the one piece of evidence which could explain the bizarre series of events in the gorge.

I look up at him. 'What murder?'

'Read on. It's all there, David,' he suggests, grinding the words out between gritted teeth.

Our investigations into *Clarion* files and with elderly residents of the village lead us to believe that Solomon Jones' father Jubal could have been involved in the death of Miss May Armstrong Smyth in August 1922. The *Clarion* further believes Solomon Jones may have stumbled on the truth, confronted his father, and could have been responsible for Jubal's mysterious death in July 1950.

Do what? I glance up at him, he glares over the rims of those half-moon specs. Me, I try and keep a straight face. Well, the guy looks like he picked eight draws then remembered he hadn't posted his coupon.

The clue to the bizarre series of events in the gorge is a painting found in Solomon Jones' cottage. A watercolour depicting a scene from *Swan Lake* painted by the noted Victorian theatrical artist Lewis Archer. The *Clarion* has discovered the last known owner of the painting was a Mrs Hermione Ham of Staplegrove, Taunton. The painting was sold along with other items from Mrs Ham's estate at a sale held in the town in 1922. *Clarion* files from the period list the buyer as Miss

Armstrong Smyth, who was found dead in the Bridge Pool, Clove, two days later. She had been raped and strangled. There was no sign of the painting she had bought and a quantity of cash had been taken from her handbag. The culprit was never found. The *Clarion* believes Jubal Jones was responsible for the murder. We believe he used the stolen cash to help fund the purchase of top field from his neighbour Arnold Mungo in June 1923. The *Clarion* also believes Solomon Jones found the picture and confronted his father over it. In the ensuing struggle we believe Jubal suffered the head injuries referred to at the inquest held in the town in 1950. Although investigated by the police at the time, no charges were ever made against Solomon Jones. The *Clarion* believes, however, that local schoolboys Rupert Jones and David Roberts stumbled on his secret when they found the watercolour in his derelict cottage. Solomon attempted to silence them for ever in Clóve Gorge four weeks ago, hoping their deaths would have looked like some kind of schoolboy prank. A spokesman for the Avon and Somerset Police refused to comment on the case, but confirmed investigations would continue. The boys, deeply traumatized by their shocking ordeal, are currently undergoing treatment at the Budgworth Neurological Institute where Dr A. Whiteman was also unavailable for comment.

I bet he was. Well go on, ask. Is that it? You know it isn't. For a start there are all these pages under your right thumb. What's that, a fucking index or something? Maybe I'll add one later, help you out a little. OK OK, don't go on, that was it. I'll admit it. That was most of it anyway. Whiteman, he made me sit in the waiting-room while he cooled out and made some phone calls. Wanted to see those damn files right then and there. Then he had me right back in there again, sat me down, eased his scrawny butt over the edge of his desk so his knee was touching mine. I didn't like him up so close, to tell you the truth.

'Well? Did you find out about the picture? Did Solomon tell you about it?'

I shake my head slowly, dumb ox again, see. 'He never said

anything about the picture. He just said he wanted it back, was all.'

'You found out. You found out and you tipped off Fish. That idiot down at the *Clarion*. You told him, didn't you?'

'How the hell was I supposed to tip him off? You've had me in here for three weeks!' I snap back at him. He rocks gently on his desk knowing he can't quite pin it on me. He bites his lip, tries another tack.

'So Mr Fish worked it all out for himself, that right?'

'His name's on the story.'

He closes his eyes. 'That doesn't mean a bloody thing. You gave him the whole thing, didn't you? You found out about the painting, realized it implicated Jubal. Solomon practically told you he was going to bump him off anyway.' He remembers, retrieves my file, flicks through.

'That time in the stream when Jubal was having a breakdown. You said yourself . . . he thought about doing his father in.'

I'm nodding with him. 'That's right. Solomon said he thought about it but then went in and fished him out. He never said anything about killing his dad,' I protest. Whiteman reads the entire page, then backtracks. It's after four already. He's losing me. Any minute now his phone will be going. Maybe my parents helped Fish out to try and get me off the hook. Maybe Silas thought it would help get Rupert released, letting the paper say all those things about his poor old brother. Christ, he was dead anyway. Blood's thicker than water after all. Maybe all the talk, all the dark suspicions, finally persuaded him the old guy was as bent as a bottle of chips and deserved all he got. Whiteman looks up again.

'All right, then. Fish had a brainstorm and worked it out without your help. Say.'

'That's right.'

'And Solomon never said anything else to you the night Rupert turned up? The night you saw him creep back under the pylon?'

'I told you what he said, how it happened. If he'd wanted

to kill me he'd had plenty of time. Look at all the times I went down to his chicken house. They wouldn't have heard me scream down there.'

Whiteman stares at me again. Thinks for a second. 'You've got it all worked out, haven't you?'

'What?'

'All this. Solomon did this, Rupert did that. What the fucking hell did you do?'

Me? Me? What I do? I've told you what I did for Christ's sake. He's shaking his head again.

'Sam tried to look the picture up in a book,' I repeat. 'She never found any trace of it at the school library. I've already told you that,' I insist. Ask her yourself, it's not going to turn her over is it, asking her a simple question like that. 'Hey, Sam, did you go see about the painting?' 'Uh-huh.' 'Find anything?' 'Nope.' There you are. Why you have to ask me for all the time? There's Rupert too. Why not ask him some questions? 'Hey, Rupert, where the hell you get to that week, huh? Rupert, you paying attention to me, boy?' Yeah, well, now he's dead too. He's dead, Solomon is dead, Silas is dead. They're all dead and good fucking riddance, says I. Me? Me I just walked right out of there. A couple of calls and Whiteman's in there with a felt-pen writing CASE CLOSED all over my file, giving it to old Cheryl to lock away somewhere. Lock away all of my secrets. And here I am spewing them all out for you, hanging all my dirty washing for everyone to see. Couple of calls from the Ministry, the police, the social services, my parents. Get that boy out of there he's had enough. I sure had. A couple of weeks off school up at the loony bin in Budgworth, hey, when I got back I was a star. Same as Fish was a star for a week, cameras down from the city and all. Exclusive bylines all over the country. Local boy made good with us local boys. When I got back I spent quite a lot of time with Martin Lawrence and his gang, like I was their *ex-officio* psychopath or something. The teachers treated me with a curious respect, half expecting me to produce diced chickens from my desk, walk upside-down on the ceiling. If I talked too much they'd uh-huh me and ask me if I would kindly keep it down. Not shut up Roberts. Abrams the head-master looked through me like I wasn't there. I was his new ghost or something. Miss De Plechon left shortly afterwards, so I had to look elsewhere for guidance, if you see what I mean. Eventually old Lorraine Lamb came to my rescue, asked me out. We spent the next eight years discovering each other. She wanted to get engaged, I wanted out. Sam came back after dropping out of college and we hit it off right away. Hit it off so long as we didn't talk about Rupert. So long as she didn't talk about Rupert. Me, I got twitchy every time somebody mentioned his name.

I used to dream about the bastard. If it wasn't him it was her. Sometimes he'd run his dreams in my head, the git. Sometimes I'd see him following me around with those tissue boxes, holding them out to me if I'd cut myself shaving or come or something. Why couldn't she just shut up and forget him? Let him lie? I mean we both went through it, me and him. Where's all my sympathy? What did my dad do as soon as I got home? Smacked me round the head. Just you cut the funny business my lad or you'll be back up that hospital quicker than you can say outpatient. Do I make myself clear? My mum looked on, rubbed her hands, rubbed her face. Rubbed her face right off, I never saw them again. I don't mean I never saw them, but I never saw them. Never saw them at all. Whiteman, he rubbed his hands of Rupert after a few hours. He rubbed his hands of me after three weeks, pretended it was no big deal anyway, told his superiors he was about to unveil the truth himself. It was only that prat Fish, jumping on in like that with all his mad theories and half-baked accu-sations, dirtying up the waters just as he was going to pick his prize shiny nuggets out of my head. He was gutted, though, I tell you he was really gutted. See, that afternoon, he'd been waiting patiently. He'd been sitting through to the final scene, the final confrontation. He didn't believe a word about old Glaistig but he wanted to hear it out to the end. See what I was going to come up with. I'd hooked him see, same as Solomon hooked me. You want to know too, if you've read this far. You want the punchline. Where was I, oh yes. Glaistig blowing her top, colours shimmering and flashing first dark and hard then misty and soft. Ah, it's no good. I keep thinking you're not going to believe me now. Boy's lied to us before, boy's told a whole pack of whoppers. Why should we listen to him now? He's bright enough to have known all about Solomon's secrets, how come he never told us? That about it? Why didn't he say at the beginning, why didn't he tell old Whiteman? Trying to make him out some kind of quack all this time. Man was only trying to help you, son. I'm not your son. You think just because Fish comes in with some cock-and-bull story, you think maybe all I've told you was a pack of lies. You think for a moment if old Jubal was still alive they'd be able to pin this Miss May crap on him? You heard the Fish guy. The police had tried to blame Jubal's injuries on Solomon, had him in for questioning and everything. Never charged him though. Fish, Fish. All he did was give them a convenient explanation. Oh yes I see, that fits, that explains everything. That's what you wanted from the beginning, some facts, some motives. Yeah, well, I'm not sure I want to tell you any more about it. You've cut me to tell the truth. I mean, shaken my resolve and that. If you think I'm just making it up there's hardly any point in going on, is there? Eh? I'm not going to tell you about Pizog and Glaistig and Rupert and me all down there up to our knees in the dishwater-dead stream, all down there staring at each other as the fog came down and the stream flowed backwards. Yeah, I noticed when I looked down at my boots. Flowing the wrong way. Going uphill, I reckon. This Trafawhatsit must be on some kind of a tilt. Maybe it was D.B. breathing, breathing the stream on in to her then blowing it back out our way. Blowing it out to bring us to her. There was Pizog dashing on out at her with his pebbles held out in front of him. There was Glaistig hanging like a pinned-out butterfly from some exotic rainforest in a glass case. There was Solomon, bent double and charging out of the undergrowth beside the stream, knocking those miserable Redcaps out of his way to duck down under the bridge after us. It struck me again, how nobody seemed that surprised to see him. Almost as if they'd been expecting him to turn up, join the party. Maybe the old geezer had been over more than he had let on. Maybe they knew him as well as he knew them. Crushed in against the cold wall, I realized they were all tiles in the same mosaic. On their own, they didn't make any sense, bits of pebble, bits of bone. Stick them together and you got a shape, a picture. Throw them in the stream, big enough pieces, and you had yourself a bridge. A crossing. They all ran together, they ran together like a kaleidoscope. They ran together and all their different bits fused for an instant, a chain reaction that had been waiting in the wings for centuries. A chain reaction she'd started when she tried to escape her world the first time. When the fisherman by the stream had prodded her naked back to the village where the Northern Jarl with his glacier-blue eyes first spied her, serving mugs of frothy ale like any village slut. She was no slut, this Lady of theirs. Yeah, I'm tired. Go on, make it up for yourself. The bridge protected us from most of it, the implosion of fog and water and colour. The little Redcaps bowled over like ninepins. The water lurching and writhing round our legs. We were huddled behind Pizog's sidekicks, we were all right. Then we were blown out by the whiplash blast, blown downstream against the flow, tumbling over and over till the stream got sluggish and we dragged ourselves up. That's when he grabbed us. Cantered through the chaos like a carthorse. Solomon had us folded under his arms, kept on stumbling along the streambed while the fireworks flared back at the bridge. Pizog's last stand. Little guy sure packed some punch in those stones of his, dented Her Ladyship, not to mention wasting half her bloody bogeymen. Great gravel guy. By the time she'd sorted him, turned him inside out and run her fingers though his jiggling eyeballs, his maybe mate Solomon was back at the cottage, pulling at those boards. We were huddled against the wall, too afraid to think further than the funny lights on the end of our noses. He dragged us in, threw us down on the shagpile, dust eddying about the living-room. I was so out of it I couldn't make out what he was up to until he struck the match, lighting up his demon face. He was striding about, cradling those stone jars as if he knew damn well he shouldn't be shaking them about.

Those little snowstorm-in-a-jar jobs. I thought maybe he was trying to douse down the dust, pouring all that stuff over the floor, over Rupert and me. The pissy stink made me gag, sit up, and rub the worst from my face. Rupert was rolling from side to side, beating himself as if he was covered in horse-flies or something. He strode into the living-room, tipping the putrid contents over the wrecked old furniture. I got a hold of Rupert's hair, crawled on out toward the door, hanging broken where he'd kicked it in. Crawling toward the kingfisher-coloured firework display, flaring and popping and lighting the dismal gorge. She was whistling on down the streambed, her gauzy cloak tugged tight round her wrong-number bones. I ducked down behind the wall as she came up the path and zoomed in the broken-down cottage after Solomon. She wasn't bothered about us. Maybe she didn't even notice us scuttled in by the wall like a couple of half-drowned kittens. It was him she was after all right. I rolled over a few times, rolled right down into the stream and splashed off, away from him and her and all the flashes and bangs. Rupert was hurrying along on tottery stick legs, his long hair standing on end. He didn't see me shadowing him down in the stream, splishing and splashing over the stones and old cans. The fires behind us flared bright, the explosion, the snap of a twenty-ton elastic band, caught us up and tossed us on downstream like a couple of empty scarecrows in a hurricane. The bright lights behind us died back to a dull orange glow in the gorge, died back until the streaks of emerald fire resolved themselves into torch beams, until the flailing claws and screaming goblins grew blue arms and turned out to be policemen, wrapping us in blankets to stop us smouldering. That's it. That's how Solomon fried himself, damn near took us with him too. Glaistig and Pizog and all their little friends must have bought it with him. Well they must.

You seen any three-foot-high goblins balancing pebbles on their fingers lately? Seen any beautiful women in flowing green gowns clippety-clopping round your corner shop in the last couple of weeks? Damn right. They lock you up for shit like that; I should know, the bastards locked me up for it for three weeks. Well as I said, if it is the end, what's all this you've still got left to read? How am I going to drag it out now, now I've told you everything? Well, not quite everything. I mean, if things were left to me this would be it, I'm telling you. Trouble is, it's not up to me. Thinking now, I should have realized they wouldn't be happy with my ending. See, like I said at the very start, at the very start when I woke up with cold balls with the hall light on, I thought things were maybe starting up again. The dreams and all. D.B. playing away in my wallpaper, waggy finger if I decide against something, reach for the erase button. All I can do to stop myself switching off and running for it. Then the phone call and the funeral. You remember that far back, don't you? Like I said, I went to the funeral, saw all the old faces. Sam, Fish, Whiteman, PC Bell. They all said I should keep in touch like it was some kind of spell or something. They didn't say who the fuck to keep in touch with, just keep in touch. Well my old friend my old mucker, well old Rupert took them at their word, decided to keep in touch after all. He's nodding there, waiting patiently while I collect my thoughts. He's smiling his old lopsided smile for me with his fringe hanging in his face the way it always used to. He hasn't come out of the wallpaper either, just smiling, nodding. Haven't really mentioned him smiling too often, have I, what with one thing and another. Strange thing is he looks exactly as he used to back then, as if I cut him off in the middle of puberty, in the middle of growing up. He never made it like I did. He looks exactly as he did the night I hit him over the head with that rock, damn near knocked his fucking eyes out. OK, OK, I might as well get it over with, that's what I'm here for after all. Rupert reckons we needed a rethink. All my endings are in the bin now, we're taking it from here, freefall improvization with Rupert holding the baton in his dirty twitchy fingers, Sam ready to wail any time now. Oh yes, she's here too. Sitting in on our little case conference and not looking too happy about it either, to tell the truth.

In fact, she's looking pretty pissed off with things in general. I'd better rewind a little, fill you in, keep you abreast of developments so to speak, seeing as how Rupert's insisting I tell the whole thing as it was. He looks so silly there with his little boy's body and his dark hair flopping over his eyes. He looks so small against Sam, and I told you she's not exactly built like an Albanian all-in wrestler. The way she's crouched there, though, makes her look like a child too, clutching her knees that way in her white-knuckled hands, looks as if she's got plastic joints or something. See, that night, the night of the funeral, I drove off like I said, drove off and left them all behind me like before. OK, so I dropped in for a couple at the Boar for old times' sake. Got a six-pack from the Paki on the corner when I got home. Kaz, the one I told you about, she works nights down at the hospital, so I didn't have to go through the *how was it* routine. The *Did you see that bitch Sam* routine. I kicked my black shoes off, they'd been pinching my feet something cruel. Made myself comfortable on the couch watching a re-run of *Carrie*. Yeah, predictable but good stuff. The ending's nothing to compare with D.B.'s, what they've got in mind for me I bet. I'd left the lights on, and just pulled the tab from the fifth can when the phone went. I thought I'd leave it, let it ring. Then I changed my mind, hey, it was Sam again.

'Look, David ... I know ... I know you don't ... can't talk. But ... see ...' She's muttering and crying all over, leading me up the garden path again. I don't know whether it was because we were together all those years or because of what happened when we were kids but she thinks she has this right to me, a right of the last night. Always there when she gets stringy, help her out some.

'Is Jerry there?' Hey, he could save me a sore throat, what the hell. He's living with her now, he gets the thrusty tits and the hair-do, it's only fair he puts up with the rest of it. Let him stand there with the tissues and stiff drinks.

'He's had to fly out early. He won't be back till Tuesday. David, you really must come over. We ... I really need to speak to you.'

'Sam, I've told you a million times' – I lower my voice as if Kaz is there giving me one of her *Tell the bitch to fuck off* looks –

'I can't keep dropping everything to try and sort you out. He's dead now, you'll have to try and forget him same as me.' That was nice of me really, don't you think? Nice of me to think of him. Sam kept on at me, kept saying we ought to go and see him more often. I thought, go once, she'll never want to again. He hadn't changed much. Still in his restraint suit, glaring at the wall as if he was trying to think the bricks out. Little flick of spit at the corner of his mouth I kept wishing he'd lick away. His hair was lank and greasy, they'd given him a good trim, got rid of that fringe once and for all all right. Looked like they'd maybe used a hedge trimmer on it.

Frankenstein wouldn't have let his monster look like it, I can tell you. It's funny, that's how I thought of him, locked away in there. Our monster. We'd made him after all, we'd made him like it. He was duller than a toilet wall. Sam looked bloody good that day, short skirt, stockings, high heels. Not too tarty but I spotted a couple of junior doctors doing double takes and the porter who gave us directions to Rupert's room could hardly push his eyes off her. If there was any life left in him she'd have brought it out for sure. His eyes would have given him away in an instant, if there'd been anyone at home. Not a sausage. He sat and stared. A pudding with currants for eyes, pasty skin, somebody else's trousers. Tweedy things with turn-ups. Couldn't they find the guy a decent set of strides? It upset me, seeing him in a dead man's trousers. I thought we'd done our bit, shown willing. No point in driving all the way over to see some fucking vegetable, eh? She was all for seeing him every Sunday, making a day of it, maybe take him out, a stroll down the stream. I didn't see the point and I told her so. Maybe that's where I went wrong. Maybe she needed the visits as much as she thought he did. All the memories that rushed in on her, rushed in on her like the tide on a stranded ship. Timbers all rotten, letting the cold waves flood in and wash everything around. He crushed her keel in, gutted her. I was just the coat of paint she used to cover up the cracks. From the day it started she was going to go the same way. 'I can't forget about him, David, you know that.' Here we go.

'He wants you to come over, he's been asking for you.' What is she on about? Did she mix her pills, take a swig too much vodka?

'Sam . . . It's really difficult for me. You know . . . with Kaz and everything. I can't talk,' I plead.

'David, he's asking for you. He wants us all to have a chat.' Now she's pronouncing everything as if she's reading it from a blackboard twenty yards away.

'Take one of your specials. Get yourself to bed.' Me and my phoneside manner, eh? Old Whiteman, he could take a few tips from me. By the time we finished he had her on three. Everyday white, periods blue, bumping headaches green.

'Take a green one. Don't shake them out, just take one. With a glass of water, nothing stronger. You'll feel fine.'

'David, you're not getting this, are you?' Is she taking the piss or what? She's abandoned the schoolgirl tremor that was getting her nowhere she sounds just like that bastard – 'This is Rupert. I think we should talk. I'm so sorry you two haven't been hitting it off lately. We should talk.'

PRINCE RUPERT DROPS IN

My arms feel like brambles, they're tearing my shirt to pieces,
all the little hairs are standing stiff as thorns. I can feel each
immaculate shiver run up my spine rattling my frozen brain,
racing thoughts racing heart. I get one of my grips, then get a
grip. She's taking the piss. She's trying to get back at me, she's
got someone there.

'Samantha and I would like a word.' It's him. It's Rupert all
right. Sounds just like him, how he used to be. He can't be. I
watched them shove his coffin into a bloody great incinerator.
I tried not to gulp too much of him when I got out of there.
She's got some kid in, doesn't know what he's let himself
in for.

'David, you still there? Come on over, do. There's so much
we need to catch up on. Sam doesn't seem to know about the
gorge. Didn't you tell her? Tell her what really happened? She
is so looking forward to hearing about it.'

'Very funny, Sam. I'm splitting my sides here, I really am.'

'Splitting your sides, eh, David? That sounds quite painful
actually.' *Actually.* This kid, he's got Rupert off pat, I'll give
him that. Give her something to think about next time I see
the conniving bitch. The tone is vintage Rupert, crowing it,
lording it, as if one day he'll do me a favour, look me up, try
and get me in the golf club type of thing. Rupert's friend. The
fat one.

'Fuck off and die, sweetheart. Don't bother ringing again.
Enjoy your pills and mind you don't take too many. What a
loss for mankind that would be.' I slam the receiver down,
crack the handle I'm so mad. I tried to be nice to the crazy
bitch, you heard me. I tried to help her out as much as I could.
What does she do? Hires some kid to try and freak me out. **219**

Well, I was the one who came through this with all my marbles, baby. Me and Solomon, we know how to hold on to our wild horses. We don't need quacks or bottles of pills. He never tried to kill us. You know that as well as I do. He never had a clue about the picture. He stuck it on the mantelpiece back in the cottage, never knew it was probably driving his old man nuts. He never worked it out, see, not like me. Thought it was Rupert, the smarmy git, thought Rupert had figured it all out? No chance buster. It was me. Sam tried to identify the painting at the school library. I went to the big municipal library in Budgworth, asked the assistant, got some professional advice. Dead helpful she was too. Certainly young man, come this way. We know what you're looking for. I found the book, found the page, found the artist and a list of his known works. I thought I'd wait till we were all together, spring it on them. Chalk one up over Rupert. Never got round to it, what with one thing and another. Anyway, I was nosing round the *Clarion* office looking up the old files, checking up on old Solomon, when I saw the artist's name again, put it all together. I'd pulled out the editions for 1922, fished through it to check the details on this Miss May Solomon had been involved with. There it was. Lewis Archer. She'd bought a Lewis Archer watercolour from the farm sale in Taunton but never got it home to hang up. Disappeared along with the ninety quid she'd been carrying. I figured it all out for myself, no matter what that rat-fuck Rupert says. He's sitting there now grinning, one arm crooked over the back of the couch, dirty hand dangling loosely against Sam's shoulder. Cold shoulder. I'd banged the phone down and tried to get back to the film. No good. I poured lager down my throat to try and soak my thoughts a little, wash them out of my system or something. They were whizzing round in my head faster than I can write. I'd had a few, OK. Then the doorbell went. It could have been Kaz home early, forgotten her key. What time was it? 12.25 a.m. I crossed to the window, lifted the curtain and peered outside. Two shapes in the shadow under the porch. The one in the long coat looked around, gave a little wave. Yeah, I know it's going to sound stupid. Bizarre. But it did look exactly like Rupert. She must be mad, going to all this trouble just to try and fuck me over. What I ever do to her she wants to try stuff like this? I was angry, I'll admit it. I wanted to smash her face in. My ears were pounding, blood jamming my eyes, blurring my vision, dulling my senses. I stepped out into the hall, flung the door open. It was her. And him. It *was* him. No kid, nobody else, no disguise. It was Rupert. She was wearing her green mac, the one I got her in Paris. She looked like shit. He must have picked up one of Jerry's cast-offs, wrapped himself up in it.

'Hello, David. Mind if we come in for a bit?' He winks, nods his white head toward Samantha's white head. She looks drunk, her eyes are a mess, won't focus properly. Has he been hitting her already? He has tied the coat tight up to his neck, top button and everything, but the arms hang empty by his sides. He's carrying something. I take a quick peek over his shoulder, there's nobody else there. Just the dustbin I put out this morning before I drove down to Clove.

'Are you going to leave us standing here or what?' he asks, jocular, friendly. I glance at her.

'Is this some kind of—' He hits me. There's nothing ghostly, ephemeral about it. His arm shoots out of his coat, catches me on the side of my head. I crack my ear against the doorframe, double up in pain. He pokes me in the eye, damn near jabs it out. I fall sideways against the door and he kicks me hard. God knows what he's wearing, steel toecaps kick chunks from my bones. Christ, that time I got kicked by a big piebald at old Mungo's place, lying in the shit flapping like a fish, winded and sick. Bloody thing hadn't packed Rupert's punch. I flop and flap into the hall and as he steps over me I smell him for the first time. He reeks. He's the lion house at the zoo, it's the worst thing I've ever smelt. He pulls the coat tighter as I grovel away into the hall, clutching my eye. He could have blinded me.

'In here,' he barks at Sam. His voice has changed, crackles in the cold air rushing in through the open door. She pulls the door to mechanically, steps in, and takes off her coat as if she's dropped in for tea and a chat. Old times. He watches closely, behind me. I can half see him crouching over me to reach for her. I launch myself at him. I can't see him clearly but his smell is concentrated in front of me and I go for that. I go for the misty raincoat. The coat flaps as I knock him down, crack his head against the wall. A picture shatters, Sam screams once. I clamber to my feet and he kicks me in the balls. That's it. My breath catches and clogs in my throat, I clutch myself, reel back choking and crying. He's up and on me, he's got me by the face, fingers filled with mad strength. He's tearing my face into a joker grin, pulling the sockets from my eyes.

'I can kill you,' he croaks, filthy graveyard breath assaulting my smashed senses.

'I can kill you like a maggot,' he snarls, wrenching my hair back and cracking my forehead against the hall wall. He releases me and I sink to the floor, crushed all over. I think I must have passed out for a second because the next thing I'm looking at the light swinging overhead, tears running out of my eyes. He's dragging me along the passage, all fifteen stones of me and he's just like a little kid. A little kid packed with brutal strength. The strength of some fucking Jap guard with a load of starving POWs to hound to death. Bushido bullshit. Pulling wings from flies. He drags me past her, she's shivering as if someone's got her on spastic strings. He dumps me on the living-room rug, peers down at me. It's like he's ten feet tall.

'Still the fat bastard, eh?' He cracks his bloody boot into my ribs again, I double up some more, curling the rug under my body, twisting in it like I'm just fibres too. I roll over as he aims another kick so this time I get to see the foot. Hoof. That mean wall-eyed old piebald, ekeing out its last few days in Mungo's death-row field, waiting for the knackers and taking it out on me. That bastard horse has unglued his hoofs, sent them for the boy the way they send bits of bodies to the pathologist. Cloven hoofs and thick brown hairy little satyr legs to prance about on like the fucking demon bastard he is. Small brown hoofs, they must have shrunk in the post. The kind deer have, and do they come tight. The fur is shot through with grey hair. Tough grey hair like Brillo pads. I can hear Samantha whimpering now, takes the heat from me. I rock slowly feel the pain ebb a little as he looks up, grins at her with his mad mouth stretching in all directions like a monkey.

'What I want to hear,' he tells me, 'what I want to hear is you telling her all about it. Tell her exactly what happened,' he says quietly, precisely. I shake my head, try to focus. Jumble and wreckage, flotsam and jetsam. I'm swirling round with the dishwater in the plughole. The last spoon.

'I want to hear you tell it the way it was,' he says nastily, rolling his eyes and his tongue around on his screwed-up face. I peep up at Sam. She's transparent. I can see my haunted wallpaper behind her eyes, behind her face.

'Take it from the time we took the picture. You went to the library, didn't you, Sammy?' She nods. 'But you didn't get anywhere, did you, lovie?' Fake baby smile. 'But David had a little bit of luck, didn't you, David? David found out all about the painting. He found out about little Miss Muffet and how the nasty man strangled her and took the painting for his very own. And he realized Solomon could have known about it, could have had a motive for maybe wanting to bump old Jubal off. Clever David then realized Solomon could have had a motive for bumping us off too. If we found out all his secrets and he didn't want us to tell. Poor little Miss May, face-down in a ditch. What a terrible waste, eh?' He crosses to Sam, lifts a loose hunk of hair from her face, gives her his lopsided grin. She twitches her lips in response. 'Absolutely beautiful,' he murmurs. I can barely hear him when his back is turned.

'No clothes on at all. All white and pale,' he hisses, flicking his eyes to me and back to her. 'They found her in the bridge pool. Right there under the cliff. I mean, it gets deep just there. Really deep by the crack, where the stream goes nobody knows,' he recites quietly.

'The stream took everything else, her clothes, her bag. Funny how Solomon came by the picture. I suppose he must have found it out walking the dog one day. Maybe if he'd realized its significance he would have tossed it right back in himself. He would have preferred to let sleeping dogs lie, eh?

He really wouldn't have wanted his family dragged through the mud any more. We had a bit of respect in the old days, we did.' He pulls Sam down beside him on the couch, eases his thin white arm round the back of her neck, the tiny tendrils of hair I used to blow about, close my mouth on her neck to make her shiver like she's shivering now.

'If old Solomon found out we knew, who knows what he might have been capable of. Who knows what he might have done to us. He might even have tried to kill us. Bash our heads in and roll us into the stream for her. I mean, it doesn't make any sense to us, but a man in his mental state?' He shrugs ironically, draws the hem of Jerry's mac together over his mad goat legs, his little satyr trotters. I'll stick him like a pig and bleed him slow for this. Coming back to haunt me, the everlasting bastard.

'I never said a word,' I say flatly. 'I never said anything about the painting to Solomon.'

'You didn't need to say anything directly. As soon as we took it there was a risk his secret would be out. Maybe he hadn't actually thought of it that way until we took it. Maybe he figured it was safe where it was. Hanging up to challenge her all that time. But you realized, didn't you? You realized what the painting could mean to him, for him. I must admit I wouldn't have thought you were up to it, thinking it through like you did, thinking motives up for him. What did it take you, a few days to piece it all together? Work out what you were going to do? By the time you went round to see Sam that night you must have had it all pretty well figured out.' He shakes his head as if he can't believe it.

'I walked straight into it. I turned up to tell you Solomon had been rummaging around for the picture in my bedroom, you realized your time had come. I've got to hand it to you, David, it's almost too clever for words. It's too clever for you to have worked it out on your own. So I was wondering who'd helped you?'

Nobody helped me, buster, I figured it out for myself. For once in your life, death, whatever it is, give me a little credit.

'Anyway,' he says, twisting one of Sam's curls in his dirty

hand, twining it round his miserable fingers. 'You said we'd better put it back. You said we'd get a real hiding if we didn't. You said we'd go to court, you said we might end up in Borstal. That's what you said, didn't you?' He glares at me, I can make out the tiny pinpoints of light in his eyes from here on the floor, glaring down at me. I straighten slowly, sit up on the mat. I glance at Sam. Her eyes are on me but they're not registering a thing. Typical of that bitch, things go wrong, switch off and abandon ship. Leave me to deal with the bastard. 'So we went round to Sam's house, didn't we? We got her out of bed, I think.' His dirty hand drops to her shoulder, his fingers play up and down the stitching on the seam of her dress. Her lips are still fluttering like she's talking in her sleep, reciting her dreams.

'You dropped it down to us and David smashed it against the wall. Almost got caught right there and then, only we didn't. We ran for it. You and me. Over the field, down towards the cottage. And then . . . and then I want to hear it from you. I want to hear your reasons, you conniving fat bastard. I want to hear your reasons before I squeeze your eyes right out of your lying head.' His hands are twitching on her shoulder, his fingers flex in and out, delving absent-mindedly beneath the shiny black silk of her dress, giving her a bony hunchback. She's not worrying though. She's out of there.

'I want to hear why you did it, left me for dead, left me out there for her.'

I swallow slowly, edging back across the carpet. I don't know what this bastard can do, maybe he can zap me with green bolts from his fingers, freeze me with a stare, turn me to stone or shit. Way I feel, he's already started.

'Tell Sammy what the nasty man did then,' he drools.

'I hit you over the head with the stone, you were going on so much.' He recoils a little, feigns shock. 'Trouble is your head was so frigging thick it didn't kill you,' I spit at him. Yeah, OK, I'll get back to you later. I'll tell you the whys and wherefores. Let me deal with this bastard first. It's true, in case you were wondering. I did hit him. I hit him right after he called me a clumsy great prick. I knew I was going to sooner or later. I knew one day I'd do the bastard. Him going on like that, dropping the picture, fear of getting caught, I suppose it all ganged up on me, made me do it. Made me stop, pick up a half-brick somebody had been using to hold down their cucumber frames. He was trotting on unawares into the night. I lurched after him, held it behind my back, ran with him some more.

'What a whack you gave me,' he simpers. 'What a flaming headache I had in the morning. Only the morning was a long time in coming. A hell of a time in fact.' He turns, slips his hand out of the top of her dress to wrench her chin round toward him.

'It's a miracle I didn't just drown. Our little playmate whacked me by the cottage. Whacked me right into the water. That's where she came and found me, took me back with her, took me back under the cliff.' He strokes her cheek slowly, little circles under her fuzzy eyes.

'He left me for dead. He'd figured out a motive for Solomon, figured if he stuck with the old boy they'd think he was protecting him. Nobody would ever think it was David all the time. And if they ever looked like getting close to him he'd hand them the old man on a plate. That's what happened, eh? What you do, post a letter to the paper? Ring somebody? That big guy at my funeral, reading comics while they burned me up. No respect. I tell you what though, it was sweet, David, I've got to admit it. Sweet.' His hand slips under the shoulder straps of her dress like a pale serpent. The fucking smartarse. The little wiseguy. I'd like to finish him. Smash his head flat. I'll maybe try a breeze-block next time. Pop his eyes out for him, bash the teeth out of his yapping jaws. I reach the wall, slide myself up against it as he tilts his head and studies Sammy. Studies her face like it's a secret document and he's a master spy.

'But why did he try and kill you?' It's Sammy. She opens her mouth as if she's struggling to form the words, as if he's finally getting through to her. Rupert smiles.

'For you. He did it for you. He wanted you all to himself, isn't that right, David?' She's staring at me, I shrug, watching them. Waiting. 'He got you, she got me. The funny lady in the green dress. She shook me out, gave me my life back. Maybe I was already dead. Maybe she gave me the kiss of life. I had to repay her, see. I had to make it up to her. She was concerned about you, Sammy, same as I'm concerned about you. All the time we wandered round the cold rooms with the tattered flags, all the time she was going on about you. She thought maybe David would harm you too, one day. If he could do that to his best friend . . . who knows what he could dream up for you.' Who knows? He's full of shit. Full of watery shit. His veins are full of it, he's got it all wrong, he's all wrong.

'She said better bring Sammy to me. She'll be safe with us. We can all live together, under the cliffs with the rest of them. She liked the outdoors the best, but she'd come and visit us, take us for walks in the woods, walk with the weather.' His eyes have glazed a little but I can still see the sharp points on me, a pot of shiny pins pointing me out.

'She brought me back to the pool. She was going to tell me something when Pizog's people attacked us out of the woods. She pushed me down, she probably saved my life, or the part of it she owned. I fell in the pool, dragged myself out the other side of the bridge. I could hear the shouts and see the water running red over my feet. I thought I'd been dreaming, my head ached, I felt faint. Then I thought of David hitting me like that. I didn't know where to go or who to see. I thought I'd go for the warmth, the safety. I didn't know where but I started running. My head ached like mad. I couldn't even remember where I lived. All I could think of was Sam's house on the corner of the lane. You'd take me in, you'd look after me. I remember going past the pylon, like it was talking to me, telling me where to go. I thought of climbing up and walking along the wires like an acrobat, but I couldn't climb the shiny legs. They were so cold, they cleared my head a little. I remember going past the dustbins, I remember a light on in your window. I was supposed to go to you but I couldn't remember why. All I knew, it had to be you. I had to climb up, climb up your drainpipe. Then they started shouting and all the lights went on. I couldn't get to you. I was scared. I didn't know where to run. Then I thought of the lady in the green dress with the nice car. She'd give me a lift if I could get to the road, see her again. It's got beautiful seats, that car of hers. Like leather armchairs. It goes without making any noise, just glides like a hovercraft, floats down the road, floats on the water. I knew I'd have to run through the woods. I was running when he caught me.' That's right buster, I caught you. What's all this crap about Lady G. wanting everybody to live together? Is she – is anybody – going to believe shit like that? What, Dream Bitch just wanted a bit of company in her old, old, old age, did she? I stood in the stream when the water flowed backwards, I heard her spell it out. She wanted us to get the girl. Sam was her passport out of there. She tried once, just dropping in on us, and they sent her back with brass knobs on. No thank you, not round here. She needed to go over in someone else's body. A horrid clicky hermit crab looking for a tasty shell. Like the time she found little Miss May – the proper Miss May – floating face-down over the bright gravel. How she do it? Osmosis? Crawled in through the open mouth with the wretched water? I'm not big on the technical details, buddy. She just wanted a body, in the stream waiting. Rupert was going to take her down to the bridge and slide her under, slip her under to the other side where she was waiting in her fuzzy green dress with those dumb-ass Redcaps. Didn't they figure it? Did they reckon she'd take them with her? Those boys weren't too hot on quarantine rules, I'd say. Sure, that's what Rupert was up to that night, that's what Pizog and his scrawny sidekicks were so determined to prevent. Glaistig should have known her place, grass is greener kind of thing. She should have stayed put and shrivelled like the rest of them. Maybe they're all running around on four legs barking like doggy-lizard crossbreeds with long flicky purple tongues. Hey, maybe I'll find out. I lick my lips. He shakes his head, smiles.

'I'd never have thought old fatso would have caught me. Not carrying all that weight. He did though. He tackled me and dragged me back down with him, back to her. Straight to her.' His voice tails off, he's looking at Sam, hand flexing and coiling under the shoulder of her dress, his glove-puppet poppet. There's a small table lamp on the mantelpiece. I could reach it, whack him all over again. His eyes flicker again and I freeze.

'She was waiting in the stream with the rest of them. Schmelker, Tilekin. I'd seen their dens. I'd seen their pups. I'd seen her rooms behind the cliff. Great tall rooms with flat sides hung with old banners. So cold. Right inside the cliff, right in the guts of some giant crouched there with the stream between his legs. She'd shown me round but she preferred being outside, the wind and the weather, singing through the trees. I could hear her chiming in my head but I couldn't go to her. They had me. Pizog's things.'

'You were unconscious,' I say, edging along the wall an inch.

'That's it. I was out cold. In cold. So cold.' He shivers, looks at Sam. 'Then Solomon came back. I heard her shout his name, round and round my head. What happened then?' he asks dreamily, as if he's forgotten what he's supposed to be. 'He barged them aside. Just when Pizog dashed forward with his stones out. They thought it was his last throw, summoning a demon. Remember that time I wiped out your Imperial Guard doing that? You sulked for weeks. Remember? No? I suppose it was her magic. You could only cross when she stood in the stream with you. I don't know.'

But I do. I'm a bloody expert on inter-Faery-world expressways, me. She was in the stream same as she'd been the time Solomon tried to burn her out. She was in the stream so he landed slap-bang in her lap. He knew all about her lap, old Solomon. He'd been round a few so he knew what he was about. It wasn't right. She wasn't right. Sam's looking at me again, her eyes are focusing slowly. He's stroking her back under her dress, feeling the tiny ridge of her bra strap maybe, letting his fingers run this way and that. I edge closer to the mantelpiece. Get a grip on that lamp and then we'll see how quick you are, pal. See how you take it this time. I shan't hold back, I'll make damn sure. I'll get all of him, I shan't close my eyes this time. I'll aim it true.

'I remember the small one . . . that Pizog. I remember him dashing out with those stones held in front of him. They all jumped together, they all hugged each other like old friends. They were firing arrows everywhere until the flash, I can remember all her bones sticking out under her dress. She was all wet. I can remember the strings of spit in her mouth as she shouted to them. I think I fell over, one of the creatures ran into me. I didn't see what happened. I saw the flash. Huge flash. White green red. It was lucky we were under the bridge. Then Solomon was dragging you and you were dragging me. You could feel the heat rolling over the hill, the ground buckling under your feet. I could feel it but I couldn't hear it. I just saw him mouthing at me.' He points to me, still against the wall.

'We saw the flash. I was chasing after Dad. We thought there'd been an accident. Thought a plane had crashed or the pylon had come down. We could feel the ground shaking. Dad had gone running out after you. You ran so fast he couldn't keep up so he went after Solomon instead. Down toward the bridge. Mum and me came after in our night-clothes. We saw Solomon running out of his hut. Dad said he hadn't ever seen him move so quickly. For an old one. He ran into the woods and we all came after. We were still looking when the night went away and the sky opened up. Dad told us all to lie down. Then we saw the big flash. The really big one. You could see all over the hill it was so bright. It was bright and tight as if it was going to split up, explode in pieces like a jug dropped on the floor. We could see the pylon drooping over, the cables were flashing and buzzing. We saw it totter on top of the cliff, watched it fall. It was so loud but you could hardly hear.' He watches her mouth, her red tongue tripping over the words.

'And then we saw you two tottering toward us in the torchlights. All the smoke. You were both all black and sooty. We could only see your eyes. I couldn't hear what you were saying, David. Dad was shouting about what Solomon had done. I could see him shouting and pointing. I couldn't hear properly for weeks afterwards.'

'It was tough, wasn't it?' Rupert smirks. He turns, sneers

at me. 'Have second thoughts did you, dragging me out?'

'I don't know. He grabbed us, dragged us on back to the cottage. We got out just before she came in on him. She'd destroyed Pizog and she was going to destroy him. He knew she was bound to come after him, taking us with him as bait. Bait to get her inside the cottage, inside with all that old scrumpy. Might as well have been petrol he was swilling around.'

'We could smell it on your clothes,' Sam says flatly. Rupert raises his eyebrows, gives us a stupid grin.

'Wasn't it exciting?' He chuckles. 'So the three of them destroyed each other and we all got away, just a little bit singed,' he says quietly.

'We were lucky,' I say.

'Lucky? Lucky? Aren't you forgetting something? Like you'd left me in the stream, left me for her?' He leans forward, letting me see his yellow teeth. Lean closer, old pal, and I'll knock your fucking block off. His face contorts as if a demented child had decided to twist him round a little.

'What do you think I'm here for, anyway? Talking over the good times? Do you think I'm going to let you get away with it, what you did?' A thin dribble of spit runs from his colourless lips. Sam is digging herself back into the couch like it's going to swallow her up.

'You left me to her, you leave me like this, and you think I'm going to forgive and forget? Go and find a little playmate down at the farm?' His voice breaks, he recovers, snarls.

'You've stolen my life, you fat bastard. You stinking lying fat bastard. You stole all my life and you stole her. And when you'd got her you decided she wasn't worth having after all. Cast her off and got a nice nurse in to look after you instead. Well, who the hell's going to look after me, eh?' he croaks, eyes brimming with stinging tears. 'I'm supposed to be grateful for her, am I? What life have I had? What have I got to show for it? These—' He tears the coat apart, shows the thick matted fur over his bony satyr legs. Bristling black bones, small deer hoofs. It's like a sick pantomime. I never did like pantomime. He kicks them slowly.

'Take a good look. Her present to me. The little maggot she

laid inside me. The little maggot that went all hard and shiny, turned into something else. Her little butterfly. Only I didn't get the wings, see, just these. And you had her and you had all your fucking life and I had nothing. Until now.' He grins wolfishly, leering at her and sneering at me. He whips round and grabs her face, wrenches her to him. She yelps, face buried in his coat.

'So beautiful. So beautiful but David still didn't want you. Didn't want you after all the trouble he went to to get you.'

'What are you going to do?' she whimpers, cowering against him.

I inch myself closer to that lamp. It's got a heavy base, I can grip it in my fist, I can swing it at him.

'Well, what are *you* going to do is more to the point. Don't you feel you owe me something, for old times' sake?'

'What are you going to do?' She's teetering. Hang on in there.

'Well, I never had the chance. Not like old fatso there. I mean, in all the circumstances.' He jerks her chin up to stare at her face.

'You owe me,' he says quietly, a little boy lost in the woods, asking for sweets. Lady G. had a soft spot for children, same as the stream. Look how she cared for Solomon before he went all hard and horny on her. Before he worked out what you did with your dick.

'You owe me that at least,' he tells her, his naughty schoolgirl.

'What do you want me to do?' she asks flatly. He glances up at me. 'You watch. That's part of it. You watch me like I imagined you all these years, all my life.' He wrenches her forward again, pulls her so hard a button pops across the room. The dishevelled black dress she wore to his funeral.

'Take it off,' he barks, fixing me with his mad stare. His voice has dropped to a guttural growl. Wait a second, wait a second.

'Take it off. Take it all off,' he orders. Samantha stares at the wall behind my head, a bored stripper in some seedy club. Tugs her belt open. Rupert is fidgeting, his eyes flit nervously from her to me then back quickly as if he's afraid of missing something. He pushes her forwards so she drops to her knees on the rug, her hair hangs horribly and there's a ladder in her stocking.

'What are you waiting for?' he rasps. 'Some music? Take it off.' I'm still waiting for him. She straightens, mouth slack. 'You stay still,' he hisses. Dull eyes, cold flints. 'Stand up, Sammy,' he says idly, as if he's seen it all before, auditioned dozens down in the stream. Samantha climbs to her feet, she's maybe been here too.

'The dress. Let me see what I've been missing. Go on, you owe me, Sammy,' like he's been playing cards with her. 'She's beautiful,' he observes. 'She's so sexy. But not good enough for you, eh, David?'

'We saw things differently,' I say quietly, waiting for him to fix his goat's eyes on her, fix them on her one moment too long. That's all I need you to do, get him looking at you. Wiggle your bum you silly bitch. She's not seeing any of it, she's standing there swaying, reaching mechanically for the catch at the back of her neck.

'There's a hook,' she says.

He nods to me. 'Undo it for her.' I cross to her, she turns slowly, and I undo the tiny catch holding her together. I see the tiny fair hairs curling on her soft neck as she leans her head forward, holds her hair up out of the way. Over her shoulder I can see him grinning and twitching, running his eyes over her. I tug the sharp tab of the zipper down, all the way. She shrugs forward and it peels away from her like a second skin. Black bra straps, red marks on her pale skin where she's had it on too long. She's a dirty old man's dream, so small, so slight. Stockings, suspenders, knickers. She's cold to touch but she smells warm enough. Rupert's slavering. His eyes are glued on her. She's so slim, dark, tempting, despite the vacant expression, the wandering eyes. The eyes that have had all their life bashed out of them. She strips as if she's alone in her bathroom, getting ready to wax her legs or something. His tongue flicks over his pale lips, eyes glimmer with a leaden intensity, drinking her in. Her elbow catches me in the chest as she reaches back to unhook her bra. I shove her forward as hard as I can. She sprawls over him screaming, cracking her head on his mouth, hands flat on his dirty coat. He lurches back, the couch tips and spills them both against the wall. I step to the lamp, grab it, and pull it away from the wall. The flex whips round my wrist but I'm OK, I'm in control. I don't fumble it the way I fumbled the picture. He rolls her off and I step over precisely, I'm like a big bloody panther. He lifts his arm and manages to deflect the blow from his head. Manages to take the full force, crumples against the wall. I crash in on him, knees to his chest, pinning him down, crushing his splayed arms by his side. I wrench at his hair, take a good grip, hold him as he buckles and whips frantically. I bring the lamp in from close range as hard as I can against the side of his head. He's snapping at me like a dog, ear smeared with bright blood. I bring the lamp back as far as I can, bring it down on the bloody smear. This time he wriggles free, wriggles under my legs. Sam is cowering against the wall, spots of blood over her chin, chest. She's smeared some of it over her mouth as if she was trying to shut herself up, shut herself in. Rupert is crawling toward the door, clutching the side of his head. I get up, cross the room after him. The bulb is smashed, splashed with blood, red shards. I up-end the lamp, step over him and drive the bloody shards into the back of his head. His face splashes into the carpet, he writhes weakly. I bring it up again and drive it into the stretched fabric of his coat. His arms are flapping but he can't get me now. I'm safe, I've saved us. He's mine. His little cloven hoofs beat a tattoo on the carpet but it won't do him any fucking good now. He's dead meat, he's mine. I sit on him, turn the lamp heavy-side up and whack him again. I don't want to see him suffer. I want him dead like a freshly flapping mackerel with a bright feather barbed in its mouth. He can't take it. His head gives up. I whack him till I'm not sure what shape his head is any more. He can't spell me now. He can't get me with his squashed head. His hands open and close like he's kneading dough. His body ripples under me. Blood and the other stuff all clogged in his hair. I'm amazed he had so much. It's so long, so luxurious only I've been and gone and spoilt it now. Trickles, spots, gouts of blood all over the carpet. Kaz'll go mad when she sees this mess. The lamp holder rolls out of my red fingers. He can't move. He can hardly raise a decent twitch. Sam must have run for it. I look around, the door crashes open, pictures drop from the walls. It crunches his hand against the wall. I look up, breathing hard, ready for them, the police whatever. Whiteman even. This time he'll have to sit up and take notice, I've got the bastard right here. What are you going to say to that, eh, you old quack? I'm sitting on the fucking evidence, aren't I? It's Kaz at the door. She looks flushed. Maybe she met Sam running down the road, wondered what the hell was going on. Her coat is open over her mauve uniform. Her hair is tied back in a neat little bun. I always think of her as Victorian, matronly. My little George Eliot. She's looking hard at me, hard and stern. I had to kill him, for Christ's sake. I couldn't leave him, could I? She'll be OK when I've got my breath, had a chance to explain. I'm good at explaining. She'll see, as soon as she stops looking at me that way, stops shouting whatever it is she's shouting.

'What have you done?' I make out. I hold up my bloody hands, all runny with Rupert.

'It's him. It's Rupert.' She can see that. She's seen pictures of him. Can't she recognize him or something? Have I hit him that hard?

'What have you done? What have you killed her for?'

'He came back. It's Rupert.' She's backing off, gone after Sam I expect. She'll tell her, she'll vouch for me.

'What the hell did you kill her for?' Kaz is yelling at me now, hysterical. What's she yelling at me for? She should be down here helping me up, helping me clean up. She's a nurse, she's seen blood before. She knows why she's here, why I had her here. Maybe she was expecting this. Not 'What's she doing here?' but 'What have you killed her for?' Like D.B. by the bridge when Solomon turned up, ruined the fun. She didn't waste time with 'What the hell?' or 'Who the hell?' She'd been expecting him, same as Kaz, if she'd been paying any kind of attention at all, should have been expecting this. Observant, see, that's me. Even now, right this moment, I'm no slouch, I can think faster than the lot of them, thinking they're so fucking clever. If she won't stop bawling maybe I'll give her a whack as well, just to keep her quiet. I look down. Where's that lamp? Rupert's hair . . . that's not his hair. There's too much of it. I know that now. I'm trying to focus, trying to think. Who did I hit? I hit Rupert by the stream that time. Then I hit him again. Only it's not Rupert, is it. I stare down at the mashed head. Blood is pouring slowly from the rents in the skull. Other stuff must be brains. I reach down, turn what's left of the head to see the face. Hang on. This isn't right. It's Sam. Something's slipped. I'm fucking slipstreamed again. It's like déjà-vu only worse, it's like the planet's gone soft on me, gone all mushy. Made the walls wobble in and out. I hit him, not her. I never touched her, I saved her. You saw me. I never hurt her in my whole life. I pushed her at him, I stepped over her she must have scuttled away. I didn't want to hurt her. She's gone. Kaz has gone. She's run for it. I can hear her shouting. What's she thinking of, leaving me here with him? With her. I jump up. Kaz has gone. Gone.

EPILOGUE

My dreams are numbered, one to ten. I don't have many variations but I dream quite a lot. In my dreams Rupert comes to me, holds the tissues, shakes his head. He's a right mess. He ought to use the things on himself, get himself cleaned up before he comes out of the walls after me. I really made some kind of a mess of his head, dug big chunks out of his back. He can't sit straight and his head hangs forwards on his chest at an awkward angle. He has to squint at me sideways. To be honest I don't like to catch his eye but where else am I supposed to look? I've bashed him pretty bad, I know that now. Sometimes he just sits and squints, sometimes he goes on like Whiteman used to. Very occasionally he'll talk about the old days, before we fell out over Sam. Before Solomon told us all his stories. Dream number one, though, he runs on about Glaistig. He reckons he's with her all the time now, says he's her right-hand man. She lost most of those rotten Redcap creatures when Pizog popped his clogs and Solomon blew his top. Maybe she hasn't got much choice when it comes to staff. I grin at him but he gets chilly, says he's the one. He likes to tell me about a fisherman who went to catch some trout in the pool under the cliff. He doesn't seem to know dates, you know what I am for detail like that, but it was a long time ago. Before we came along for sure. He has a willow fishing pole and some twisted gut. What does the guy use for hooks? I ask. Rupert says a bent pin, something like that. I mean, can you imagine trying to catch a trout down at the Axeheads Reservoir using twisted gut and a bent pin?

'But he was using worms, not some dinky little fly. He wasn't doing it for the sport, he was after his lunch,' Rupert snaps. He gets annoyed if I try and trip him on the details, see.

'Anyway, he was fishing, under the cliff there, when he sees this beautiful woman floating in the waters held in the crack. Nothing on. He waded in and dragged her out, dragged her up the bank getting her all dirty. Smearing her with red earth. When she woke up and coughed up a lot of water and sick, he took her back to his village. His chief was pleased, he thought the girl beautiful too. If it hadn't been for the chief's wife he'd have taken her there and then. But he'd changed wives once already. He'd got rid of his first wife to marry this slave girl from the south, and she was no push-over apparently. She was jealous of the stranger, said she must be a witch. Said some other tribe further upstream must have sacrificed her to their water gods. Stuff like that. All the women shook their heads, said that's what must have happened. They were all for chucking her right back in. This chief though, he wasn't going to let her slip away just like that. He'd think of something once he'd signed the treaty, got the Northmen off his back. The chief wasn't about to let her get away. Maybe when he'd drunk a few horns of mead with the Northern Jarl things would be clearer to him. Maybe he'd stumble on the right words for his wife. They talked and laughed and argued until the night was done and the drink was running out.' Rupert leans back, gingerly examines his back and gives me his lopsided grin.

'Next morning they hugged each other in front of the whole assembly, peasants, housecarles, and Northmen. They all gave a great cheer and the Jarl went to mount his pony. Just then, by some chance (and we know all about chance, don't we, David?) the girl Rush had found in the stream woke up. She'd worked hard swaying between the rows of drunken warriors, pouring drinks and fetching food. She'd been mauled by the men and abused by the sweating women. They'd all seen how their husbands had looked at her as she passed. She'd been sleeping in a corner with the dogs, missed all the shouting and cheering. Just then she rose, stretched like a cat. The rough sacking gown she'd been thrown had slipped from her shoulders, she'd casually fastened it together but not before she'd reminded the Jarl he had meant to ask after her. The blonde girl in the brown shift. He took his boot from the stirrup, turned back to the chief. "The white-haired one is not of your people?" he asked in his mangled West Speech.

'The chief glanced at the girl. "She is but lately come to us." He was uneasy now. He'd struck a bargain, let them go. He would worry about the girl later. He would worry about his wife later.

' "Well then, let us seal our treaty once more," the Jarl suggested. "Let me have the woman and you shall have twenty suits of mail we took from the Frisians. Then your housecarles will be as well equipped as any. They will have armour to match their courage." His wife had appeared in a fine white gown as if she had been anticipating developments.

' "This is an excellent proposal, My Lord," she said, laying her dark hand on his arm. He could hear his own warriors fidgeting and whispering behind him. Rush, the poor fisherman with the crooked arm, found himself pushed forwards.

' "The girl should stay, My Lord. Stay for one of us, even as you have said," he stammered, looking about him nervously, holding his crooked arm as if to remind the village how he had come by his job. The young men nodded, fingered their weapons. The Jarl swept his ice-blue eyes over them. Dozens of strapping farm boys in smocks, leather belts, holding their weapons as if they were weeding rakes or hoes. He cared little for them or their muttering.

' "I have promised my men," the chief said heavily. "Any other prisoner, any other slave that catches your eye is yours, without the mail." It was a mistake. The Jarl weighed it as he climbed aboard his pony. This chief was a fighter, not a talker. He had already agreed a treaty which benefited the Northmen more than the hill folk. Now he was dropping his end of the deal, admitting weakness, admitting uncertainty. The Jarl smiled a little, comfortable with twenty fully armed men at his back. His best fighters. They could cut their way through this crowd as if they were hacking stubble in the fields at home.

' "Why not take your woman's advice? Let the girl come with us." It was a calculated insult. Would such a chief be advised by his wife?

' "I make my own mind in my village. The girl stays for my warriors, as I have said. My wife is too generous to our guests."

' "Must we spoil our new friendship so quickly, arguing over such a trifle?" the Jarl asked.

'The chief shrugged. "Our treaty stands, even as we agreed it last night."

' "But I want to amend our treaty. I want to trade this miserable girl, this miserable scrawny pale thing, for twenty suits of mail. Mail for your brave boys." There was a fresh outbreak of muttering. "I have a fancy for the girl." He smiled.

' "You have heard my mind. Does the treaty stand or must we fight?" The chief bristled, stood his ground. What a fool this Jarl must be to think of jeopardizing the treaty now. He had obtained terms far better than he had dared hope. The sight of the girl stretching, the sight of her gown opening invitingly, the sight of her small white breasts, had robbed his wits. The Jarl could see his men levering weapons out of belts, loosening swords. The standard-bearer gripped his raven banner, they closed up on their shaggy ponies, surrounded on all sides by jostling villagers in the middle of their own stockade. The messenger gripped his horn to his chest, ready to blow a warning to the rest of the host who waited down the hill in the drizzle and mist.

' "I have a fancy for the girl," the Jarl repeated slowly.

'The chief's wife hissed in his ear. "Let the witch go. There will be bloodshed else."

'He ignored her, pulled the axe from his belt, weighed it. "Do not make me break our oath," he said. His men crammed up behind him, clutching whatever weapons they had. The Jarl leaned forward slowly, straightening his boot in the stirrup. Rush the fisherman saw what all the warriors had not. He hurled himself forward.

' "He's got a knife!" Before he'd finished the Jarl had flicked his wrist and sent the black dagger into the middle of the chief's broad chest. He staggered back with a cry into the arms of his wife and his startled housecarles. The Jarl drew his axe and hacked at the outraged villagers as they rushed forward.

The women screamed and grabbed their children, ducked indoors. The men bellowed oaths and closed in with whatever weapons they had to hand. Slowly, the furious crowd pushed them closer, biting, kicking, stamping, shouting. The women-folk passed daggers and knives over the heads of the crowd to the fighters in front. They eagerly grabbed the smaller, craftier weapons, jabbed and slashed at the frantic riders. Just then the rest of the Northern host struggled up the hill to the blaring horn and shrieks of battle. They scrambled over the undefended stockade and fell on the villagers from behind, hacking left and right. The furious villagers gave way before the heavy axes and locked shields, ducked into doorways or climbed on to the roofs. The mass combat dissolved into dozens of murderous individual fights. The women fought beside the men, the chief's wife flailed about her with her husband's axe, wrenched from his dying fingers. The Jarl cut his way to the main body of his men. Together they fell back to the wall, helping their wounded comrades to their feet as they went. They linked shields, levelled spears, jabbed and hacked at the villagers as they closed in cautiously. They made their way back through the alleys between the hovels, reached the wall and began to climb over, keeping the villagers at bay on the far side of their shieldwall. One by one they turned and clambered over the stockade until only the Jarl and a handful of his lieutenants kept the bawling mob away. Rush waited on the roof of a hovel, a light spear in his good hand. He waited until he saw the Jarl climb the wall, protected by his men. Then he threw with all his might. The Jarl looked back at the same moment. The iron spearpoint scored the Jarl across the face, taking his nose and smashing his teeth, filling his mouth with blood. He collapsed behind the struggling bodyguards who were backing off in the face of a furious onslaught from the toughest and best-armed villagers. They fought on, ground down by dozens of blows, hacked and spitted on bloody forks. The mailed men retreated from the walls in ones and twos, hurried on down the hill.

'There was a ragged cheer when the villagers realized they'd won. Realized they had beaten the mailed men. Twenty of them lay hacked and bloody in the mud alongside thirty-seven dead and dying villagers. The chief's wife watched her husband being carried into the great hall by the few bodyguards who had survived. Rush blinked at the solemn blood-splattered procession as they filed in. The chief's wife saw him, pulled him out in front of the stunned crowd.

"Your catch has cost us our chief," she told him. "Would that you lay there and not him." But she hadn't finished, not by a long chalk. That night they burned the bodies in a great fire on top of the cliff, lighting all the trees around the gorge. Away on the coast, the Northmen watched the flames and made their new chief. In the smoky village the chief's wife called the women to her, for they outnumbered the men. Their eyes were red from loss and ruin and from the smoke from the roaring bonfires of their husbands. They brought Rush and the girl before them, arms tied behind their backs. They announced the punishments for them. Rush to be drowned in the stream in which he fished, for surely it was he who had brought the witch to their hearths. She . . . she was to be returned to the stream from which she had come, but she was to take the mark with her. The mark of the beast who came in the night to lie with their menfolk and steal their souls. The mark of the Beast with Two Backs. They left the last dozen men on the walls, the boys and the old men beside them to fill out the woeful ranks. They stole out over the hillside and down to the stream. The chief's wife's rage knew no bounds. The tragedy, the enormity of the day had overwhelmed her, gnawed at her mind. Her chief was dead and thirty of his men. Half a dozen would die of their wounds before the week was out. If the Northmen didn't come back the Saxons would. Their neighbours would soon hear of the calamity and arrive with their own consolation in mind. That morning, with a new treaty signed with the raiders, their future had looked as bright as ever. That night they were little more than brigands, waiting for the spearmen to come for them out of the mist. If they could not hold their walls they would have to move west, cross the great river and follow their comrades to the mountains. The hills were not safe for them any more. The women wept for husbands and sons and for themselves. And it was all the fault of this miserable cripple and the filthy witch with the staring eyes. The witch who had caught the Jarl like a lure traps the lark. A thousand deaths, a thousand agonies, would not have been enough for her. She had silently shattered their lives and dreams. Bewitched the men so they had fallen to slaughter and shambles. She had been the Judas goat, leading them all to bloody death. The chief's wife, blackened with smoke, lead the way along the stream. The prisoners gagged and bound, a dozen women with red eyes and red hands, pulling a bleating goat. Rush thrashed like a fish on his rope, implored them with his eyes, implored them to let them be but their hate knew no bounds. It reverberated around the gorge, bounced back, redoubled itself. Grew, twisting and coiling like a sleepy snake in each mind. Snorting and prancing, a ferocious drooling beast dragging the prisoners down to the clearing by the stream where they stopped to talk over their washing.

'They tied him to a tree, bound his arms as he thrashed against the cold bark. They tied his head tight so he couldn't look away, held his hair hard in their smoky claws and jabbed daggers into his arms in case he tried to clench his eyes shut, in case he tried to look away. The women dragged up the old logs they used to sit on, forced him to watch as the chief's wife butchered the bawling goat with ruthlessly efficient strokes of her husband's axe. Now, all their hate was focused on the pale girl who cowered in the red earth at their feet. Blonde hair matted with dirt, pulled tight in vicious hands. The chief's wife looked at Rush, pleading with his eyes, shaking his head as far as he was able. He closed his eyes and clenched them tight despite the knives that speared and pricked his arms, that opened a dozen deep cuts. He felt the blood run down his arms and trickle over his bound hands. He heard the axe falling, biting, tearing. He could smell the coppery tang of blood in the cold night air through the filthy rag they had tied round his mouth. He could hear their hoarse breathing, gasps of horror and astonishment. But he dared not look. He dared not see the busy demons dart around the butchered carcasses, the slaughtered meats. Wiping hair out of their mad faces, smeared to the elbows in bright hot blood. The chief's wife worked furiously, dementedly, as if any moment the Jarl's men would rush in and stop the horror, put them all to the sword. Cackling and whispering to herself as she worked with demonic precision. She fetched the heavy darning needle and a length of gut, the length of gut they'd found in Rush's tunic with his awkward iron hooks. How they hooked, how they fished. How she worked, shapes swirling in a red mist. Her fear welled in her throat, choked her like a stone. Rush clamped his eyes. Clenched them tight till thin trickles of blood seeped between the creased skin. He would not look when the breathing had subsided, when the anxious moans had given out. When he heard the shape writhe in its blood on the blood-red bank. He crushed his head against the tree, felt his skin tear and his muscles rip as he pulled his head against his bloody bonds.'

Yeah, and about then I always turned away too. I didn't want to look, look at what they did to her. It wasn't her fault, it's never been her fault. I'll tell her when I see her, when I've got her attention, when it comes down to just the two of us. Because that's what it's all been about, really. Her and me. Solomon's had his turn, Rupert's had his turn, maybe you've been wondering, all this time, all these brushes, why I'm still so keen, still waiting for mine. I think she knows, she knows I've loved her from the beginning. You know, the idea of her. She's come out after me so many times, scared me ragged, dragged me down kicking and screaming into my dreams you'd think I'd have tried to get away, get some help, some therapy.

Call in old Whiteman, let him inside my head with a whip and an upturned chair. I kept that old quack away all these years, palmed him off with my patented teenage ignorance and superbly studied, fully grown resentment. Treat old D.B. the same she'd never have stood a chance. I could have washed her out of the walls, swilled her down her own plug-holes, flushed her back under Hillstones with those funny blind fish and the shopping trolleys. If I'd wanted to. But I could never bring myself to hide from her. Call it what you like, fickle fascination, reluctant repulsion. She's my dream girl, I've waited long enough for my turn, to talk with her face to face, find out what she's really like. No matter what Solomon says about her tricksy ways, the masks she'll show me. That's where Sam and Lorraine and Kaz came unstuck. Lorraine didn't know shit, Sam suspected, and I reckon Kaz knew. Thought she knew just about everything about my dripping dreams. Kaz had her own reasons, her own motives for sticking to it. Her stake in the trendy lounge lizard she'd met at my club in Budgworth that night. It hadn't taken her long to figure there was another woman, that I was already spoken for. She could have put a name to my problem, but it wouldn't have been the right one. Remember her bursting in, asking why I'd killed Sam? Not 'Why are you sitting on top of your naked ex-wife' but why had I killed her. Sam, well, she'd had Rupert, clinging on to her guilt like a crab in a rock pool. He was her motive. Maybe Sam, if she'd been here with me now, would say the same, agree with me: it's easier to love an idea, an ideal, than real solid everyday people with minds of their own and axes to grind. I don't care what face my dream girl shows me, what she's like under the green dress with the fancy runework. Sam and Lorraine and Kaz and all the others in between, they couldn't come close. They couldn't stay the distance like she could. Always there, with me always. To the grave and beyond. My Dream Bitch Eternal Girl. Dream Girl Eternal Bitch. Glaistig. I'd turn away just like that Rush guy, the poor crippled bastard. I reckon he knew, I reckon he loved her too, don't you? Sticking by her like that. Who's going to stick by me, eh? You? When they realized he wasn't looking, they cut off his eyelids, held his hair in their bloody claws. When they'd finished they cut him up and rolled him in the stream after his mistress. I bury my face in the contour on my bunk that passes for a pillow. They figured, give me a real one I'd choke myself, eat it, something crazy like that. I scream and scream at him when he tries to run number one dream through my head. Run it in your own head you fucking bastard, I yell at him. He laughs, gives me his lopsided grin and looks at me out of his mashed-up eyes.

'I'd like to, old pal,' he says gaily. 'I'd really like to. But look at the mess you made of me. How am I supposed to dream in this, eh?' He holds up his bloody hands, he's been fingering his wounds again. 'How could I dream in this?'

Leave me alone. I don't want to hear about it. Each time though, he comes back again and tells me a little more.

'After they finished, they rolled the red and white and brown mess over the bank into the stream. The Beast with Two Backs they told their children about. The waters ran red round the rocks and red over the little rills of pebbles and stones.' Shut up about the stream, can you? I don't want to see it. I've seen it myself, remember? I've been down in the blood when the stream goes backwards. I've been slipstreamed too, Christ, we all have. Telling me about their faces like people slowing down to look at an accident. Fickle fascination, reluctant repulsion. It was no accident. None of it was. Rolling down their windows to take a good look at the smashed metal and the torn bodies. Like they roll the observation panel back and squint in at me, giant-eyed.